I0727463

THE HOUSEWIFE ASSASSIN'S HOSTAGE HOSTING TIPS

JOSIE BROWN

A BOOK BY

SIGNAL PRESS

Praise for Josie Brown's Novels

"This is a super sexy and fun read that you shouldn't miss! A kick ass woman that can literally kick ass as well as cook and clean. Donna gives a whole new meaning to "taking out the trash."
—Mary Jacobs, *Book Hounds Reviews*

"*The Housewife Assassin's Handbook* by Josie Brown is a fun, sexy and intriguing mystery. Donna Stone is a great heroine—housewives can lead all sorts of double lives, but as an assassin? Who would have seen that one coming? It's a fast-paced read, the gadgets are awesome, and I could just picture Donna fighting off Russian gangsters and skinheads all the while having a pie at home cooling on the windowsill. As a housewife myself, this book was a fantastic escape that had me dreaming "if only" the whole way through. The book doesn't take itself too seriously, which makes for the perfect combination of mystery and humour."
—*Curled Up with a Good Book and a Cup of Tea*

"*The Housewife Assassin's Handbook* is a hilarious, laugh-out-loud read. Donna is a fantastic character–practical, witty, and kick-ass tough. There's plenty of action–both in and out of the bedroom… I especially love the housekeeping tips at the start of each chapter–each with its own deadly twist! This book is perfect for relaxing in the bath with after a long day. I can't wait to read the next in the series. Highly Recommended!"
—*CrimeThrillerGirl.com*

"This was an addictive read–gritty but funny at the same time. I ended up reading it in just one evening and couldn't go to sleep until I knew what the outcome would be! It was action-packed and humorous from the start, and that continued throughout, I was pleased to discover that this is the first of a series and look forward to getting my hands on Book Two so I can see where life takes Donna and her family next!"
    —*Me, My Books, and I*

"The two halves of Donna's life make sense. As you follow her story, there's no point where you think of her as "Assassin Donna" vs. "Mummy Donna', her attitude to life is even throughout. I really like how well this is done. And as for Jack. I'll have one of those, please?"
    —*The Northern Witch's Book Blog*

Novels in The Housewife Assassin Series

The Housewife Assassin's Handbook (Book 1)

The Housewife Assassin's Guide to Gracious Killing (Book 2)

The Housewife Assassin's Killer Christmas Tips (Book 3)

The Housewife Assassin's Relationship Survival Guide (Book 4)

The Housewife Assassin's Vacation to Die For (Book 5)

The Housewife Assassin's Recipes for Disaster (Book 6)

The Housewife Assassin's Hollywood Scream Play (Book 7)

The Housewife Assassin's Killer App (Book 8)

The Housewife Assassin's Hostage Hosting Tips (Book 9)

The Housewife Assassin's Garden of Deadly Delights (Book 10)

The Housewife Assassin's Tips for Weddings, Weapons, and Warfare (Book 11)

The Housewife Assassin's Husband Hunting Hints (Book 12)

The Housewife Assassin's Ghost Protocol (Book 13)

The Housewife Assassin's Terrorist TV Guide (Book 14)

The Housewife Assassin's Deadly Dossier (Book 15: The Series Prequel)

The Housewife Assassin's Greatest Hits (Book 16)

The Housewife Assassin's Fourth Estate Sale (Book 17)

The Housewife Assassin's Horrorscope (Book 18)

The Best Way to Prep for a Party!

Every great hostess knows that the key to a successful soirée has nothing to do with best intentions, and everything to do with attention to details.

So that your next gathering is the talk of the town (in the right way), do as much as possible in advance. That goes for picking the date of your event, making your signature hors d'oeuvres, and getting dressed early, so that you're ready to meet and greet those guests who always appear ahead of schedule.

Of course, for the early birds, you can always hire guards with MP5s. A few rounds fired over their heads will certainly make them think twice about their obsession to arrive ahead of the crowd!

As for any guest who is rude enough to whisper under her breath, "Boooooring…" invite her to see the newest room in your house—the wine cellar! The fact that it doubles as a dungeon can be revealed after you've drugged her with whatever Kickapoo Joy Juice you've injected into that very expensive Chateaux Margaux 1995 she's been dying to try—

"Dying," of course, being the operative word.

His body, encased in a black body bag, lies on a marble-topped table in the morgue.

The room's chilly temperature sends a shiver up my spine, but the coroner–a beefy, barrel-chested guy named Jerry–thinks it is widow's nerves that are undermining my stoic composure.

Jerry waits for my lethargic nod before zipping open the bag–from the bottom first, to read the toe tag. "Yep, the ID is correct." He gives a half-hearted chuckle. "It's never good when the attendant pulls the wrong corpse–er, body–"

I stiffen at his idiotic attempt at humor.

The coroner stutters through his faux pas. "I–I meant to say *loved one*. Really, I did."

I pat his arm to indicate that I forgive him for his mistake.

He zips up the bag at the foot, and steps toward the head of the bag, where the zipper pulls down.

Slowly, he opens it.

My reaction is the same as that of any widow who is looking at the waterlogged body of her husband–I stifle a moan as my knees buckle.

The coroner catches me in his arms before I collapse. "There, there," he murmurs sympathetically. "It will be over in a moment."

When, finally, my composure returns, I lift the short black veil that barely covers my eyes with a gloved hand in order to wipe away my tears. Choking on my sobs, I turn my head.

In truth, I'm doing my damnedest to keep from laughing at the corpse in front of me.

Oh yeah, that's him all right.

May he rest in hell.

Although drained of blood and life, his once proud and handsome face is now pocked with blisters, made even more hideous because of its greenish-black hue. Three weeks at sea without sunscreen will do that to you. I hope the tourists who first spotted him while they were joyriding on the Princess Cruise Line on its way to Alaska take this lesson to heart.

At least his lids are closed. I guess that's a good thing, considering that they caved into his sockets, once his eyes were ravaged by sea critters. They also nibbled away at his skin, which was loosened as it absorbed the naturally chilly water found this far north in the Pacific Ocean.

What is left is embalmed in waxy body fat.

What a way to go.

And yet, I feel no pity.

I do feel hungry, though. In the little French bistro around the corner, there's a filet mignon with my name on it. Very rare.

And certainly no fat.

Time to move this charade along. I bow my head. As I wipe imaginary tears from my eyes, I whisper, "If–if you don't mind, I'd–I'd like a few minutes alone with…with him."

Jerry hesitates. Finally, he shrugs. "No problem at all, ma'am. Take as long as you want." He lumbers toward the exit. The door closes behind him with a small click.

Time's a wasting. With both hands, I wrench open the mouth of my supposedly dearly departed. The force snaps his neck in half. *Yowch!* My bad.

Well, hopefully, I'll be long gone before the coroner notices that this corpse is now a bobblehead.

His mouth is open just wide enough for me to slip my hand into it. I reach for the second molar on the left side of his upper jaw–the maxilla. Wrapping my fingers around it, I twist as hard as I can.

Nope, it can't be the right tooth because it's as solid as a rock.

On to the next molar–no movement. The third try is also a bust.

I hit gold–make that porcelain–with the fourth tooth, a premolar with a cap. While it twists, I can only get it halfway off.

Believe me when I tell you that I'm not a sadistic necrophiliac (or for that matter, a desperate housewife who's obsessed with the *Twilight* and *Fifty Shades* series), but rather an agent on a black-ops mission to protect the free world from terrorism. Inside the crown is a microdot with locations of well-placed terrorists–saboteurs planted in key defense administration positions in governments throughout the world: England, Germany, Japan, France, and yes, the United States, too.

However, they've yet to learn that one of their puppet masters was, until recently, fish food.

"Speed it up, Donna. The coroner is looking at his watch," Jack Craig, my mission partner, warns me through my remote ear bud. Between it, my 5MP cam feed contact lenses, and the hack job our tech-op, Arnie Locklear, did on the security feed here at the morgue, I've got some coverage.

I pull out a pair of needle-nose pliers, but the handle is so big that I can't fit it and my hand into his mouth, so I take a wild guess which way to turn it in order to loosen the cap, and twist.

It comes off–not the cap, but a tooth–

And the wrong one at that.

"Oopsy," I murmur, as I toss the tooth over my shoulder.

The fact that I'm strapped into four-inch stilettos and a short flouncy black dress doesn't stop me from scurrying onto the morgue table in order to straddle my dead darling. This puts me in a better position to see the target tooth.

It also allows me to feel something I might not have noticed before, because of the draping of the body bag:

To my amazement, he has a hard-on.

Jack is laughing so hard into my ear bud that I have to pull it out of my ear.

"Jeez!" I mutter. "I didn't know a corpse could do…*that*."

"Happens all the time–especially under the circumstances. When he went overboard, he got tangled up in the mooring rope; he died by strangulation as opposed to the fall. It's called a post-mortem priapism, or a death erection."

The fact that he somehow got snagged in a Japanese trawler's net meant for Bluefin tuna and choked to death shows you just how polluted our oceans have become.

All of a sudden, I'm hungry for sushi.

I frown. "That doofus, Jerry, could have warned me."

I've just wrapped the pliers around the right tooth when Jack tells me, "Better hustle. He's coming your way."

I twist the pliers with all my might, but the crown doesn't move.

"Three seconds," Jack mutters. "Two…."

I hear the click of the morgue's heavy door.

I'm left with no alternative except to suck face with the corpse of a despicable terrorist.

I've had worse kissers.

It helps that I'm thinking of all the great ones in my life– Jack, first and foremost. Okay, yeah–admittedly, my dead (so it seems, albeit still hard to believe) ex-husband, Carl, curled my toes a time or two.

But that was before I knew he was a terrorist, and certainly before his many attempts to kill me.

This is neither the time nor the place to reminisce about the man who haunts my nightmares. When it comes to Carl Stone, I'll never think, *Rest in peace*. Instead, I declare, *Good riddance*.

The last laugh is on him.

Okay, maybe it's on me. As it turns out, the coroner can't

help but stutter when he sees me. I guess it's the first time he's walked in on a widow having a make-out session with one of his corpses.

I glance over, feigning surprise, then sigh loudly. "Excuse me–*do you mind*?"

He takes the hint and skedaddles. This time, the door closes with a bang.

I wipe yucky grave wax from my lips. Seeing it on the back of my hand makes me sick to my stomach.

"Are you okay?" The sympathy in Jack's voice is all I need to buck up and get back to work.

"Don't worry, I've got it covered," I assure him.

To speed things up, I put both hands in Dearly Departed's mouth, and wrench his jaws wide open. Except for his emerald hue, he could have modeled for Edvard Munch's painting, *The Scream*.

Well, well, whattaya know? In addition to the crown, he has loads of fillings, too. Note to self: set an appointment for my children–Mary, Jeff, and Trisha–as well as Jack and myself, with our local dentist, Dr. Yarborough.

"Oh, hell, Donna, the coroner is headed back your way, and he's got company. He doesn't look happy, either."

It's now or never. Once again, I position the pliers over the tooth. I tug. I yank. I jerk. "I've–almost..."

For inspiration, I hum, *Hit him, baby...one more time...*

With both hands, I yank up as hard as I can–

And topple over backward onto his thighs.

"*Got it!*" I mutter jubilantly. Then, "Ouch! It feels as if I've got a knife in my back."

It's not a knife. Instead, I was speared by Dearly Departed's hard-on.

Jack sighs. "Now, seriously, get the hell out of there! He's on his way in with Hardy Higginbotham's real widow!"

Hardy, whose business cards call him out as an international financial consultant based in Vancouver, British Columbia, was on his yacht, circling Vancouver Island.

In truth, Hardy headed up new business development for the Quorum, an international conglomerate of businessmen who finance terrorism around the globe. Their investments in these unusual start-ups reap big bucks in the munitions businesses they own, such as banks used for money laundering, and companies in the transportation, construction, and prison management industries.

Hardy had just pulled in a whale of an account: an already well-funded terrorist group known as the Islamic State of Iraq and the Levant, or by its acronym, ISIL. Right now, its primary source of income is hostage ransoms.

The microdot has the deets about an imminent mission that takes place in some major city outside its usual 'hood. My employer, a CIA-sanctioned black-ops company known as Acme, wants to stop it before it happens.

Unfortunately for Hardy, late one night, he fell overboard.

Make that *pushed*–by Jack.

Had Hardy gone to the bottom of the sea, the mission would have ended right then and there–somewhere around Latitude N 55" 51' by Longitude W 140" 37'. As luck would have it, he got pulled up in a trawler's net, so now I'm here to help Jack finish the job he started. It's my last gig before retirement.

"Yeah…okay." For some reason, he finds it hard to believe.

That's okay. I enjoy proving him wrong.

Kindly reader, if you presumed that the corpse herein referred to as my Dearly Departed was anyone previously known to you as–Carl Stone–let me set the record straight, here and now:

It is not.

Six weeks have passed since creepy Carl went overboard. In the meantime, acres of northern Pacific waters have been scoured by both boat and helicopter, and voluminous hours of satellite footage have been scrutinized for anything that may prove Carl survived the explosion that took place during his escape.

We've come up with zilch, nada, bupkis.

Yes, I am relieved too. Unlike Hardy here, Carl apparently made it to the bottom of the ocean.

Let us rejoice together–champagne, fireworks, dancing in the streets, the whole nine yards–but first things first–

I've got to get the hell out of here.

I jump off the table and look around. The room has no windows. "But…where will I go?"

"I hate to say it, but…"

I know why he paused: the morgue drawers. I've got no other choice than to hop into one.

Preferably empty.

I shudder at the thought that it will be anything but.

There are forty of them: twenty each on two facing walls, in rows of five drawers, stacked four high. I run to the far corner of the room. In the farthest column on the left wall, the three bottom drawers hold bodies. The two above them are empty, but I'd have to use the lower handles as steps to climb into one.

In the same column on the opposite wall, every drawer is occupied. In the column next to it, the top drawer is the only one empty, so it won't do, either.

I run back to the other side of the room. Pay dirt! The very bottom drawer in the second column is empty. I leap into it, as if it is a luge and this is my one and only chance for Olympic gold, and scoot toward the wall. This is all the motion needed to give the drawer the momentum needed to slam shut.

And just in the nick of time.

Jack is relaying the morgue's web cam feed into my wireless contacts and my ear bud, so that I can hear and see what is happening outside my drawer. Jerry stands in the threshold and looks around. Realizing that I'm nowhere to be found, he does a double-take, then cranes his neck down the hall.

Angrily, Widow Higginbotham pushes past him. Like me, she's a platinum blonde. She's also dressed in what passes for widow's weeds these days: a black Versace dress that hugs her curves, black stiletto heels, and a hat with a veil.

I could claim that my ensemble was somewhat more innocent. Then again, sucking face with a corpse was a slutty thing to do.

By the way Jerry stares at Widow Higginbotham's cleavage and heaving breasts, I'd say he agrees with me. She has got a rack on her that would make any male corpse rise up and take notice.

The one on the slab in front of her is already at full mast, so he doesn't count.

She glances around the room warily. "I thought you said someone else was here too–and claiming to be me."

He nods vigorously. "There was! Strange…"

Before he has a chance to do it for her, she unzips Hardy's body bag and wrenches open his mouth. No doubt she sees the hole from the missing tooth. She raises her veil to get a better look. When she also notices the spiked tooth is missing its crown, she curses, and storms out of the room.

Jerry looks around one more time, then runs after her.

My teeth chatter as I ask, "Want to take bets that she wasn't Hardy's old lady?"

"Not a chance," Jack murmurs. "In fact, I recognized her the moment she lifted her veil. She's a Russian operative named Tatyana Zakharov. I owe her a bullet to the back of the head."

Odd. He had never spoken of her to me. I rack my brain for

some tidbit I may have heard, but it's no use. I can't think when I'm famished.

"Donna, listen up! Don't–"

His audio and visual feeds are breaking up. Instead, I get a loud whistle in my ear.

I'd reach up and pull out the ear bud again, but the drawer doesn't give me much room to maneuver. When I'm hungry, I'm cranky. When I'm cold, I'm cranky. And when I'm locked in a three-foot-by-seven-foot stainless steel refrigerator, I'm downright ornery. I ask my fearless mission team, "Hey, how soon can you get me out of here?"

No response.

"Hello? Jack? Arnie?"

Still, no response.

Instead, I hear the following, in this order:

The morgue door opening.

A woman's voice, purring "No! You really don't want to do that, do you?"

The whoosh of a bullet, silenced by a suppressor.

The thump of a dead weight, hitting the floor. I presume it is this Tatyana person.

Footsteps–Jack's, I suppose, as he as moves through the room.

I holler, "Yo! Over here! And it's about damn time!"

I listen as the drawer immediately left of me opens with a click.

"You're getting warmer," I jibe him impatiently.

When you're inside a box made of stainless steel that is three-quarters of an inch thick, eight bullets from a semi-automatic hammering a wall next to your head makes you feel as safe as a piñata in a shooting gallery.

The fact that I'm still breathing means the bullets weren't able to penetrate the drawer. I consider myself lucky.

The gun must have jammed, because the shooter lets loose with a litany of blush-worthy cusses, and the exclamation–"I don't get paid enough for this crap!"–in Russian.

Really, I've given you a very loose interpretation of a phrase that uses a very common English word beginning with the letter *F*. I'm sure you agree with me that mine weighs lighter on sensitive ears.

Apparently, Tatyana is alive after all. *Does this mean she killed Jack?*

The next click I hear is my drawer being opened and pulled out, and the next face I see is Tatyana's. She's holding a gun, and it's pointed at me.

Rage blinds me to the reality of the situation: That her smirk indicates she'll use it without any hesitation. And that I have nothing with me to defend myself against the woman who just killed the love of my life.

"Where is the tooth with the microdot?" she asks. British accent, veddy posh.

Ah, well, so much for the simple nicety of a formal introduction, perhaps one of the few things that separates us humans from other species.

Then, surely, I can be excused as my own animal instincts kick in. The fist holding the needle-nose pliers swings back over my head, stabbing her in her gut.

Her scream is a shrill squeal, akin to a bonobo in heat.

The bright red blood flowing out of her is the color of cherry Kool-Aid, but has the consistency of a glaze.

In other words, it's made a mess of her chic black sheath.

Instinctively, she reaches for her wound. It's only when she stares down at it, though, that the reality of her situation hits her. Shivers run through her body. Her eyes grow big and glassy. She grits her teeth and forces herself to shift her gaze directly at me–

And to take one more shot.

The only way to defend myself is to flip over and squeeze myself as far into the right side of the drawer as possible–

And just in the knick of time. The bullet slams into the left side of the drawer, only to ricochet up, hitting the drawer's roof, then down–

Into my ass.

I groan from the pain.

Tatyana smiles, even as the light goes out of her eyes. As she slumps to the floor, the weight of her body shoves the drawer back into the wall.

I hear it click shut right before I pass out.

I'm awakened by the sound of my pounding heart.

I take that as a good sign.

"Doc, she's coming to," says Jack.

He's speaking to Doctor Fleishman, I presume, who happens to be Acme's around-the-clock no-questions-asked medicine man. He works out of an urgent care center in the building next to Acme's, which picks up the tab for it, him, and his staff.

Just hearing Jack's voice puts a smile on my face. And feeling his lips on mine is all the encouragement I need to attempt to open at least one eye again. He's laid his head next to mine, so that we're nose to nose and I'm staring into his sweet green peepers. The concern in his eyes is all I need to know I'll be alright.

"Ouch," I mutter.

"I'll bet." Jack is trying not to smile. "At least you took it where it could do the least damage."

"I guess you're right." I crane my neck to see what the

doctor is up to, but before I turn, Doctor Fleishman stops me with a gentle tap on the lucky cheek without the bullet hole. "Whoa! I've got a few more stitches to go!"

"Oh…sorry." Blushing, I ease back down.

Time to change the subject. "Jack, what's the prognosis on the Russian widow?"

Jack's smile fades. "You pierced her pretty hard. She lost a lot of blood, and she's still unconscious. The doc says it'll be touch and go. We've got her under lock and key. The moment she wakes up, I'll be questioning her." He shrugs. "Abu is at the morgue, cleaning up after her."

"I presume Jerry was DOA."

"Sadly, yes." Jack winces. "I wish I'd gotten there sooner."

From behind me, Dr. Fleishman declares, "You're good to go, Donna. I leave you with two souvenirs." In one hand, he holds a pill cup. I look inside. It holds the bullet that pierced my rear. The other hand holds an inflatable donut–not the greatest fashion statement.

"Take it easy for the next couple of weeks," Doctor Fleishman warns me.

"Will do," I promise, as I ease myself off the gurney. Gingerly, I step forward. Pain pulses through me, but I force a smile through it as I make my way to the front door. "Now that I'm benched, per doctor's orders, I guess it will make it easier for Ryan to learn to live without me when I formally turn in my resignation."

"He'll whine at first, but he'll get over it," Jack assures me.

"I didn't realize I'm so easily replaceable."

Jack raises a brow. "No one says you are. But you've made up your mind, and that's that. Acme will have to go on without you."

"I do feel right about it," I insist.

"As you should," he assures me. "Frankly, your timing couldn't be better, with what seems to be coming down."

"What do you mean by that?"

He shrugs. "Tatyana's reappearance is not a good sign of things to come."

"You mentioned that you have a history with her."

"Just a couple of run-ins. She's a former SVR sparrow. These days, she's freelancing for the Quorum, which is why she was also coming for the microdot."

"I see." I pause.

Nothing else. Apparently, he doesn't want to talk about it.

About *her.*

"Nothing to worry your little head about." He forces a smile on his lips. "As of now, you're off the clock, right?"

We're in a business in which some intel, even between lovers, is only divulged on a need-to-know basis. Apparently, Jack thinks this is one of those times.

I pretend to respect his wishes, and drop the matter.

Still, I wish my aim had been just a little bit better.

2

Choosing a Theme for Your Party

Throwing a posh soirée? Give it a theme!

For example, choose a decade. How about the nineteen-thirties? Hand out tin cups to your guests, put Ruth Etting and Ethel Waters blues albums on your retro turntable, and wear chiffon dresses with cap sleeves (to cover up your jiggly batwings). As for food and drink, make revelers stand in a soup line, and dole out gin you really made in your bathtub, out of pure grain alcohol and juniper berry juice (as opposed to holly berries, which may turn your party into a wake for the first to imbibe). Talk about authenticity!

Another example: commemorate a movie. For example, you can have fun with Hitchcock's "The Birds." Stage your living room with taxidermic crows. Invite your guests to put their hair up in a French twist and to dress in jacketed sheaths, like Tippi Hedren. Your buffet can include hard-boiled eggs and roast quail. For authenticity, hire a falconer and have him do tricks with his trained peregrine–

Well, his ad claimed the bird was trained.

Last one into the phone booth is a rotten corpse!

I'VE SPENT THE NIGHT SLEEPING ON MY STOMACH. AT LEAST JACK'S arm was around me. But sadly, I now awaken to find he's not in our bed.

Nor is he in the shower. A shame. I'd love to have joined him there.

According to the bedroom's mantle clock, it's only six-fifteen. I slip on a robe and head downstairs.

Jack is standing at the kitchen counter, where Mary, Jeff, and Trisha's lunch boxes lay open. He's already made sandwiches from last night's leftover roast chicken. A sandwich bag filled with chips is also tucked into each box. He's chopping a carrot: first the tip and the end before slicing lengthwise once, then again, so that the carrot is quartered. He lines up the pieces so that the next cut halves all the slices at once.

Without turning around, he murmurs, "You're up early."

But of course he'd know I was behind him. All senses working at all times. It's second nature for spies like us.

He turns and smiles. Leaning against the counter, he teases, "Between the day you had yesterday and the painkiller Doc Fleishman gave you, I expected you to sleep in until at least noon."

I steal a carrot stick and take a bite. "I'm too restless. As they say, 'This is the first day of the rest of my life.'" I hold what's left of it out to him.

He takes it in one bite. As he munches on it, he admonishes me, "I still insist on making breakfast this morning, and taking the kids to school."

"If you're offering to make your world famous French toast, how can I refuse? But why don't we split up carpool? You take the girls. I wanted to attend the middle school PTA meeting anyway."

"It's a deal." He must not mind that I have carrot breath because he goes in for a real kiss–long, deep, and oh so sweet.

When I open my eyes, I notice that his eyes have shifted toward the kitchen table, where his laptop sits open. Nonchalantly, he positions himself so that he stands in my sight line.

Why?

I turn toward the cabinet and open it for a coffee mug. After pouring myself a cuppa, I reach for the morning paper. Pretending I'm immersed in an article about Hilldale's local bake sale, I murmur, "Oh…sorry, darling, I forgot to mention it, but I'm pretty sure I woke up because your cell phone was buzzing."

"Oh?" he frowns. "I guess I should check it, to see what's up."

I nod absentmindedly.

I wait until he's all the way up the stairs before I click onto his computer, using his password: my measurements. (At least, the ones I swore to him were mine.)

He's been reading an Acme file that includes an update on Tatyana's condition. Apparently, she's regained consciousness, but refuses to speak to anyone.

No surprise there.

His footsteps are heavy enough that I can hear him in the hallway above me. Before he makes his way to the stairs, I position myself back at the counter with the newspaper back in my hands, as if the latest shenanigans of the Hilldale city council are of grave importance to me.

Too late, I realize that I closed his laptop.

Oh. *Shit.*

If he notices, he doesn't show it. Grinning, he starts on his next carving project, an apple. "I presume that, after PTA, you'll stop by the office to formally tender your resignation to Ryan."

"Of course." Does he notice the catch in my throat?

I'll admit, it won't be easy leaving my Acme family. But I've accomplished what I set out to do when I started this journey:

save my children from the harm that was imminent when Carl disappeared.

More to the point, I saved my children from Carl.

The world would be a safer place, too, if his demise meant that the Quorum was also dead. Unfortunately, Hardy and Tatyana's machinations prove otherwise.

To be honest, it bothers me that Jack doesn't also feel the need to get on with his life.

By that, I mean our lives together.

I force my lips into a smile. "I'll be in the office before noon. Let's have lunch together, somewhere off campus. That way, we can play catch up."

He's about to say something, but whatever it is, he decides to wait because Mary is tripping down the stairs, rubbing her eyes. Seeing her, he reaches for the square skillet–a sure sign that the family Stone is to be treated to his celebrated French toast.

She hesitates before giving him a hug on the way to the fridge for a glass of orange juice. Of my three children, Mary took the news of Carl's death the hardest.

As if the blow of Carl's death wasn't bad enough, the press has been having a field day dissecting the data files–courtesy of the straight-shooting data thief known the world over as the Mad Hacker–that accompanied a Clark Kent Justice League article. It detailed Carl's attempt to auction off security intelligence while in his position as the U.S. Director of Intelligence.

Jeff's mourning is mitigated by his classmates' taunts that his father was a terrorist, whereas Trisha's teacher, Miss McGonagall, and her principal, Miss Darling, have done a good job of tamping down the parents' gossiping in front of their children. No bullies at any age are tolerated at the school.

As for Mary, her initial response was a shrug, but every night for a week, I heard her crying, usually right before dawn.

We didn't tell her how it happened, since there is always the tendency to shoot the messenger. Granted, if she knew the truth, she'd have just cause.

Then again, if she knew that Carl almost killed Jack and me, maybe she would have shot him herself.

I married evil. Taking him down was my way of dealing with it. His child might see it differently.

Speaking of evil, I wonder if Jack will mention Tatyana's status to me, or if he'll honor my resolve that all Acme business stays out of my life from now on. I hope it's the former. I mean, hey, who doesn't like a little office gossip now and then?

Especially when it's about the person who put a bullet in your ass.

"WHY IS YOUR MOM SITTING ON A WHOOPEE CUSHION?" JEFF'S BEST friend, Morton Smith, points at me.

That's what I get for leaving the car door open as I position my inflatable donut.

My son's face turns candy apple red. "She…had surgery."

Stupid me. I should have taken Jack up on his offer to drive the boys, too. But he's got enough on his mind—even if he won't tell me exactly what that is.

"Let me guess," declares Cheever Bing, Jeff's other pal, "hemorrhoids."

"No," I growl, as he climbs into the middle seat of my Toyota Highlander Hybrid. I pull away from the curb with a jolt. He takes the hint and buckles his seatbelt.

If he were smart, he would have read my tone as a warning: *subject closed.*

But the child is not the sharpest pencil in the drawer, which is par for the course, considering his mom, Penelope, is just as dull and twice as obnoxious. Cheever wrinkles his forehead, as if using his brain is hard work. Finally, he ventures another guess: "Prostatitis?"

Jeff shoves him. "Women don't have prostates, you moron."

Cheever shoves back. "Prostatitis is a disease sluts get from the johns who pay for them."

Morton leans over the seat from the back row. "What…you mean, like, paid toilets?"

"No, jerk! Johns, as in men who pay for sex." Cheever leers at me through the rearview mirror, then hits the seat hard enough that Morton retreats back into his corner.

Jeff grabs Cheever by the neck and puts a fist up to his nose. "Are you calling my mother a hooker?"

Cheever breaks free and shrugs innocently. "I'd never do that. On the other hand, my mom says that any woman who's got two husbands must be making them both pay through the nose for *something*." He nudges Morton.

Morton's face twists from a complete lack of comprehension. "I didn't know your mom was a bigot!"

"You mean *bigamist*, you idiot," Cheever snorts.

"She isn't a bigamist! And she's not a whore, either–" Jeff grabs Cheever by the collar and swings his arm back.

His fist is within pummeling distance when I screech to the curb. Catching Cheever's eye in the mirror, I say, "Out. *Now*."

He looks back at Morton, as if he doesn't believe I'm addressing him. Morton heads for the door. My two-fingered whistle puts him back in his seat, fast.

"I mean *you*, Cheever–you little perv." I jump out in order to slide his door to one side, then I grab him by the collar and pull him out.

He's actually whimpering. "But–but it's two miles to school from here!"

"Not quite. A mile and two-thirds, to be exact." I squeeze

his plump cheek until he winces. "A nice long walk may help you lose some of this baby fat."

He's so frantic that he's practically clawing at the car. "But– I'll miss first period history class!"

I climb into the driver's seat. Revving the engine, I shout out the window, "Not if you jog!"

He's still staring after us as I drive off. Make that, glaring.

I'm curious, so I ask, "Why, all of a sudden, does he give two hoots whether or not he makes first period?"

"Because of Gabrielle Mathews." Morton holds his hands chest-high and hefts them, as if they cradle a bounty. "Capisce?" he asks.

Jeff leaps over the middle seat in order to slap Morton's hands back down into his lap. "Not only are you not Italian, you're disgusting."

"What did I do?" Morton whines. "You know it's true! She's got 'em, and Cheever wants to get ahold of 'em."

Angrily, Jeff shakes his head. "Oh yeah? Like *that'll* ever happen!"

A part of me is proud of Jeff for standing up against derogatory remarks aimed at the opposite sex. But another part of me suspects there's a reason for his gallantry.

Maybe two. Chest high.

"Why do you care, anyway?" Morton mutters, just loud enough for both Jeff and I to hear him.

Catching my eye in the mirror, Jeff turns bright red.

Who is this Gabrielle Mathews, anyway?

A quick scan of his Facebook page's friends list should answer a lot of questions.

MY QUICK CURB STOP MAKES ME A FEW MINUTES LATE FOR THE PTA

meeting. I get the evil eye from Penelope's sergeant at arms, Hayley Coxhead. She waves me to a seat in the back of the room.

My walk of shame takes me in front of the podium. As I pass Penelope, she mutters, "Well, surprise, surprise! Mrs. Stone has graced us with her presence. Or shall I say, Mrs. Craig? ...Oh! Forgot, you aren't married to him. You're just living in sin. Ah, what a *wonderful* example you're setting for your three children."

Hayley chuckles at what she perceives is Penelope's wittiness, whereas Tiffy Swift, Penelope's other sidekick and usual whipping girl, lets loose with a very unladylike snort.

Angered, I freeze.

I can do one of two things now:

The first option is to kill her. I would never carry a weapon into a school building, but that is a minor inconvenience for someone with my skillset. I could just as easily get her in a headlock and snap her neck, causing her cervical vertebrae to shatter, and severing her spinal cord–

It takes four seconds to rule this out as a viable course of action, the primary reason being that there are too many witnesses. Alas, my inevitable incarceration would defeat my plan to spend as much time as possible with my family.

My second option is to hold my powder and bide my time for the right opportunity in which to show up Penelope in her own fiefdom: here, in MomLandia.

With head held high, I glide graciously toward the back of the room, but I eschew the last empty seat.

I forgot my donut, and the last thing I need is yet another pain in my arse.

~

I SMILE THROUGH THE HOUR-LONG MACHINATIONS THAT ARE PART and parcel of Penelope holding court. She chastises the group because bake sale revenues are down. ("We need more gluten-free treats, people! Who's handy with almond flour? Raise your hand! ...Not you, Lorelei. Your cookies taste like lead doorstops.") She berates the SCRIP team because their tallies were off. ("Maybe you ladies need to take the remedial summer course in sixth-grade math. One more error, and I'll sign you up for it myself!") And apparently, too many parents are skipping the mid-semester parent-teacher meetings ("Just because your children aren't the budding geniuses you'd hoped doesn't mean you should throw in the towel. If you show up, at least you get an opportunity to blame their teachers, right?")

No wonder everyone flinches when she proclaims, "Okay, now for some new business–something that will need another volunteer. All those who want to chair the middle school prom committee, raise your hands."

Instead, most of the women in the room sit on their palms.

Penelope scrutinizes each face, one by one. "Oh, come on now, don't be shy. This is a chance to showcase your hostessing skills! To show real leadership!"

In unison, everyone slumps down in their chairs.

I don't blame them. Dances have so many moving parts, including the coordination of volunteers to decorate, make and serve refreshments, arrange for entertainment, and to monitor the students most likely to spike the punch or to sneak off and make out.

Then again, if you pull it off, the kids have a memorable event.

And your child is proud of you.

This is especially important at a time in which his friends are insinuating that his mother is a slut.

I am not a slut.

However, I am the best hostess ever.

If I pull this off, Jeff will be so proud of me.

My hand shoots up.

Seeing it, Penelope frowns. (At least, I think it's a frown. Her brow is smooth as glass, but even from where I stand I can see a line of sweat where a wrinkle would be if she didn't have quarterly Botox appointments.) Her eyes sweep left, then right, in the hope of finding someone else's hand, to no avail. "I'm being serious, people! WHO WILL TAKE THIS ON?"

I wave both hands, as if sighting a rescue plane from a deserted island.

She looks right through me, then points to Allison O'Connor, in the third row. "What's that you say, Allison...you'd love to do it?"

Allison bolts upright in her chair. "What? Who...*me*?" she stutters. "No! No way! I–I'm late–to catch a flight, to Bolivia! Yes...Bolivia! We're moving!" She grabs her purse and is out the door before Tiffy can beat her there.

No matter. Now that Tiffy is standing guard, no one else can escape.

The mumbling among the other moms should have Penelope worried. I hear the phrase "make a run for it as a group..." and "can't catch all of us..."

Before the stampede begins, I shout, "I'll be glad to head it up!"

Everyone freezes.

All eyes turn to me.

In some, I see relief. In others, pity.

In Penelope's, there is red-hot anger.

Finally, she bares her teeth and purrs, "Why, Donna, how kind of you to take this on. By this afternoon, you'll be receiving the criteria handbook outlining the specifics."

I'm tempted to ask if it will be delivered by her army of

flying monkeys, but I hold my tongue. Instead, I nod. "No problem."

Through her gritted grimace, she hisses, "Meeting adjourned."

I doubt that rats jumping from a sinking ship could move as fast as these women.

I do my best to play it cool as I stroll past Penelope and her posse. I'm almost out the door when Hayley mutters, "She was married to a terrorist. Does that mean she aided and abetted him? Isn't there something in the PTA bylaws about that?"

Tiffy adds, "I hear she's close to President Chiffray. Maybe he pardoned her"–she nudges her girlfriends–"and I can only imagine what she did to get it."

A better person ignores such taunts. A better person proves herself with great deeds, not retaliation.

In times like these, I wish I were a better person. Alas, I'm a dame with great aim, a mean right hook, and a long memory.

I'll wait until the dance to show them just how bad–I mean good–I can really be.

Three Tips for Trimming Your Guest List

Dear, oh dear! Looks as if the number of potential guests for your next party rivals that of a Boeing 747 manifest, despite the fact that your living room is the size of a puddle jumper. Who should you cut? No problem! Just follow these three simple rules…

Cut her if…she's tried to steal your boyfriend or flirted with your husband. This also goes for anytime she's (a) borrowed anything and never returned it; (b) paid you too many backhanded compliments; or (c) implied you could afford to lose a few pounds. (Yes, you know it's true, but it's not her place to say so. That place belongs solely to your mother.)

Cut him if…you haven't heard from him in over a year. Was his phone on the fritz? Did he have amnesia? Is he trying to disengage because you're no longer friends with benefits, but friends with spouses who now share awkward silences? None of these excuses make him a keeper. Should he show up anyway, have the bouncers throw him out on his ear. Better yet, leave that honor to someone who'll enjoy it more: your husband.

Cut them if…they've never invited you to anything other than their wedding, or for that matter, their child's circumcision, baptism, bar or bat mitzvah, confirmation, or graduation. This isn't to say that they only think of you when they're looking for a handout, or that they want to rub your nose in their happiness–

Ah hell, okay, yes: they love it when you're pea-green with envy. Now you can return the favor. Just make sure every friend you share with them is invited, even if they aren't.

Okay, time to peruse the list to see who's left on it…

Your mother.

Sigh.

Expect a blatant hint that you're diet isn't working–again.

ACME INDUSTRIES TAKES UP A THREE-STORY CUBED AND MIRRORED building in one of the sprawling, ubiquitous office parks abutting the 405 freeway on the west side of Los Angeles. There is no sign out front. All employees enter via an elevator coming up into the lobby from an underground parking lot two buildings away. The cars in the lot fronting the building belong to no one, and therefore no one is ever seen going in or out.

In other words, from the outside, you'd never know it's home to one of the world's most active black-ops organizations.

Sometimes the mandate is something as simple as an exfiltration of a diplomat in a dangerous situation. Then again, it could be the complex extermination of a political enemy. The one guiding criterion is that the client is either one of the U.S. government's many intelligence arms, or an intel agency of one of its allies.

When it comes to discretion, we live by the rules set by our clients. When it comes to methodology, Acme is given a very wide berth. It is the true meaning of the phrase *don't ask, don't tell.*

As I wait for Ryan's high sign that I may enter his private

office, I gaze out into the analysts' pit. The rows and rows of five-foot-high cubicles are too tall to see the heads of the analysts who oversee the missions in play. But if you listen carefully, every now and then, you can make out a word or two from the low drone that comes when a hundred or so people are muttering into headphones–giving directives, warnings, intel, or encouragement to their charges, Acme field operatives. They are our eyes and ears.

But the heart and soul of Acme is the man who will soon accept my resignation.

I look around for my heart and soul–Jack–but he's nowhere to be found.

Finally, Ryan beckons me. Strapped to the small of my back is Acme's latest standard-issue to all of our agents: a Sig Sauer P226R. I'll be turning it in, along with my resignation. There is an ache where it sits, in the small of my back. I'm sure I'm imagining it.

The one I feel in my heart hurts more. It's real, and not going away anytime soon.

As I enter, Ryan rises from the chair behind his desk to walk over and give me a peck on the cheek. "Care to sit down?"

I shake my head.

"I thought you'd pass on the honor." Then realizing his eyes have slipped down toward my wound, he blushes. His way of compensating is to maneuver me over to the window. There is a slim greenbelt between Acme headquarters and the steady stream of cars flowing down the 405. In another hour or two, it will slow to a standstill.

Life in LA is one big traffic jam. Life in general has its detours. One of mine brought me here, to Acme.

Now it's time for me to get back on the main road in my personal journey.

I tamp down the urge to blurt out that I'm leaving, that I

will always appreciate the opportunity he gave me to prove to myself that I had a life after Carl, and more importantly, to right Carl's wrongs. Instead, I ask, "How is Tatyana's interrogation going?"

Ryan shrugs. "She's close-lipped, as expected. But that should change any moment now." He hesitates, then adds, "At least, I hope so. The cipher team has yet to crack the microdot's message. For all we know, the mission is already underway. But now that Jack is in there with her…" He shrugs. "Well, I guess we'll know soon what's going down."

"In there" refers to Club Dread, a room that's forty feet below Acme headquarters.

From street level, it can be accessed only via a secured rolling cargo door on the farthest side of the building. Should, say, a wayward FedEx driver wander in by mistake, he is greeted by a beautiful but stern woman who is trussed up in a black latex catsuit and thigh-high boots. With long, lacquered talons, she'll point to the lobby's "wall of shame," where photos of the club's "members" are shown in various states of undress and distress. She'll then hand him a flyer listing the current month's members-only punishing events, none of which are for the faint of heart.

Even if they arrive in a catatonic state (and most do), all "members" are made to sign release forms before entering the bowels of the club. It is one way in which Club Dread LLC gets by the country's annoying little executive order that ensures "lawful interrogations" and does away with extraordinary renditions of captured terrorists.

In any event, oopsies happen all the time (make that every time), and most of the members leave in body bags, through a very long, very dark tunnel just wide enough for a van that can carry a body or two.

The tunnel ends somewhere on the other side of the Pacific Coast Highway.

Welcome to the club, Tatyana.

On a more jovial note, Club Dread is where Acme holds its Christmas party. And during Halloween, it's decked out as a haunted house. In our business, gallows humor abounds.

"Jack mentioned he has a history with Tatyana," I murmur casually.

"You could say that." To cover his wince, Ryan pretends to be fixated on a sixteen-wheeler honking its air horn at a Porsche Boxster that just cut it off.

The fact that I don't say any more tells him that Jack hasn't divulged the circumstances of their past run-ins. The fact that Ryan feels it is Jack's place to tell me is implied by what he doesn't say.

I won't be able to convince him otherwise.

The anger wells up in me. I am not jealous, I'm tired–of the secrets, and the deliberate diversions from what could be said, but isn't.

I've proven my ability to be trusted. I've been through hell and back again for Acme.

And yet, here I am, on a "need to know" basis.

To hell with that.

I take both of Ryan's hands in mine and smile sweetly at him. "I'm here to turn in my notice."

His eyes widen, then contract as the reality of my declaration sets in. Only for a moment do they alight on the sandy shoal of disbelief before a churning tidal wave of doubt lifts them up and pitches them into the depths of possibility.

His teary blink tells me that it has finally landed with a thump, on the sea floor of acceptance.

Needless to say, I am flattered when he declares, "I wish you'd reconsider. Your leaving will be a great loss to Acme."

"I'm humbled that you'd think so. But I've done what I set out to do–avenge the demise of my marriage." Before he has a chance to argue otherwise, I add, "The fact that Carl was, in fact, the enemy doesn't alter my decision. His death last month gave me the vengeance I needed. It allows me to get on with the rest of my life–with my family."

Yes, they were his family, too. But you choose what you lose and pay the price, no matter how dear to you, or to those you profess to love.

And actions speak louder than words.

Ryan looks down at our entwined fingers and sighs. "You'll always be welcome to come back."

I sigh. "I'm flattered, and I appreciate your saying so. But seriously, Ryan, don't hold your breath," I chuckle.

I wish he'd laugh, too, but he doesn't. Instead, he lowers his head.

He's going to miss me.

Well, I'll miss him too.

When finally he gets ahold of himself, he raises his head and his eyes seek out mine. Very seriously, he says, "I presume you're giving me the requisite two weeks."

"Oh!" I hadn't thought about it. I guess it's the least I owe him. "Okay, sure."

"Good, because I'll need your help in choosing–and for that matter, training–your replacement."

Wait a minute...I can be replaced?

Missed, for sure. Mourned, no doubt. But replaced?

Seeing the shocked expression on my face, he adds, "Don't worry. I'll make sure it's something that you can do between school drop-off and pick-up." He smiles.

Hey, could be worse. Ryan could have had the bright idea of assigning the task to my mission teammate, Dominic Fleming.

The interviews would have gone on forever, and the winner's training would have all happened in bed.

Worse yet, what if Ryan had asked Jack to replace me?

I shrug. "Um...yes, okay. Sure. It'll be...an honor."

For my replacement, anyway.

"Good! Then it's settled. I'll send over some dossiers, and you can comb through them. Choose the best three of the bunch, and call them in."

He holds out his hand to me, his indication that the meeting is over.

What he doesn't expect is that I take him in a bear hug instead.

I've got his arms pinned, so he can't wipe away the tears brimming in his eyes. "Allergies," he declares gruffly, but I know better.

I'm at the threshold of Ryan's office door when his phone rings. He picks it up, but doesn't say anything at first. When he does, his shock and awe come out with a shout: "How in hell did she...The transfer team–is *dead*? Where's Jack? He's..."

Ryan can't keep his eyes from seeking out mine.

What I see there sends a shiver down my spine.

I must get to Jack.

Alarms clamor through the building. Ryan rushes past me toward the elevator bank.

But by the time I get to it, the door has already closed.

Everyone else has already exited the building, through the garage elevators.

I hustle to the fire stairwell, and double-time it down the steps.

THE STAIRWELL SHOULD BE LIT, BUT IT'S AS DARK AS A TOMB. IT IS only sixteen-feet-by-sixteen-feet wide, and there are ten steps between each of the four landings, each at a quarter turn.

I'm on the second landing when I hear faint footsteps, but I can't see who's coming up the stairs. Whoever it is walks quickly and quietly.

I flatten myself against the wall. I'm glad I hadn't yet handed Ryan my Sig. Slowly, I ease it out of my back holster and into my hands, pointing it downward into the stairwell. If only I had night goggles. Instead, I'll have to use my instincts to guess when my target is close enough, and at what angle to fire.

Seconds seem like hours. She's taking her sweet time to get here, but if I listen carefully, I can hear her breathing, or the creak of a footfall, but I hold my fire.

Come to me, my little pretty…

The scrape of a heel tells me what I need to know:

She's on a step that is less than six feet below me.

If I aim downward, at a one-hundred-twenty-degree angle, I'll actually hit her heart this time.

No hesitation. *This one's for Jack, you bitch.*

The shot slams into drywall–in other words, a wall, not a body.

The next thing I know, someone grabs my ankle and jerks me hard. I topple down the steps, on my back. My arm with the hand holding the gun is twisted so that the pain forces me to drop the gun. It does, but at the very same time my knee goes up, hitting my assailant right between the legs–

"What…*the hell!*" The groan is unmistakably Jack's.

Oops.

"Oh, my God! I thought–" I pull my phone from my jacket pocket and click on the flashlight app so that we can see each other.

I may be relieved, but he seems annoyed. Seeing the look on

his face makes me angry. Why isn't he happy to see me, coming to his rescue?

Granted, the fact that I fired a gun at him may have something to do with it.

Okay, yes, that and the knee to his groin.

"What the hell are you doing?" we ask in unison.

Suddenly, light floods the stairwell. We blink in its glare. Ryan is running up the stairs. "Did Donna shoot him?"

I feel my cheeks turning red. If I had shot Jack, I'd have never lived it down.

More to the point, he wouldn't either, because he'd be dead.

Jack must be thinking the same thing because he scowls at me as he turns toward the bullet hole in the wall behind him. "If I hadn't bent down to tie my shoe at that very second, I'd be a dead man now."

For the first time, I notice that the back of Jack's shirt is bloody. "Oh, heck!" I run to the wall. No, the bullet hole is deep. It's embedded in there, somewhere. Obviously, the bullet didn't ricochet into his back.

I point to Jack's shirt. "Then, where did that come from?"

I turn to Ryan for the answer, but he looks just as shocked as me. Suddenly, Abu Nagashahi runs up the stairwell. He's dressed all in white, like a medic—but his chest is covered in blood.

Arnie Locklear, our mission team's tech-op, is right behind him—and he's also dripping blood, like an escapee from a haunted house.

No more guessing games. Angrily, Ryan and I say in unison, "Will someone please tell me what the hell is going on here?"

Abu and Arnie keep mum, but their eyes shift toward Jack. Reluctantly, he mutters, "We let Tatyana get away...on purpose."

Ryan slams the wall with his fist.

Frankly, I'd be hitting Jack's nose. I stare at him. "After what she did to me–not to mention whatever grudge you're holding against her, why the hell would you do that?"

"She wouldn't break and give us what we needed–where the next terrorist act will take place, and who is carrying it off," Jack insists. "Now that she's on the loose, she'll lead us to her client."

"Are you sure she didn't suspect anything?" Ryan growls.

"I doubt it," Jack declares. "Not from the way we worked her over first."

Still in shock, I cross my arms at my chest. "So, she's chained to a bench, and her cuffs miraculously fall off?"

"We gave her the opportunity to do it," Arnie explains. "We made it possible for her to steal Abu's gun. She shot him with it, grabbed the cuff keys, then Jack and I came into the room. She shot us, too." He hesitates before adding proudly, "So that she thought she was getting away with it, I loaded the gun with fake blood pellets."

Ryan shakes his head in disbelief. "Now that she's on the loose, how are we going to find her?"

"While she was out cold, we embedded a GPS chip inside of her," Jack explains. "Dr. Fleishman got the idea when he…well, when he stitched you up."

"How nice to hear I was his inspiration," I mutter.

Ryan turns to me. "Donna, I presume I can trust you to keep all you've heard here on the QT?"

He asks this because he knows that President Lee Chiffray sometimes summons me for off-the-record intel recaps. Despite my insistence to Ryan that Lee and I have gone our separate ways, the years Ryan has spent in our line of work are reason enough for him to be paranoid about what tales others tell out of school.

Still, it pisses me off that he thinks he has to ask. I shake my head angrily. "What's wrong, Ryan? Are you concerned that my resignation means that I'll be screaming Acme's failures from the rooftop?"

"No, not at all." He frowns. "I'm just stating protocol. It's in the manual."

"Are you implying that I've never read the Acme manual?"

"Read it? Possibly. Follow it?" Ryan's eyes narrow. "That's another story."

"I know one thing that's in the manual, under 'resignation protocol.'" I look down at the Sig in my hand. It's been at my side through more dangerous missions than I can count. Slowly, I reach my thumb up and decock it. I ease the same thumb down to the release button and clear the magazine. As I take one more deep breath, I yank the slide back to clear the last round from the chamber, and lock the slide open.

I exhale as I hold out both hands to Ryan. One holds the gun. In the other, I offer him the magazine and stray round.

For the longest moment, he stares down at them. Finally, he waves my hands away. We are eye to eye as he murmurs, "Keep it. Your instincts are unique, to say the least. If there's another Donna Stone out there, Acme wants her on its side."

This is his way of kissing and making up.

For Jack's sake, I hope his is better.

4

Make Your Silverware Gleam Again!

When was the last time you checked the condition of your silver? The first Bush was in office, right?

Ha, thought so!

Listen here, missy: no matter how much time and effort you've spent hunting down and dickering over pieces of Tiffany & Co. Feather Edge sterling flatware, should your guests blanch visibly at the thought of sticking one of your pretty little festooned teaspoons in their mouths, you can stick a fork in your reputation because, honey— it is done.

And no need to worry about breathing in toxic fumes from cleaners made of harsh chemicals. To restore your precious pieces to their former glory, consider polishing organically! All you need is a pot large enough to hold your silver, filled with water no more than two inches from the top; baking soda; aluminum foil; and a stove.

First, put the pot of water on the stove, and bring it to a boil. Next, line the bottom of the pot with a piece of tin foil. (Be careful not to scald yourself!) Now, load in your silver, piece by piece, onto the tin foil. (Again, don't burn yourself!)

Shake baking soda over it all. Yes, it will bubble and foam and smell like rotten eggs. It isn't magic, but a chemical reaction. The tin foil draws the tarnish away from your cherished flatware. Keep sprinkling the baking soda until all the silver is clean, or when it no longer bubbles.

Finally, remove the silver. Any leftover tarnished spots can be removed by rubbing with a soft cloth.

One last little note: So that you don't look like a witch hovering over a caldron, don't wear black, let alone a pointed hat, no matter what kind of bad-hair day you may be having.

And by the way, a little makeup wouldn't hurt either.

"You could have told me the game plan," I state flatly to Jack.

True to his word, we're sharing lunch at a sunny corner table in Duke's Malibu, the best beachside boîte on the Pacific Coast Highway.

If we didn't have to pick up the kids in a couple of hours, no doubt he'd be on his second scotch, and I'd be on my third wine. Despite the lack of any excuse to lose our cool, it's obvious to both of us that we'll leave lunch with our stomachs in knots, and our anxiety will have nothing to do with the richness of Duke's Tahitian shrimp and poke tacos.

He shrugs. "I told you—everything about this mission is on a need-to-know basis."

"Didn't my bullet hole on the stairwell make it pretty obvious that I should have been clued in?"

He honors me with a grudging nod. "In hindsight, yes. But what we did was a spur-of-the-moment decision."

I snort loud enough that patrons at three other tables stare at us. I raise my glass at them with a smile, but through gritted teeth, I growl, "I guess you forgot to put Ryan on that short list."

Jack's eyes narrow. "He was tied up at the time—with you, if memory serves."

"Ha! Ryan. He acts as if the minute I turn in my Sig, I'll be opening my yap to everyone about my good old days at Acme." I grab a roll from the basket in the middle of the table. I'm holding it so tightly that it's crumbling in my fist. "If he thinks so little of me, why does he want me to vet my replacement?"

"Beats me." Jack downs his scotch, and signals our waitress for another. "You know, Donna, you can always tell him you've changed your mind and can't take the time to do it."

"No! …I mean…I'd feel awful if I left him short-handed."

The smirk on his face indicates he's guessed my real reason for agreeing to do so: no one wants to believe they can be replaced. But should that day come, it's better that you have the opportunity to choose your successor.

At least, that way, you're assured that you're missed.

He chuckles. "I get it. You're pulling a Teddy Roosevelt."

"What the hell does that mean?"

He leans in and whispers, "It means you've opened your yap so many times about walking away once Carl was finally out of the picture, now that it's finally happened, you feel you can't take it back."

"Who says I want to take it back?" My voice is shaking, but I can't help it.

"Admit it. You love what we do."

"Love is a pretty strong word, and certainly not one I'd use to describe how I feel about our gig." Thrilling, for sure. Challenging, no doubt about it. Heart-stopping? Yes, on more than one occasion.

Which brings up the real bone I have to pick with him.

"Living the rest of my life in danger was never my end game. But, apparently, it's yours."

His eyes darken. "You want me to retire too."

"Of course I do!" I crumble the bread roll in front of me. "And frankly, I thought you did too."

"Unlike you, my dear Mrs. Stone, I've got some unfinished business to complete under my current job title."

It's my turn to sneer. "I presume you mean the delectable Tatyana Zakharov."

He frowns. "The last thing you need to be is jealous."

"Ha! Don't flatter yourself." I toss the breadcrumbs back into the basket. "I guess it's too much to presume you're avenging her attack on me."

He waits until the waitress puts a fresh drink in front of him before declaring, "It may surprise you to know that you're not too far off from the truth."

"Then why haven't I heard about her before now?"

"Because I assumed she was dead."

"Obviously, she's got nine lives, like a cat." I take his hand in mine. "Look, with all we've been through, don't you think it's time I know how she fits into all of this?"

"Under normal circumstances, yes. But now that she's part of our–I mean *my* latest mission–"

I pull my hand away from his. "Oh. I see." I see that this is how it will be from now on. I see that there will always be things that Jack will keep from me.

At least, as long as he stays with Acme.

I grab my purse and stand up.

He looks up, surprised. "We ordered dessert, remember?"

"I can't afford it, either financially or physically. I'm no longer a honey pot. I won't be running off extra calories anytime soon."

"I thought it was exactly what all you housewives do–you know, jog, or go to the gym, or to a yoga class."

"Shows you how little you know about 'us housewives.'" I toss down a few twenties and head for the door.

"Wait! Lunch was on me," he insists.

He's got a point. I grab the bills and stuff them back into my wallet. "Sure, okay–now that you're the sole breadwinner of the family."

But that doesn't mean I'm waiting around until he finishes dessert.

I'm moving on–with or without him.

TO SAY THAT JACK AND I HAVE YET TO KISS AND MAKE UP IS AN understatement. In fact, in the past forty-eight hours, he's made no reference to our argument, which only makes me angrier.

I show my hurt with a cold shoulder to every statement he makes to me, from yesterday morning's "Hope you have a great day, honey," (My silence speaks volumes) to last night's "Pass the salt, please." (I let one of the kids do it instead.)

More to the point, my bird finger shows him exactly what I think of his happy-pappy platitudes.

It takes him all day to take the hint and get out of my hair. As he goes out for his daily jog, he looks back at me through the window, only to see me stick out my tongue at him.

Incredulous that I'd stoop so low, he chuckles as he trots down the street.

Oh yeah? Well, we'll see who has the last laugh.

I WAIT UNTIL HE'S GONE A COUPLE OF MOMENTS BEFORE LOGGING onto his computer–

Um…what the heck? The password isn't working…

Why, that son of a bitch! He's changed it!

Okay, if it's not my measurements, what else can it be?

I try my birthdate–not my real one, but the one he thinks is correct.

Nothing.

Now I try my real birthdate.

Again, nothing.

The day we met. Our address. The day we first made love.

Nothing. Nothing. Nothing.

Suddenly, it hits me: his world no longer revolves around me!

Jack Craig has crossed a serious line.

At the very least, we could have both kept up the pretense that he was sticking to protocol. I would have respected him for doing so, and especially had he pretended I'd somehow become clairvoyant and insightful when making out-of-the-blue declaratory statements about That Mission That We Dare Not Speak Of.

There's nothing left for me to do but sulk.

Should that mean his computer somehow leaps off the table and onto the floor, so be it. When he asks how it happened, I'll act innocent. Can I help it that the screen somehow got smeared with peanut butter, and our dogs, Lassie and Rin Tin Tin, knocked it over as they licked it clean?

An hour later when he returns, I'm upstairs, busily cleaning out a closet. Even from that corner of the house I can hear his curses when he sees his cracked laptop screen.

Poor Lassie and Rin Tin Tin scurry out the dog door.

⌖

It hurts that Jack so completely ignores my sullenness!

He even shrugs off the crack in his computer screen. "Time for a new MacBook anyway," he declares blithely. "I'll ask Ryan to acquisition one."

At the same time, he treats me as if I'm some petulant child who will forgive and forget because he's brought home bonbons (my favorite, dark chocolate-covered almonds) or some trinket that commemorates our last mission together (in this case, a tiny diamond-encased casket for my charm bracelet).

Talk about rubbing salt in the wound.

Under normal circumstances, we'd have shared a laugh, a kiss, a night of lovemaking. And afterward, he'd beckon me into a leisurely shower that would have left us soaped up, sexed up, puckered-up and rosy, and eventually squeaky-clean.

But now, as I pass Jack in the shower and he teasingly suggests that I join him, my answer is a long, lingering kiss–

Right before I reach in and turn the shower's handle to freezing cold.

His curses aren't exactly terms of endearment, but at least he no longer can pretend he doesn't know where we stand.

Or where we sleep, for that matter.

He slams the door to the guest room.

I already miss him, but before we kiss and make up, he's got to show me a little respect, some real contrition, and give up at least a pound of flesh.

As for Ryan, he's wasted no time in linking me to Acme's secure cloud that holds the dossiers of my possible replacements.

I may think I'm irreplaceable, but considering that there are seventy-two of them, it's obvious he's got a very different opinion.

As I flip through the dossiers, I delete the ones that for any reason don't meet all four very specific criteria.

My first mandate is that she must be a crack shot, and already highly skilled in tactical maneuvers and weaponry. I don't have time to teach her how to point a gun and squeeze a trigger, let alone break a man's neck. And next, whereas I'll give strong consideration to someone with military experience, I won't discount those applicants with academic or tech backgrounds, acting experience, or street cred.

(Yes, doing time won't be a deterrent, either–depending on the circumstances that put her in the clink, and why the parole board deems her reformed enough to be released back into society.)

This alone knocks twelve of the candidates out of the box, six of which have never held a gun in their lives. Considering that a large part of my job is exterminations, I can't understand why Ryan included them in the mix. Was it because they wrote a great personal essay? My God, this isn't a college application!

A first kill is never easy. Very few of us can turn off that compassionate side of ourselves. Whether you've sliced a jugular vein, put a bullet in someone's heart or given them just enough poison to watch them gasp at the realization of their last breath, it's not easy watching another human being die.

Which brings me to my second mandate. It's much better that a sparrow has no emotional attachments. Quickly, I delete another twenty-four files–those with husbands, fiancés, and long-term lovers. I mean, let's face it. Even if the man in her life is aware of what she does for a living, a man is lying if he declares it doesn't bother him that she's sleeping with the enemy.

And for the clueless significant other, it's inevitable that someday he'll find out that part of her job description is whore and killer–both of which can be deal breakers in any relationship, especially if his mom gets wind of it.

Having a license to kill puts your odds of survival at an all-time low. The fact that you don't have a man in your life doesn't mean you don't have other very important attachments. The next to be eliminated are those candidates with children and living parents–those who you love dearly who will grieve your all but inevitable tragic demise. Another eleven dossiers hit the trash. Someday, these women will thank me.

The third mandate is that you be physically fit, because the job is more strenuous than most people might presume. Sorry, ladies, I'm not running a fitness boot camp for the well intentioned. I'm seeking those who are ready and able to fill my shoes–a cross-training-slash-hollow stiletto heeled hybrid with a poison-dart tip. The flatfooted and fainthearted need not apply.

In that regard, I can immediately ditch nine of the dossiers because the women are either too thin (not all catwalks are fashion runways), too thick (there will be many tight squeezes–another reason why sometimes a female is needed on a mission), or has too many miles on her (if she's got a cracker-jack mind, promote her to mission control. No need to assure she ends up with cracked ribs), or too dumb (this variety also includes quite a few brunettes).

I also eliminate the eight trust fund babies and the socialites. Acme isn't a charity or a hobby, thank you very much.

And last but not least, no matter what her last gig, there has to be some demonstration that she can think on her feet, and certainly out of the box. For that matter, it would help if she doesn't panic when she's out on a ledge.

That being said, any candidate who admitted on her application that she's afraid of either fire, water, heights, tight spaces, the sight of blood, or getting naked and doing the nasty when the situation calls for it is deleted too.

Okay, now, I'm down to only three possible candidates:

The first is Tally Lloyd, a tall, gorgeous brunette who also happens to be a former Marine Corps pilot, as was her father, and his father before him. In fact, she had an ancestor who stormed the shores of Tripoli. Her last tour of duty put her in Marja, Afghanistan. Since then, she's worked at the DOD as an aviation analyst. From the way her application reads, she's already bored of being a desk jockey. Who can blame her, after the adrenaline rush of dropping a six-pack of five-hundred-pound Mark 82's from an AV 8B Harrier jet on Taliban rebels?

Another likely candidate is Jenny McDougal. For the past eight years, she's worked in the Intelligence division of the CIA as a terrorism analyst. Whereas she's a desk jockey, her dossier also points out that she is an excellent marksman, speaks Mandarin and three other Chinese dialects, and is a skilled in martial arts.

Oddly, no picture of Jenny is included. That's okay. I'm sure it's just some oversight.

The final prospect is Pucci Tedeschi (formerly Luciana Giovanni), a sultry New Jersey housewife who went gaga over a big handsome lug who just so happened to be a made man with the Carducci Syndicate. Unfortunately, her husband, Knuckles Giovanni, was also a sick pedophile. When Pucci caught him jumping into the bunk bed of her ten-year-old little sister, she nailed him with one shot to the heart, from a distance of fifty feet. Thank goodness the kid never woke up, not even as Pucci dragged Knuckles' body out of the room.

At her hearing, she refused to let the girl speak on her behalf. She was too worried that the poor kid would be scarred for life. With no evidence to back up her claim, she was facing first-degree manslaughter until she cut a deal with the district attorney that put her in Witness Protection. At the same time, a raid on Carducci footmen put several of them behind bars with murder raps. Did she turn state's evidence? Only she, her priest, and her hairdresser know for sure.

Ryan is quick to get on the line when he hears I'm on the other end. "So, does anyone measure up?"

I laugh uneasily. "That's a loaded question, and you know it."

"By that, I mean in your mind. If you ask me, it's a foregone conclusion that there's only one Donna Stone."

"Well, thank you for that." I cough in order to pretend that he didn't make me choke up. "In fact, I've got three possibilities. How would you like me to proceed?"

"Why don't you start with the least likely? That way, if she lives up to your expectations, you can put her on ice as you vet the other two. Better to have more choices than less."

"Good point." I hesitate, then ask, "Is the winner being considered for the current mission?"

There's a long pause. Finally: "Despite the fact that I could use all hands on deck, I doubt your replacement will be up to speed in time to do us any good."

Talk about a guilt trip.

To mitigate the sting, I send a secure email to the candidate I feel is least likely to be chosen, Pucci. It reads:

Dear Ms. Tedeschi,

Your application has made it to the next step of Acme's acceptance process, skills assessment. With that in mind, arrangements are being made for you to join me here, the day after tomorrow. I look forward to meeting you then.

D. Stone

In the twenty minutes it takes to ready myself for my next task–a meeting with Penelope to go over the details of the dance–I've already received a reply from Pucci. It's short and sweet:

With relish. –PT

I've been retired just three days, fourteen hours, and six minutes, but it seems like a lifetime.

5

Selecting the Perfect Venue

Yes, everyone loves visiting you in your quaint little abode. (In all honesty, it's a careworn hovel—but then again, it's sooooo you!) But let's face it: there are times when your next soirée should be held somewhere more accommodating. (As in, a place where your neighbors won't so readily call your local police department's SWAT team.)

That being said, when, how, and where should you choose your next venue? Here are three easy-peasy answers to this question:

- *Answer #1: Let your theme lead the way. For example, if you're throwing a Tarts and Vicars party, rent out a church reception space! (Warning: This is truly the worst place to have an orgy. That being said, don't let your guests use the confessionals or the altar for making out or getting it on.)*
- *Answer #2: By all means, make it work within your budget. If your budget is unlimited, rent a hotel rooftop and let the champagne flow. However, if you have next to*

nil in your party till, consider a free park, where you can choose from a slew of event themes, including "Roaring Twenties Croquet Party," with real bathtub gin (again, a cost-saver if you make it yourself), retro duds (second-hand store couture) and the croquet set your grandma bought you when you were ten. (Helpful Hint: if you can't shoo away the local bench bum with your mallet, place a sign on him that says, "A LOOK INTO THE FUTURE: THE 1930s!")

- *Answer #3: Book your space on the day the event manager is willing to give it away. The fact that it's a sex dungeon and he's been tipped off that there will be a raid on that night shouldn't deter you from choosing it as the location of your knitting club's annual holiday party. Just be ready to explain that the sweaters being exchanged in the Secret Santa contest aren't straightjackets, and the circular knitting needles aren't cock rings.*

"FANCY SCHMANCY!" I GIVE A LOW WHISTLE AT OUR surroundings–the lobby of Beverly Hills' newest hotel, the Savoy. "So, why are we here again?" I ask Penelope.

She arches a brow. "Didn't you read my memo?"

"Yeah…um…sure." No, not really. Frankly, I've been avoiding all of her texts and emails, which are usually marked EMERGENCY!!!!!

As if. Seriously, this woman needs a life.

Until she figures this out, I'll play along, in the hope that it buys me the goodwill my children will need as long as we stay in Hilldale.

"Then I'm sure you'll find this handy." Penelope reaches into her valise and hands me a three-inch binder. It's so heavy that my hand drops practically to my knees. "It's the prom committee handbook you were supposed to pick up three days ago. Remember? You can thank me later. We'll sit over there to go over the fine points of your task." She points toward the middle of the lobby, where settees surround a gushing fountain. An exquisite glass sculpture graces each table. I recognize the pieces as the work of Nikolas Weinstein.

Yep, fancy schmancy, for sure.

She chooses a settee that faces the six glass elevator banks. Its publicist is touting it as the latest and greatest Mecca for stars behaving badly. The fact that it's almost an hour out of our way for something that could have taken a phone call means nothing to her. I've no doubt that Penelope arranged for us to meet here just so that she can have a few star sightings to tell the rest of her coven.

As if by magic, a waitress appears. She is pushing a full deluxe tea service for two, with a three-tiered tray. The bottom tier is filled with sandwiches made of artisan breads, filled with savory delights, and cut into bite-sized wedges. The middle tier has pastries, scones and cupcakes, while the top tier alternates between petit fours and handmade chocolates.

Noting my look of surprise, Penelope waves it away. "Not to worry, Donna. It's on the PTA–part of the dance planning budget."

After the woman pours our selections–chai for me, and Morgentau for Penelope, she presents the bill to Penelope, who points at me. "Sign it, okay? It's part of your job as the committee chair."

I nod and scrawl my Jane Hancock.

"And while you're at it, you should sign your volunteer contract, too." She slides out a manila envelope from the front of the binder.

I eye it suspiciously. "Since when do volunteers have to sign a contract?"

"Only the event chairs have to do it. If you had attended more PTA meetings, you'd know it's common procedure now. Oh, don't worry, Donna! It's quite simple and straightforward. Frankly, the PTA board has found it to be the best incentive for the volunteers to follow through on their commitments. It seems that everyone likes the title, the prestige, and the accolades, but no one likes to do the dirty work."

I open the envelope. The damn thing is four pages long, all in small type.

I hesitate, but only for a moment–until I remember why I'm here: so that others don't snicker behind my children's backs.

As I sign it, I mutter, "I presume you and the rest of the PTA board have signed one of these, too."

Penelope's head snaps back so fast that I'm surprised she doesn't have whiplash. "Hell, no! I'm no fool."

Apparently the court jester's role is all mine.

I take the binder and heave it onto the table in front of us. It lands with a thud. I notice that its five pounds of pages are separated by six dividers labeled VENUE, TICKETS, PROMOTION, ENTERTAINMENT, REFRESHMENTS, and SECURITY.

So far, a piece of cupcake. Soaked in brandy, in fact. Here's hoping it makes the rest of what she has to say go down easier.

I take a bite before complimenting her. "Well, it certainly looks as if you've done your homework."

"You mean, I've done *your* homework for you," she retorts.

Whatev. "I appreciate your two years of experience in planning the event." Duh, lady. *In the middle school gym.* It's why the gig is a no-brainer.

"Ha! Thought so! You never even opened my memo!" She shakes her head as she clicks her tongue.

I point to the book. "This isn't a 'memo.' It's a doorstop."

She shrugs. "Donna, you've got to trust me on the seriousness of this event. After all, I'm doing my bit to nudge your acceptance back into polite society."

"Oh? Pray tell, what exactly does that mean?" The advantage to still being on Acme's clock means I can access the security feed of many places. Take this hotel, for instance. By hacking into the reservations manifest, I noted that the eighth floor has only six of its ten guest rooms occupied, all at the end closest to the elevator. Should I elect to torture Penelope for any reason (and that seems likelier by the second), no one would hear her begging for mercy as I waterboard her in the suite's Jacuzzi tub, which boasts a Moen Velocity vertical spa oil-rubbed rainshower head.

Penelope opens a compact in order to check her lipstick. "Admit it, Donna. Haven't you noticed the chill in the air when you're in the presence of the other mothers?"

"Come to think of it, I have." I cock my head to one side. "Perhaps it has something to do with all the nasty rumors being circulated about me."

At first, Penelope feigns shock. But seeing my frown, she shrugs. "I must admit, I've heard them too."

"Heard them, or spread them?" With a click of an iPhone button, I can book Room Eight-Sixteen, touted on the Savoy's website as "a suite that affords guests the level of privacy found only in the highest reaches of power. Because of our patented 'Walls of Silence' not a peep can be heard, either from within, or those seeking the quietest venues for intimacy…"

Good to know. Should Penelope make me any angrier than I already am, I'll be testing that claim with all sorts of little tricks that are used at Club Dread.

"Puh-*leeze*, Donna! You know me better than that." Penelope bats her eyes at warp speed, which causes one of her false lashes to flutter onto her cheek. "If anything, I've been making excuses for–I mean, *standing up* for you. Considering all the times the SWAT team has shown up at your place, it hasn't been easy tamping down the rumors that you abetted a terrorist." As she pats the lash back into place, she continues, "My gawd, anyone who knows you realizes you're not some sort of evil mastermind. If anything, you're naïve when it comes to men."

"Me–*naïve*?" Suddenly, I look forward to testing the claim that the Savoy suite's bidet has "Niagara-force cleansing power" by holding Penelope's head in the bowl for a good four to five minutes.

"Well, duh–*yeah*!" Penelope takes a dainty bite of asparagus. "You marry a man who stays away for so long that half the neighborhood thinks you've lied about being married in the first place, and the other half presumes that you're such a lousy lay that you drove him off."

"Is that so? And which side did you take?"

"I was in the Runaway Hub Club," she insists emphatically.

I murmur, "Founding member, I presume."

Involuntarily, she nods. Suddenly realizing she's just copped to it, she says defensively, "What else could it be? To start with, you're not that good of a liar. Secondly, since your kids all look as if they came from the same father, I just assumed he ran away because you were a lousy lay." She leans in conspiratorially. "But then, when that hunk, Jack Craig, shows up claiming to be him, all bets were off."

"Sorry we ruined everyone's fun," I say dryly.

"Oh, trust me, a whole new betting pool began when the news broke that he wasn't the elusive Mr. Stone after all. You'll be happy to learn that no one ever won the pot on that one."

"What was it for?"

"How long he'd stick around. That's because none of the bets went beyond the first year."

The crest of my pinky ring is hollowed out and filled with enough aconite to bring on a fatal heart attack. If I tap on the band's center diamond gem, a tiny needle pops out. One prick with it and Penelope is artisan toast.

I'm still contemplating the odds of the movement being caught on the hotel's security camera when she adds, "If I haven't said so before, let me assure you that I appreciate that you've taken on this arduous task. No one else had the gumption, and heaven knows, had I lateraled it to either Hayley or Tiffy, it would have been botched for sure."

"Gee…thanks for saying so."

"I mean it!" Penelope insists. "I figure that anyone who can juggle two handsome men who both insist they're her husband–not to mention booty calls with President Chiffray–must be great at time management…or something."

"Let me assure you–and by proxy, the rest of Hilldale–that the president and I are merely friends." Some sleight of hand with the teapot will give me the coverage I need to drop the Sux in her cuppa. "May I pour you some more?"

To my disappointment, she declines my offer with a wave of her hand. "I'll admit it, Donna, I went overboard in compiling all my notes from past dances, but considering it's being held here–"

I pause, teapot in hand. "You want the dance to take place here?" I look around at the Savoy's opulent setting. "But…why?"

Penelope holds her nose. "Who wants to dance in a smelly old gym? My son–that is, our sons, deserve a more fitting setting for their very first prom! Cheever's new girlfriend, Gabrielle, is sure to be impressed."

Ah, so that's why we're here. Talk about being a helicopter parent.

I drop my teacup back onto its saucer. "Penelope, using the Savoy's ballroom has got to cost an arm and a leg!"

"You're wrong about that. The place is so new that right now, they're begging to have events here," she declares smugly. "As a matter of fact, I pummeled the hotel manager, Henry Massey, so hard over the contract, he was practically in tears." She hesitates. "Of course, there are some strings attached."

"For example?"

Delicately, she glazes a scone with apricot jam. "Well...there is the tiny little issue of thirty guaranteed room rentals."

I choke on my cupcake. "Even a closet here has to go for, what, four hundred dollars a night?"

She frowns. "Okay, yes, the rack rate starts at five-hundred-and-thirty dollars. But I figure the kids can sleep four to a room–"

"A class sleepover, here at the Savoy? Are you crazy? No way! Not with all those raging hormones!"

She slumps into her tufted throne. "Calm down, Donna. We're not talking coed dorms. And, of course, there will be an adult chaperone on each floor."

Adamantly, I shake my head. "I don't know of a parent who would consent to it!"

"No? If you'd taken the time to open 'the doorstop,' as you so caustically call it, you'd discover that last week's parent survey proves you're wrong. Or, as one parent wrote, 'I'll do anything for one night away from my little pituitary gland in heat.'"

"Oh, great. So tell me: have any of the parents volunteered to chaperone?"

She rolls her eyes. "Are you kidding? Unlike you, none of

these women are helicopter parents. They want their children to have new experiences–"

Like, say, jumping off balconies, or raiding mini-bars? Or playing Truth or Dare?

"–to spread their wings–"

For the girls, hopefully not their legs, too.

"–and to have the most memorable night of their young lives!"

I've no doubt it will be that, and more, especially when the hotel calls the cops and the kids do their very first perp walk.

When she realizes that I'm not buying her malarkey, she shrugs. "Look Donna, some parents will pay through the nose for a night without their kids around. Not only will we earn enough to cover the event's expenses, we'll double the PTA's revenue from last year."

I nod slowly. Look at it this way: should any of their little scholars pull a fast one, they'll have me to thank for saving their kid's ass. It'll be great to have a few chits to call in.

"It won't exactly be a cakewalk. For example, we'll have to keep a very close watch on *die kinder*, what with all the alcohol floating around," Penelope points out.

"Alcohol? But of course we won't allow the kids to spike the punch!"

"How quaint, but no one said anything about 'spiking the punch!' I'm talking about the minimum amounts of liquor, beer and wine purchases that are written into the contract."

I wince. "Can the hotel at least leave it in bottles, so that the PTA can resell it?" I'm sure the parents will need a swig or two after they get the bill for damages to the rooms.

She sighs mightily. "Must I ask for everything? I'll let you negotiate that niggling detail with Henry." She nods toward the reception desk at a tall, courtly gentleman with a pencil-thin mustache. He's perhaps in his mid-forties, and buff beneath his custom double-breasted Brioni suit.

Seeing us, he rolls his eyes. Yep, Penelope left a lasting impression.

To sweeten her wave, Penelope licks her lips seductively.

Finally he waves back. If anyone got pummeled, it was her. No doubt, she enjoyed every minute of it.

"Seriously, Penelope, maybe it's not too late to get out of this deal."

Her eyes narrow like tractor beams. "You're wrong. Your signature just now was the PTA's co-signature. We are locked and loaded."

This new little bombshell makes my trigger finger itchy. To tamp down the urge to reach for my gun, I use the finger to motion her closer. When only she can hear me, I whisper, "You owe me big time for this. And by that, I mean no more innuendoes about my love life. Do you understand, Penelope Bing?"

Maybe it's the way I hold my head high and proud. Or perhaps it's the look in my eyes. Or maybe it's the fact that I'm holding her wrist in such a way that she knows one little move will snap it, like a twig. In any case, she nods and mumbles, "I…promise."

Slowly, I release her wrist. "Good! Glad we understand each other. I'll call Henry later this week, to set up an appointment–alone."

She frowns, but at least she knows better than to argue with me.

I hold up one hand and start counting down fingers. "As for chaperones, you and I will be there, so that's two. I presume Hayley is volunteering, too–"

"Hardly! Do you remember what happened the last time Hayley was around so much alcohol?"

I wince. "The father-daughter dance, two years ago? Actually, it was pot, not alcohol." I take a closer look at her face. "If it's any consolation, your eyebrows grew in nicely after the flash fire."

"Thank you." The way she's smiling reminds me of a feral cat. "Still, her substance abuse issues are not something we'll want to test on the big night."

"Agreed. Okay then, it'll be you, me, and Tiffy, of course–"

Penelope frowns. "Fortunately for her, if not for us, she and the mister are taking a much-needed couples getaway. In fact, I recommended Fantasy Island to them."

I shudder at the thought. It might have been where Penelope got her groove back–with and without her husband, Peter. Still, it would have been far off my bucket list, what with the pygmies and their poison darts and the slave trafficking, the place has bad mojo. Considering that Tiffy's marriage has more downs than it has ups, a place with less going on is certainly in order.

"At the very least, we can count on Peter," I insist.

Penelope shakes her head. "Wrong. He claims he's going hunting with his pals that weekend."

I've seen Peter when he's on the hunt. It's usually in a bar, where he can prey on two-legged, large-breasted birds perched on five-inch heels and sipping fruity drinks out of large glasses with tiny umbrellas in them.

"Speaking of husbands, I presume at least one of yours will be here–Jack, for instance?" Penelope practically salivates at the thought.

I shrug. "Lately, he's been working nights, so we shouldn't count on it." She need not know that his dance card might already be filled with whatever terrorists may be on the loose between here and New York.

"'Working late?' How…original." She tries to hide her smirk

by munching a sandwich wedge, but we both know what she's thinking.

Well, she's wrong. Jack is nothing like Peter. He's sweet, and loyal and loving and hardworking–

Soon, with a new partner.

I'd prick Penelope with the Sux if it weren't for the fact that so far she's the only other chaperone on the big night. Lucky us.

Lucky me.

6

Entertaining on a Budget

Few of us have a billionaire's budget for parties, or can write off our parties as business expenses. Just because your own measly bank account falls somewhere between barely there and nonexistent doesn't mean you can't show your nearest and dearest a good time. Here's how to slash your budget without cutting corners:

First, invite others to bring the food. Gauche, you say? Not if you make it part of the fun–say, give a prize for "Best Dessert" or "Best Appetizer" or "Best Main Dish."

Of course, every dish gets a prize–proof yet again that you only hang with winners!

(And for those who show up empty-handed: they are stripped naked, collared, and chained to a wall, where they must beg for scraps from those who followed the rules.)

Next, make your guests the entertainment. Have the one with the best musical taste play deejay. Better yet, invite musicians and singers, and encourage them to jam. Or stage a live reading of a book or play. A good time will be had by all! (And if you're smart, you'll charge admission in order to fatten your bank account.)

Last, but not least, make it a no-host bar. Yes, people will actually pay for booze–or they'll BYOB, in which case, feel free to charge a corkage fee. Cha-CHING!

"OH, MY GOD, DONNA! BLACKENED SALMON SANDWICHES WITH fried green tomatoes? And your world famous apricot brandy pound cake? I'm in heaven!" Emma Honeycutt hands me her six-week-old son, Nicky, as she digs into one of the sandwiches with both hands.

Acme's ComInt manager has been on maternity leave for about six weeks. I came bearing a picnic basket because I figured–correctly, as it turns out–that, by now, the mind-numbing joy of holding her newborn son has finally worn off, and she's ready for a little adult company.

Don't get me wrong. Taking care of a newborn baby is no prance through the posies. Nicky–formally christened Nikola Franklin, in homage of two of the world's greatest technological visionaries, Nikola Tesla and Benjamin Franklin–has just now locked into a sleep pattern that allows his parents a little shut-eye. That being said, a day in which the highlights are breast-feeding, diaper duty, laundry, grocery shopping, and keeping house in the two-bedroom apartment she shares with her betrothed–Acme's very own Arnie–won't frazzle a woman who is used to tracking insurgents via satellite surveillance, providing geospatial intel to field agents, and managing Acme's crack team of cryptologists.

In other words, she's primed for some office gossip.

I know this, because I've been retired just over four days (two hours and sixteen minutes) and I'm climbing the walls.

Sadly, with Jack and me in Cold War mode, all I have to offer her is my gourmet cooking. Seeing her reaction (not to mention the boxes of cereal lining her cabinets, as Emma isn't much of a cook), I'm hopeful that it's enough of a trade-off.

The way in which she gulps down her sandwich makes me laugh. "Considering you've just had a baby, you're looking pretty svelte–at least, in all the right places."

They say that pregnant women have a certain glow. Frankly, I think the light in a new mother's eyes is even more spectacular. There is no smile wider than that of a woman who has witnessed one of her child's many firsts–be it an adoring smile, a tenuous step, or an unintelligible word.

There is no sigh as content as that of a mom who holds her sleeping baby in her arms.

And for that matter, nothing swells your heart quicker with love than when your newborn infant wraps his tiny hand around your pinky finger, the way Nicky's does now, around mine.

In fact, Emma looks happier than I've ever seen her. As I stare down into Nicky's eyes, I say a prayer of thanks that Nicky is now a part of her life.

Pre-Mama Emma had been wary of love. She approached the acceptance, respect, and adoration of others as if they were landmines that could blast through the steely armor of her disaffection that, for some unknown reason, encased her heart. The Emma who now sits in front of me is beaming with the kind of joy found in women whose hearts are open to unconditional love.

My joke about Emma's figure has her instinctively turning toward the mirror over the foyer table. A half-turn sideways allows her to scrutinize her postpartum chest. Shrugging, she mutters, "Yeah, well, I guess there's one advantage to breast-feeding. At least, Arnie thinks so. Frankly, I hate the fact that I'm stretching out my T-shirts."

"Speaking of Arnie, I guess he's excited about this latest mission, right?"

"That's putting it mildly! But he was sweating bullets while they waited for Tatyana's GPS feed to go live."

"Jack felt the same." Even as I rock back and forth on my heels with her cooing son, I widen my eyes as if I know what the hell I'm talking about.

"I'd hate to think how Ryan would have reacted if Jack's plan hadn't worked. I mean, Tatyana, of all people!"

I nod, but keep my head down as I shift Nicky into one arm so that I can cut her a nice healthy slice of the apricot brandy cake. Sliding the plate in front of her, I murmur, "Yes, of course! Then again, you know Jack's feelings about her in general."

"Tell me about it!" she exclaims through a mouthful of cake. "The history they share is something else! And to think, if Jack hadn't gone to that party with her, how much longer would it have taken us to learn about the Quorum?"

Jack was partying—with Tatyana?

Emma reaches into the fridge for a carton of milk and pours it into two short glasses. Handing one to me, she tips hers toward it so that we can toast our reunion. I'm in the middle of my sip when she adds, "So, tell me the truth—does it change how you feel about…you know…"

I can't let her in on the little secret that I don't know what the heck she's implying, so I simply shrug. "What do you think?"

"I don't know. I guess if I were you, I'd feel…betrayed." She looks closely at me.

Oh, I get it now.

I wish I'd killed Tatyana when I had the chance.

"Of course I feel betrayed," I say angrily. "I also feel…" I'm hoping my pause gives her the impression that I'm at a loss for words, so that she'll keep talking and shed some light on what the hell she means.

"Pissed. *I know.*" She pats my arm. "Heck, who wouldn't be?"

I don't think I'm too successful keeping the bitterness out of my voice as I say, "Sometimes our business makes for strange bedfellows, doesn't it?"

"You mean, he confessed about sleeping with her?" Emma's eyes open wide. "Well, look at it this way. If it hadn't been for her going after Carl, we might never have known about his role in the Quorum–"

Wait...

She went after Carl? How? When? Why?

To cover up the fact that I don't know where the hell Emma is going with this, I nod slowly.

"–not to mention what she did to Jack." Emma nods knowingly.

I want to scream, *Tell me, damn it! Just tell me...*

Instead, I take another gulp of my milk.

Emma stares at me, waiting for me to say something, so I mutter, "Well, if she leads us to her clients, we'll have our payback."

Emma frowns. "But she did, yesterday in fact. That's the beauty part."

"Oh!" My exclamation elicits a funny look from her. To cover my tracks, I add weakly, "I guess I missed that memo."

"Are you sure? I wrote it up myself. And I know Ryan had it distributed the moment the DOD confirmed it." She heads to her computer.

"*You* wrote it up? But...you're on maternity leave!"

"I've been working from home for the past two weeks now. But, of course you knew that...right?" She's clicking through emails on her computer. I watch as she halts to scan one.

"Wait…Donna, you're not copied on any of these!" She stares up at me.

Busted.

I shrug. "I thought Arnie would have mentioned that I turned in my notice–on the day Tatyana pulled her disappearing act, in fact."

She nods slowly as she takes this in.

She knows I've played her.

"I'm still on payroll," I insist. "In fact, I'm now assigned to vetting the candidates for my replacement."

"But you don't have clearance on this mission." She's not accusing me, she's just stating a fact.

"Well, to be honest…no." I take a step closer. "You said it yourself, Emma. Tatyana is the key to everything that happened in my life since Carl walked out on me. And yet, Jack won't clue me in!"

"Had you not retired, you would have been part of the mission," she points out.

"Look, I didn't even know about this Russian hussy until she waltzed in as Hardy Higginbotham's widow–and put a bullet in me!" Emma winces at the anxiety in my voice.

That only makes me all the more desperate as I add, "And now you tell me that she's the key to everything that changed my life–that she has some hold over Jack–"

"What I meant was…" She shakes her head sadly. "Look, Donna, it's not my place to tell you. I could get fired! In fact, I've said too much already."

She's right. We both know it.

"I'm sorry I misled you, Emma. It's just that Jack refuses to discuss her." I wipe away a tear. "To be honest, even if I hadn't turned in my notice, I don't know if he'd have told me how she fits into the big picture."

She nods sympathetically. "I wish I could help you, Donna.

Really, I do. But the rules—"

In unison, we sniff the air. Something smells rotten. This is no figure of speech.

In my arms, Nicky stretches, then cries.

Emma rises to take the culprit from me. "Sorry about that! My guess is that he's hungry, too." She heads down the hall. "I'll be gone for a good twenty minutes. Of course, I don't need my computer in the nursery with me." She turns around to give me a wink.

Thank you, I mouth to her.

I wait until she closes the door before I open the only file on the computer's screen.

The dossier for Tatyana Zakharov is one of the documents within it.

With one click, I'll discover how this woman changed my destiny.

THE DOSSIER IS FAIRLY SLIM. IN FACT, ACME ONLY HAS A FEW pictures of Tatyana, and the two reports are just a few pages long at best.

In the first photo, she is several years younger. In it, she's a redhead, and she's wearing a turquoise sundress and a matching wide, floppy hat. It looks as if she's stepping out of a sleek motorboat onto a dock alongside a Venetian canal.

Jack is on the motorboat too. At least he's not the man helping her off the boat while giving her the once-over. And, to his favor, he's also not one of the many men giving her admiring glances.

As I read the report attached to the photo, I understand why. Later that night, Jack was found along the canal with a bullet in his shoulder. He lost a lot of blood before a couple of good Samaritans took him to a nearby hospital. He was sent to retrieve intel at some private party.

Apparently, she was too.

The accompanying report puts it this way:

The photos enclosed herewith, obtained via public security cameras, provide formal verification to Acme Agent J. Craig's eye-witness report that Russia FSB agent Tatyana Zakharov was onsite and carried out the extermination of Irina Romanov.

A. Locklear

Jack succeeded in obtaining what he came for, but the price was precious: an innocent bystander's life. Thank goodness it wasn't his.

In the third picture of Tatyana, it's obvious that she's in Paris because she's descending in one of Charles de Gaulle Airport's famous escalator tubes. She's so gorgeous that she draws the attention of many eyes–those of strangers from some of the other tubes. Jack owns a pair of them. I spot him in a tube that seems to be ascending to the gate she must have just left.

They seem to have spotted each other. Whereas he glares at her, she smiles supremely back at him.

The last photo of Tatyana must have been taken a few moments before the last one, at a departure gate. The sign over it indicates the plane is headed to Los Angeles.

The security camera only caught her from behind. She's kissing someone, but her head is tilted so that you can't make out his face.

I don't need to see it. I already know who it is: Carl. I recognize him from his Burberry raincoat, now slung over one arm. His valise is open because of a toy jutting out of it.

A Wolverine action figure.

He'd brought it home from a trip right before Jeff's fifth birthday.

Why, that son of a bitch.

He'd been in Paris, and yet he told me he was in Chicago.

None of this should surprise me. Still, Carl's lies and betrayal sting after all these years.

The report with the photo says, simply:

Obtained via public security cameras, provide formal verification to Acme Agent J. Craig's eye-witness report that Acme Agent C. Stone conducted unauthorized contact with the suspect, Russian FSB agent Tatyana Zakharov.

E. Honeycutt

Unauthorized contact? That's putting it mildly.

Well, at least now I understand what Jack meant when he said he has some unfinished business to take care of before he can walk away from Acme.

Go for it, Jack. You have my full support, for as long as you need it.

THE FINAL PHOTO IN THE FILE IS ONE THAT SHOWS TATYANA AS I last saw her: high cheekbones and almond-shaped eyes the color of a bright cloudless sky, white blond hair, and dressed in her Versace widow's weeds.

Apparently, Arnie captured her via the morgue's security webcam during my face-off with her. Knowing him, I presume he erased all video traces of both of us from the web feed.

It is attached to a report that was filed by Jack. It is a surveillance map, studded with coordinates listing dates, times, addresses, routes, and descriptions of contacts made since she left Club Dread.

There is also a video feed of her Club Dread stay.

It ain't pretty. Her initial torture, which was carried out by Abu, gave her orthodontic surgery without anesthesia–the most pain, leading to quick gain–if they don't have a heart attack first.

Several teeth later, she still hadn't broken down. On the upside, she won't be smiling for quite some time.

Jack's turn up to bat gives her a blood-striped back to go along with her jack-o-lantern grin. I wince with each slash of the cat-o-nine-tails. On the other hand, Tatyana seems to enjoy it. Why am I not surprised?

However, when he hits her kidney with his fist, she coughs up blood. Thank goodness the video is soundless, so that I don't have to hear his jeers and taunts, or her screams and pleas.

I have to close my eyes when, with one twist, his pliers break the first bone in her pinky finger.

I can read his lips: *That one was for Donna.*

Not as romantic as the casket charm and bonbons, but it's certainly comforting to know how far he'll go to defend me. I'll have to show my appreciation to him later tonight–only no S&M roleplaying.

If he hadn't let her go in order to track her, her latest accessory would be a nine-millimeter bullet, which she'd be wearing somewhere deep in the gray matter of her cerebral cortex.

There are better fashion statements.

I've got to face it. Honeypots are part of the business. I know this, firsthand. But as far as Jack is concerned, if she goes after me or anyone else he loves, he'll treat her just like any other enemy.

Talk about true love.

ALSO IN THE REPORT IS A HYPERLINK OF A MAP. WHEN I CLICK ON it, I see that it is live, and in real time.

The object being tracked is initialed *TZ*. By its coordinates, I pinpoint her location as Mosul, Iraq. If so, it means she is meeting with ISIL's leaders.

The Intelligence Community can't decide which is the bigger terrorist threat to the United States, ISIL or Al Qaeda. But ISIL is certainly in the lead, what with impressive military tactical planning. Currently, it controls of half of Syria, two-thirds of Iraq, and enough of the rolling desert within Lebanon and Yemen to make the rest of the Middle East quake in fear.

Worst of all, it's got very deep pockets, thanks to the very lucrative resources located in the lands it now controls. The region's oil fields gush out forty-thousand-barrels-each day–at least two million dollars.

If you think any of it will go toward the care and feeding of the region's eight million citizens, you truly are living in a fantasy world. This money is used to recruit those with a deep hatred of Western culture–a hate cultivated during a life spent in a country occupied by Western armies whose leaders care less about the blood spilled on the parched earth than about the oil flowing under it.

Oil creates money. Money is power. Control the oil and you have the power.

The big question: Is ISIL the threat facing my mission team at Acme?

As I stare at the computer screen's glow, I envision Tatyana's smug smile. According to its coordinates, she's been in the same location now for the past sixteen hours. That doesn't seem right. If she was running a mission that takes place on U.S. soil, she'd be here, not there. Even if she's only acting as a carrier or cutout, she'd be on the move within a few hours of touching base.

I've just run after Emma in order to point this out when I hear the back door open.

For the life of him, Arnie doesn't know how to make a graceful entrance. Today his excuse is that his arms are filled with five bags of disposable diapers, which fall out of his arms in his attempt to juggle them while, at the same time, closing the door behind him.

When he sees me, he does a double-take. "Donna! What are you doing here?" The guilty look on his face proves he knows that Jack never told me Emma was part of the team, and that he never clued her in to the fact that I wasn't.

"Having an impromptu lunch with Emma." In a flash, I turn to block her laptop on the counter in front of me and I say brightly, "What are you doing home so soon?"

"I'm using my lunch break as a diaper run. Before I left for work this morning, I noticed that Nicky was down to just one." He attempts to hold up the boxes, only to have them tumble out of his arms again.

"You're a very thoughtful dad and father. Here, take this as a reward." I move toward him, the other sandwich in hand. "It's blackened salmon on focaccia, with an aioli sauce."

As I suspected, his eyes lock onto my offering like tractor beams. While he tears into it, I close the lid on Emma's laptop, and head for the door. "You made it just in time. Emma is changing Nicky's diaper, and I think it was the last one in the house. Please let her know it was great seeing her, but I have to run. I still have some grocery shopping to do. Feel free to eat my piece of cake too." I hold it up and watch his eyes water in anticipation.

He's still thanking me through a mouthful of fried green tomatoes as I sashay out the door.

7

How to Stuff a Wild Canapé

The most memorable thing about any party is its food! (That is, unless a dead body pops up.) A delicious tray of canapés is a must—especially if the ingredients are farm fresh and organic. A tried and true favorite:

Wild Mushroom Caps Stuffed with Blue Cheese

For these mouth-watering morsels, use sustainably farmed or foraged ingredients. Your guests will be begging for more (as opposed to for their lives).

Ingredients: Onion, Wild Mushroom, and Crumbled Blue Cheese.

Directions: Slice an onion, then grill it. After popping off the stems of the mushrooms, fill the cap with an onion round, then add crumbled blue cheese, and grill the mushrooms until they are soft.

How do you know the mushrooms are wild? Why, you picked them yourself! How do you know they're not poisonous? You don't—

Which is why you have the guest you like the least take the first bite.

I'm making Jack's favorite dessert: double fudge cherry brownies. When they come out of the oven, I'll let them cool before forming them with a heart-shaped cookie cutter, then icing them with chocolate, whipped cream and a cherry on top.

It's the perfect act of contrition.

Well, that and what we'll do with the whipped cream later tonight.

I've just placed the brownie pans in the oven when the doorbell rings.

I open the door to find the mothers of Mary's two closest friends standing on the front veranda–Babs Groves' mom, Janine; and Wendy Sims's mom, Loretta.

Neither is smiling.

Oh no–what has Mary done now?

I do my best to keep my sunny side up. "Ladies, so good to see you. To what do I owe the pleasure?"

Janine and Loretta exchange awkward glances before Janine takes the lead. "Donna, we wish this were just a social visit– Heaven knows, it's been ages since we got together just to play catch-up. But the truth is that something is going on with Mary. We feel you should be aware of it before it gets out of hand."

"Please, come in." I usher them over to the living room couch and take one of the facing chairs.

Loretta hesitates before taking a seat, almost as if she's afraid she'll catch something. Instead, she perches at the very edge of it. "We might as well come to the point. Mary has been slipping off campus during lunchtime."

For anyone but seniors, doing so is strictly forbidden at Hilldale High. I sink further down into my chair. "But...the school would have called me about it!"

"Wendy and Babs have been covering for her," Loretta

declares. "They sign her into the lunchroom, and buy a meal with her lunch card."

A cold chill runs through me. I rouse myself, only to stutter, "How did you find out?"

"I overheard Wendy talking it over with Babs on her cell phone." Loretta frowns. "Of course I was angry that they'd even cover for her once, let alone every day for more than two weeks–"

"Two weeks! ...When you confronted them, did they say why?"

"Apparently, she goes off with some boy," Janine says quietly. "From what Babs has told me, he's a couple of years older."

"But she's not dating anyone–" Even as I say this, I realize how foolish it sounds. The looks Loretta and Janine exchange confirm my fear:

If Mary hasn't brought him home, it's because she knows I wouldn't approve of him.

"What else do they know about him?" I ask.

"He doesn't go to Hilldale High. In fact, from what Wendy said, I don't think Mary's mystery date is in school at all." Wendy's right brow rises to her bangs. "I have to be honest with you, Donna. I'd never blame Mary–or you, for that matter–for your husband's atrocities against our country. But Mary's own indiscretions are making it hard for me to condone our daughters' friendship."

Janine must find Loretta's tone just as irritating as I do, because she frowns. Noting my tears, she takes my hand in hers. "Donna, the reason we're here is because we care very much about Mary, and about you. My goodness, we've known you both since the girls met in second grade! We love and respect you, as we know you do us. That being said, if the shoe were on the other foot and you knew if our girls were going through a rough patch–well, we have no doubt you'd let us know, before it escalated into something regrettable."

Janine is right. In fact, last year when the girls began their freshman year, Babs caught the eye of a senior boy. His very jealous girlfriend made it her full-time job to encourage Wendy and Mary to break off their friendships with Babs. She almost succeeded.

Mary came to her senses only after stumbling upon my teen diary. In it, I'd detailed my own experience with my school's queen bee mean girl, CeeCee Connolly. It was an eerily similar situation. Her boyfriend, Bobby, showed me too much kindness. It didn't help that I had a crush on him. It also didn't help that, at the time, my mother was dying of cancer, and without my knowing it, she'd hired CeeCee to hang out with me.

To quash my feelings toward him and his kindnesses in return, CeeCee ruined my reputation while burnishing her own–with my mother's famous apple pie recipe.

After college, CeeCee and Bobby got hitched. By the time CeeCee ran for Congress, she was going by her married name: Catherine Martin.

When she ran for president, I was one of the Acme bodyguards charged with safeguarding her California whistle stops.

But when Bobby–by then called Robert–decided Catherine's political supporters had the wrong agenda for the country and decided to divorce her during the campaign, she had him murdered.

Playing the grieving widow bought her the sympathy vote. But with the evidence secured by their teenage son, Evan, we were able to bring her to justice.

Janine was grateful that Mary stood beside her daughter during that tough first year of high school. Since then, despite bone-wearying shifts as a registered nurse, this single mother has shown her appreciation with random acts of kindness toward Mary, me, and the rest of the Stone family. In fact, she was one of a few neighbors who knew better than to believe Penelope's gossip when it was revealed that Jack wasn't the real Carl Stone.

Loretta rises–her way of signaling that the ball is now in my court. "Sorry I had to be so blunt, but we've got our own daughters' reputations and futures to consider. We know you respect our motives."

I mean it when I tell them, "Thank you for your candor. I appreciate you coming straight to me about this."

Even before we reach the front door, Loretta gives me a peck on the cheek, but she strides quickly to her car.

On the other hand, Janine stands there as if she doesn't have a care in the world, except for me. Leaning in for a hug, she murmurs, "Your family has been through so much in the past year, what with the reemergence of Mary's real father, and his recent death. Once you and Mary clear the air, you may want to consider family therapy. In fact, I could suggest someone. When Don and I went through our divorce, Babs, Don, and I saw Dr. Bonnie Ramsey."

"Thank you, I appreciate the referral."

Janine's goodbye hug is warm and real.

By the time I get back into the kitchen, the brownies are charred and hardened. I'm so angry that when I reach in to pull out the pans, I burn my pinky on the red-hot rack.

Angrily, I dump the pans in the sink.

After a good cry, I pull out the flour, chocolate, and cherries, and I start all over again. I'm not going to let this news about Mary's antics ruin the rest of my day, let alone my night.

And I pray that whatever she's doing won't ruin her life.

Mary is scanning the carpool line for Jack's Lamborghini. Her eyes widen with surprise when she spots my mommy mobile instead.

"Oh! ...I thought Jack was picking me up today." When she hops in and realizes that she's the only passenger on the Donna School Express, her eyes narrow suspiciously. "You didn't have to worry about me. I'm sure Wendy's mom would have dropped me at the house."

I smile and nod. "It was no problem at all. Jeff has basketball practice. It's Penelope's turn to carpool. And Trisha went to ballet after school. I had errands to run out this way. You don't mind taking a little detour with me, do you?"

She purses her lips, but nods anyway.

It's a thirty-minute ride to our destination. The whole time, Mary's declarations to my innocuous questions and polite asides are only either yes or no. To fill the void, she takes control of the car radio, clicking around from one rock station to another.

I'm surprised that she doesn't ask about our destination. Even more so, I'm disappointed that she is so oblivious of our route and her surroundings. Only when we turn onto the placid street in Santa Monica where we find the tiny cottage we owned prior to moving to Hilldale do her eyes register the memory.

It's the first time I've driven by since we moved to Hilldale, just before she turned eight. From the way in which she tears up, my guess is that she hasn't seen it in some time either.

Nor has she forgotten it. Instinctively, her eyes move to the window of the room that was once her bedroom.

Ah, good times. Simpler times. Happy times.

I park across the street, and turn off the engine.

At first, neither of us says a word. Finally, she turns to face me. "Why are we here?"

"Because it started here. At least, I presume it did."

She doesn't say anything, but she knows what I mean:

The beginning of the end of our happiness as a family.

"Your father had just returned from one of his business trips. While he was in the shower, I picked up his phone, by mistake. The man at the other end of the line spoke German. It was a language I'd never heard your father use, and it surprised me. By the time the man asked for someone named Simon, your father was out of the bathroom. He grabbed the phone out of my hand. He was angry." The memory makes me wince. "No, in truth, he was terrified. It was a few weeks later that he suggested we look for a new home, in Hilldale. I presume he felt it would be safer for us."

"From his enemies," she mutters.

"Yes. I've no doubt he knew he'd have to leave us–to disappear. It was several years later that I joined his old firm, Acme. I did it to avenge his death. I did it because–because I felt we needed more than a panic room and a security system in a gated community to keep us safe. At the time, I hadn't known what he'd become."

She nods slowly.

"Mary, I'm leaving Acme. His death made it possible for me to put aside my concerns–my fears–that he can harm us, or break us apart as a family, physically or legally. I'm resigning because I want to be here for you and Jeff and Trisha–always."

There is no relief in Mary's face, only wariness.

I've got to make her understand that I'm doing what I can so that we can heal and move on, as a family. "I think you're old enough to know this. Should you have other questions about your father or me, I will answer you truthfully." I pause, then add, "In return, I'll always want the truth from you too."

The blood goes out of her lips, as if stunned from an unexpected blow.

"Mary, where do you go at lunchtime? Who's the boy?"

My openness isn't enough to win her trust. I realize this when she slumps down into her seat and turns her head toward the window to avoid my eyes. "To the mall. He's just...a guy."

"Tell me about him. In fact, I'd like to meet him."

She shrugs. "When the time is right."

"The time is right, now. Before...before you both do something you'll regret."

Like being teased into having sex–and getting pregnant.

Or being urged into trying pot, or Oxycontin, or worse–say, coke and heroin–and end up with a lifelong addiction.

Or letting her depression over her father's death get the better of her, so that she ends up hating herself–and if she hates herself enough, she may also end up dead.

Mary's head whips around in my direction. "How about you, Mother? Do you have any regrets?"

Right about now, I regret having this conversation.

Keep calm. "Let's stay on topic. If I can't trust you, I'll have to–"

She turns back around. Her eyes glitter with scorn. "You'll have to what, Mother? Track me via my cell phone's GPS? Initiate satellite surveillance? Embed a tracker in my wrist?" She laughs cruelly. "That's okay. To tell you the truth, it doesn't bother me in the least that you don't trust me–*because I don't trust you.*"

I slap her cheek–hard.

Instinctively, her hand rises to the heat she feels on her face.

My face feels as if it's on fire too. Anger can do that to you. So can shame. "I'm sorry, Mary. I shouldn't have done that."

"You want the truth?" Her voice quivers–from fear or rage, I can't tell. "Okay, you asked for it! I'm glad I made you angry with me! At least it's an honest emotion–not like the lies I've heard from you my whole life."

"I'll admit it–I didn't tell you everything. But at the time, I had legitimate reasons. Sometimes it was the privacy conditions that went along with my job. At other times, you were too young to comprehend what was happening."

"I'm not too young now. So, tell me the truth! Who killed my father? Was it you, or was it Jack?"

Her tone says it all: *Do you want to earn my honesty? Do it here and now.*

Okay, then–let's see if she can handle the truth.

"You've got it all wrong," I say coolly. "Your father rigged it so that Jack would die in an explosion in a cabin. When I came looking for Jack, your father promised to let him live–if I went with him on a boat. As we were out to sea, the cabin blew up anyway. I thought Jack had died. I threw the item your father wanted so badly overboard. He was so angry that he tied me up and threw me off the boat. He didn't know it was rigged to blow up if it went above a certain speed."

Truth walks a tightrope. It can tilt too much toward disbelief on one side, or hatred on the other. No need to shoot the messenger when the odds are she'll stumble into the bottomless abyss of distrust on her own accord.

From the ice in Mary's eyes, it seems I've shot myself in the foot and am in a free fall–and that I may never crawl out of it.

Finally, she growls, "I knew it! I knew you killed him."

He was a terrorist; a killer; a deserter of his company, and his family.

And a deadbeat dad.

And yet, somehow, I'm the bad guy. Well, to hell with that. "You're grounded. Hand me your phone."

She sits there, stone-faced.

"Now," I warn her.

She reaches into her school bag and tosses it into my lap.

I growl, "And just to be clear, no Facebook or texting, either,"

She slumps further into her seat.

On the way home, neither of us says a word.

Neither of us cries either.

And we certainly don't say we're sorry.

Like mother, like daughter.

"DELICIOUS," JACK DECLARES, AS HE DIGS INTO A SECOND chocolate cherry brownie heart.

I'm not surprised that Mary skipped dinner, pretending that she wasn't hungry. As for Trisha and Jeff, they gobbled down my spaghetti and meatballs. By now, Mary's moodiness is taken for granted by everyone. I guess I should be relieved that my younger children have less pressing issues. In Trisha's case, whether or not she'll be chosen as the ballet recital's fairy queen. On Planet Jeff, I can't tell if he's more concerned whether he'll be the starting forward in his next basketball game, or if this competition over the infamously well-endowed Gabrielle Mathews bothers him.

Frankly, I hope it's the former. The last thing the Family Stone needs is more relationship drama.

Eventually, they'll ask questions about Carl's death. Mary's reaction is good preparation for when that time comes.

"So glad you enjoyed my little treat." It's nice to be appreciated, even for something as small as a homemade dessert. "And...thank you for picking up Trisha and Jeff."

"And for putting up with you, too, as you go through separation anxiety with Acme," Jack adds as he licks his fork clean.

I nod grudgingly. "Call it what you will."

"What would you call it?"

"Not jealousy, if that's what you're thinking," I declare primly. "I have complete trust that you know exactly what you're doing as it pertains to Tatyana."

He drops his fork with a clatter. "Oh, yeah? Since when?"

I can't exactly tell him, *Since you crushed her pinky and stripped the skin off her back.* So instead, I say, "Let's just say I've known you long enough to trust your actions, motives, and instincts." I slump down in my chair. "Which is more than I can say for my daughter, as it pertains to me."

Jack pulls me into his lap. And in a totally unnecessary attempt to turn my frown upside down, he spoon-feeds me a bite of brownie. As I chew on it, he murmurs, "I suspected that Mary's grief over Carl's death would explode somehow. I'm sorry it was directed at you, Donna."

"Better me than you." I wince. "Although, to be honest, you're right alongside me in the Mary's mad-at-mommy doghouse."

He kisses my forehead. "I can't think of a better place to be."

That gets a laugh out of me, but my smile fades as I hand him back his fork. "Doesn't she get it? What if we'd died instead of Carl? That was the alternative!"

"Donna, remember, she's still a kid. If Carl had succeeded, believe me, she would have been beating him up over it–or he would have beaten her into submission, emotionally if not physically."

I shudder at the thought. As for Jack, his hands curl into fists. After a moment of silence, he takes a deep breath. When he releases his fist, it's to stroke my palms. "She's lashing out," he murmurs. "We have to bite our tongues and wait it out."

"We should do more than that," I insist. "Jack, I think we should go to counseling, as a family."

He nods slowly at the thought. "Good suggestion. It will

clear the air about Carl, and maybe about other things as well. Just name the day."

"Janine gave me the name of someone she trusts," I murmur sadly. "Ha! And all this time, I thought I was the perfect mother."

He laughs. "You're the perfect lover. Isn't that enough?"

"It means a lot that you think so, yes." I'm being serious. "But if I've let my children down in any way, I'll never forgive myself."

"You haven't. And the sooner we get Mary beyond her anger, the sooner we can get on with the rest of our lives."

"Agreed." I hesitate and add: "You know, I was thinking… about Tatyana."

Jack groans and closes both eyes.

"Please, Jack, don't jump to conclusions! What I have to say is strictly professional."

He opens one eye. "Okay, let's have it."

"I was just thinking…I mean, I don't know how your surveillance has been on her since she left Club Dread, but considering the few facts we–*you* know about her mission, I hope you realize that she'll be back here on U.S. soil as soon as she can."

"We already have all ports of entry being watched," he assures me.

"Good"–I take a deep breath–"because we both know that no one with a ticking clock is going to sit too long in one place." I smile up at him innocently.

Despite his attempt to keep a poker face, I see the corneas of his eyes grow as it dawns on him that Tatyana's stay in Mosul is now going on its second day.

This is not the norm.

I kiss him before jumping out of his lap. "I've got to clear the table. Afterward, I'm going to leave a message with the family counselor Janine suggested, so that we can get the first available appointment."

He nods absentmindedly. Not that I blame him, with all that's on his mind right now. I could have easily predicted his next step: walk upstairs to the bedroom to call Ryan and ask all the right questions:

Did Tatyana somehow discover she was tagged with a GPS chip?

And, if so, what other surveillance does Acme have on the area, to determine if she lost her tail?

Fifteen minutes later, when Jack is back in the kitchen, he isn't smiling–not a good sign. I guess my hunch was right, which is unfortunate for Acme.

He takes my hand and leads me out into the backyard, where a hammock awaits us, as does a night filled with glistening stars. I fall into it first, and he follows.

As I lay snug in his arms, we stare up into the sky, but neither of us says anything. Instead we stare up at the cosmos of constellations far over our heads.

Finally he murmurs, "You were right. Tatyana must have realized she'd been tagged with a GPS chip, and dug it out before leaving Mosul."

"I'm sorry to hear that, Jack." The angle of the moonlight extends the shadows around the features of his face. His eyes become more deep-set, and his cheekbones even more pronounced. As I stroke the one closest to me, I ask, "Were you able to pull up coordinates based on the last signal reading?"

"Yes. It's a large apartment building. The DOD already had a drone scheduled with extermination orders. If I'd called even one hour later, the place would have been a pile of rubble. I'm sure Tatyana and her hosts were hoping we'd do just that, considering all the bad press it would have generated over the collateral damage. Your fast thinking saved many innocent lives, Donna."

"I...well, I'm glad of that." I lower my head onto his chest. It's too dark for him to see me blush at his compliment.

"In fact, the chip may have been planted in that specific building after it was removed from her. As we speak, Acme is going through all satellite surveillance leading up to her arrival in Mosul. Actual sightings will help us pinpoint exactly when and where we might have lost her." He tilts my head so that we're eye to eye. "How did the thought come to you?"

"I told you–it came to me out of the blue. I figured it had already occurred to the surveillance team, but I thought there'd be no harm in mentioning it, just in case it hadn't," I say nonchalantly. "Jack, will my replacement be assigned to this mission?"

He hesitates before answering. "Probably not, unless she's already highly seasoned. My team can't afford someone who'll slow it down, or make mistakes. We're handicapped as it is, what with you giving notice, and Emma out on maternity leave."

"But Emma is still working from home–" The moment it's out of my mouth, I could bite my tongue.

"How did you know that?" Jack sits up so quickly that I'm almost tossed out of the hammock. I'm still trying to come up with a plausible answer when he raises his hand. "Wait–don't tell me. I really don't want to know." He shrugs. "Donna, I'm certainly obliged to you for catching on to Tatyana's trick and passing it forward to me."

"Thank you for saying so. I hope you–"

"Wait, I'm not finished." He takes a deep breath. "I truly believe that you've made the right decision for your–*our* future. At the same time, for both professional and personal reasons, I'll sorely miss you on my Acme team. But make no mistake: I'll be sticking to protocol as it pertains to this mission. By that, I mean you can't be questioning me or anyone else involved about its status. Are we clear on this?"

"Yes, crystal clear." I blink my tears away.

"Good. That being said, I've already asked Ryan, and he's agreed that as we both value your opinion, you'll be consulted on specific matters," he pauses to emphasize, *"on a need-to-know basis."*

I've heard that line before "Yeah, sure. But how is that different from my status five minutes ago?"

"Five minutes ago, Ryan felt you didn't need to know anything, considering you've got one foot out the door. Now it means that if and when we want your input on some portion of the mission, we'll ask for it. But your last Acme assignment is still finding your replacement."

"Understood." I add slyly, "And if I should stumble onto some insight that may be useful?"

"By all means, pass it forward." He smiles knowingly. "Just don't spend your day tripping over Emma's computer–or mine again, for that matter."

"I didn't trip. It fell."

"If you say so." He smiles as he settles back down in the hammock. The arm that isn't cradling his head finds its way around my shoulder.

What can I say? It's great to feel appreciated–

Even if it's only on a need-to-know basis.

Well, of course I need to know–everything. I want to keep my family safe, and my Acme colleagues too.

And I would die if anything happened to Jack.

It's why I'll always have his back.

Just like he has mine.

I start by giving him my mouth.

By the way he devours it, I presume he missed it as much as it has missed him.

8

Should You Use Cater Waiters?

Unless you're Lady Crawley of Downton Abbey, a battalion of butlers holding trays with each of the delectable courses served at your next party isn't a necessity.

However, should your next gathering be large enough that formal invitations are in order and valets will be needed to park your guests' cars, a few cater waiters wouldn't hurt. Whether it's for passing pu pu platters, trays of champagne flutes, or manning the bar, here's how to pick the ones who will best serve and protect (your precious china):

First, interview each one personally. The obvious ones to avoid are the ones likely to bump into your exquisite furnishings, pick their noses in front of you, as well as those who smell like a brewery, or like your ganja dealer. You can also do without the guy calling his bookie every five minutes, and the gal with red-rimmed eyes who sobs incessantly because her married boyfriend just broke up with her. The much better choices are hotties who can easily dodge your drunk, grabby guests while carrying two trays, or the naughty boys who can mix a dry martini and a mean French 75.

Next, check their references. If it turns out the names given are similar to characters in Marx Brothers movies or corpses now residing in the local cemetery, cross these candidates off your list.

And, finally, don't hire anyone whose criminal record includes pick-pocketing.

On the other hand, anyone who's done five to ten in the big house but has never snitched on his murderous bunkmate, no matter what secrets were divulged, would make an ideal sous chef during the preparation of your world famous blue cheese mushroom caps, especially if he had kitchen duty while in the hoosegow. (Added bonus: should someone try to wheedle the recipe out of him, he knows how to use a shiv and hide a body.)

PUCCI TEDESCHI IS SHORTER THAN SHE LOOKS IN HER PHOTO. I guess the mile-high honey blond bouffant threw me off. She's also thinner and has a tiny frame–except where it counts, if the hanging tongues of all the men she saunters past is any indication.

So far, she's passed every task adequately. Although her martial arts skills are limited, they're effective. Acme's MA instructor finds this out the hard way when he grabs her in a chokehold from behind and says, "Let's see how you'd protect yourself when I do this to you."

A second later, he's doubled over as she grabs and twists his ball sack. When she slams a fist into his throat, he's down for the count.

Crude, but effective.

On to her lie detector test, when she's asked if she affiliated with any known terrorists, her response is, "I know every psycho mob hit man in Jersey. Does that count?"

It doesn't, and the rest of the questions go just as smoothly, so it's on to the next task: psychological testing, with our in-house psychiatrist, Doctor Bellows.

Afterward, she's asked to leave the room so that he and I can go over the results. The good doctor's glasses fog up as she sashays out. Even after he removes them, his eyes don't leave her. I guess she cured his nearsightedness. Go figure.

When he collects himself, he reports, "No panic disorders or phobias. However, there is a touch of adult antisocial behavior, a smidge of impulse control disorder, and a sprinkling of sado-masochism."

Sounds like a recipe for trouble—or for an excellent sparrow. "In other words," I declare, "she'll make a perfect hit woman."

"Yes...except..." he hesitates, then adds: "Her narcissistic personality disorder is somewhat worrisome."

"Tell me, doc, is that something you'd find in, say, Dominic Fleming?"

At the mention of Acme's blond British Adonis, Dr. Bellows rolls his eyes. "He's a textbook example! In fact, he is *the* textbook example." Bellows picks up the latest issue of *The British Journal of Psychiatry* and leafs through it until he finds what he's looking for, and hands it to me.

It's an article entitled, *The Triple Threat of Egocentrism, Vanity, and Megalomania: Can This Patient Be Saved?*

Dominic's picture is there, all right, as a centerfold—

And sans a stitch of clothing.

I turn it sideways so that I can take it all in, pun intended. No doubt about it, he has a lot to be proud of.

I turn back to the first page of the article and notice the byline: Dr. Alfred Bellows. "Congratulations on its publication, Doctor. This photo, however..."

He nods. "Yes, well, Dominic gave me a few to choose from.

To put it mildly, this was the most acceptable. On the plus side, this issue of the magazine has sold more copies than any other since 1963, its first year of publication."

"All's well that ends well. And considering Acme's success with Mr. Fleming, I presume Ms. Tedeschi is a shoo-in."

"Certainly," Bellows assures me, beaming.

Speaking of Dominic, he insists on following Pucci and me to her next test in Acme's shooting range, if only to "make sure our comely guest is shown how to hold something as long and hard as Benelli M4." He holds his large hands apart just in case she's too naïve to get the double entendre.

Um, *hardly*. Her eyes drop below his belt buckle. They grow exponentially at the bulge she sees there.

"I refuse to take no for an answer," Dominic proclaims airily.

"I'll say," she purrs.

I sigh. "O...*kay*! What do you say we get this show on the road?"

"Sure, but can I freshen up first? Which way to the little girl's room?" she asks in her kewpie doll voice.

I point her in the right direction. "That way, and around the corner."

By the time she's halfway down the hall, Dominic's tongue is on the floor.

Before he can follow her in there too, I slap his arm. "You better behave yourself! If she becomes my replacement, she's on your mission team. How do you think your hanky-panky shenanigans will go over with Ryan?"

Dominic responds with a smirk. "I presume he'll react the same way he did when he found out about you and Jack–he'll put his revolver in his mouth for a quick game of Russian roulette."

I blush. "Ha, ha, very funny! At the very least, you can wait until she actually gets the position before you pounce."

He shrugs. "I'll call her either way. 'Commiseration sex' is the best kind. Albeit 'survived death' sex is high on the list as well. Then again, 'you saved my life' sex usually leads to a jolly good time, not to mention 'angry at my husband' sex. Talk about boisterous!"

"Let's not."

"You act as if you're strapped into some sort of chastity belt, my dear. But we both know better, now don't we?" He laughs heartily. "That one, on the other hand, is quite a saucy minx, and makes no bones about it. She told me I remind her of her husband. Can't do better than that, eh?"

I'm just about to tell him that Pucci thought so "well" of Knuckles Tedeschi that she shot him through the heart when the lady in question waltzes out of the ladies' room.

She and I head for the elevator with Dominic right on our heels.

He had better tread lightly. We'll be around guns, and accidents do happen.

"WOW, ANOTHER BULLSEYE! ...I GUESS." I STARE DOWN AT THE bullet-riddled crotch of Pucci's paper target. This time around, her weapon was a Sig Sauer P226R. So far, she's moved through a Colt 45 and a Glock 42 with similar ease. "I mean, as long as you weren't aiming at his heart, or his head. You weren't...were you?"

"Get *outta* here!" Pucci smacks her gum hard and loud. "If we shoot 'em in the gonads, they stay alive, and we can torture them to squeal on their rat bastard pals. Besides, the world needs more eunuchs. Dontcha agree, Dom?" She looks over at Dominic for validation.

Despite his bacon-crisp tan, his complexion is now a light shade of green. "In–Indubitably!" he stutters. He nods his head so hard I'm afraid he'll snap something.

I hand her the last test weapon–an AR-15. "Have you used one of these?" I ask.

She shrugs. "My old man kept one under the bed. I shot that pedo-bastard scumbag with it. Made a hell of a hole in his chest! The exit wound was even better. You could have driven a Mac Truck through it."

Hearing that, Dominic's skin tone goes from puce to ghost. His hand is shaking so much that his next shot misses the target completely.

Seeing it, Pucci's bubble pops, causing Dominic to jump out of his skin. "Yo, Duke of Earl! You can do better than that, can't you?"

He smiles weakly and points to his ear protectors, as if he can't hear her.

Bullshit. He's just running scared.

"Obviously, you're proficient with the AR-15. Here, try this." I hand her a Bellini M4.

Dominic's eyes narrow. A sly smile rises on his lips. "Here, let me help with that." He positions himself behind her–very close.

Make that too close. Either she's ticklish or just not that into him. In any event, when her finger touches the trigger, she loses her grip on the gun. A shower of bullets spray into the concrete target wall, only to ricochet in every direction.

Everyone ducks for cover.

By the time the gunfire is over, Dominic's infatuation is quelled. He mumbles some excuse to get the hell out of there.

Pucci smirks. She knows the score. But like a cat with a mouse between its claws, she doesn't mind having a little fun before the final act. As she waves to Dominic, she simpers, "Tah tah, Lord Byron! Remember, we're hooking up for cocktails after work."

Dominic freezes in his tracks. His head turns slowly. "But… I'm sure Donna has a whole evening planned for you lovely ladies," he stutters.

"Nope," I assure him. "In fact, we'll be kicking off in time for happy hour. Of course, you're welcome to join us."

"I'm sure you two have a lot of ground still to cover," he insists.

"You're right, we do." I shrug at his bad luck–but then brighten as I add, "Tell you what–I'll drop Pucci by your place on my way home."

His eyes grow big with worry. "But…I was planning an early evening. I'm going straight to bed."

"I can put away three lemontinis in under an hour! I'll be there before dark," Pucci promises him. "If you're already tucked in, don't wait up. I can pick any lock. My cousin, Moochi, was the best B&E guy in Trenton."

"Fancy that," Dominic mutters under his breath.

I've never seen him run so fast, even when under fire.

Pucci giggles. "Whattaya bet he'll spend the night in his panic room?"

"You're not offended that he's trying to weasel out of your date?"

"It wasn't a 'date.' It was a booty call." She rolls her eyes. "He may have the right equipment–and plenty of it–but he's too soft for my taste, at least where it counts most–his head." Up until now, if her lips turned up at all, it was with a forced brittleness. But at this very moment, her smile is sad.

I hand the M4 to Acme's shooting range manager. "I've got

a few more questions, but they can be answered anywhere. "Let's get that drink."

THE BARTENDER AT AGO RESTAURANT ON MELROSE AVENUE IS flirting with Pucci, and she doesn't mind it at all.

Not that I blame her. He's dark with curly hair, has a chiseled jawline with a dimple in his chin, and lets her know up front that his name is Bruiser.

"Should I ask you why?" she says coyly.

"Stick around after my shift, and you'll find out firsthand."

She shrugs. "I'll think about it."

In case she doesn't, he writes down something on a napkin and slips it to her–if I were to guess what it is, I'd say it's his phone number.

She smiles slyly as she tucks it into her cleavage. Something tells me her life is now filled with a series of one-night stands. According to her dossier, she was a virgin when she married Knuckles. I guess she figures she's got to make up for lost time.

And let's face it: sex is another way to forget whatever ails us, if only for a few minutes.

Ago was Pucci's suggestion. It's an Italian eatery in West Hollywood. Robert De Niro is one of the owners. Or as she puts it, "Now that I'm out on this coast, I've always wanted to say I went."

The rest of the crowd at the bar is older males–that is to say, not the young hipsters who cruise Sunset Strip, but the over-forties with money for great grub and a little celebrity caché. We get more than a few admiring glances. Pucci isn't afraid to stare back, or to murmur, "Hey! Isn't that What's-His-Name from that movie?"

I chuckle as I sip my wine. "That is indeed. I hope this

restaurant wasn't too far out of your way. Do you live on the west side of town, or the east side?"

She shrugs. "Neither. I'm deep in the Valley. The Feds planted me in the middle of nowhere, and I hate it. Let me put it this way, I'm not the 'suburban mommy' type–oh! No offense!"

"None taken. We choose what we lose, don't we?"

She winces. "Sure. And we make our own mistakes, too. Mine was a doozy. I married a pedophile. You've seen my dossier. How about you?"

I shrug. "I married a terrorist."

"Jeez, we're quite a pair, ain't we?" Pucci murmurs. "Well, on the plus side, things can only go up from here, right?"

"For me, it already has."

"I saw your honey–that guy, Jack." She sighs deeply. "He's *soooo* smitten with you, kitten. I should be so lucky!"

"Then let's drink to that." I clink my glass with hers. "Word of caution: Acme's line of work has a way of putting a serious crimp on your relationships."

Hearing this, the light goes out of Pucci's eyes–if only for a moment. She shrugs, "Nothing lasts forever, right?" She gulps down her lemontini, and motions to the bartender for another. "So, what are the odds I'll get the gig?"

"One out of three. Two more candidates have also made it to the next round."

"Are they better qualified?"

"You've each got your plusses and minuses."

She turns to look me in the eye. "Let me guess mine. No military experience or covert ops skills, and I'm a felon."

"I had neither, and look where I am today."

"But you're leaving," she points out. "How come?"

"I've accomplished what I set out to do–avenge the wrongs done to me. And my family needs me."

"Good reasons–none of which apply to me. I have no family, and nothing to avenge."

"Then why did you apply to Acme, Pucci?"

"To get a life." She stabs a lemon peel with her swizzle stick. "The first nineteen years of my life, I was my father's girl. When I married Knuckles, I married the mob, too. I had to put up with his wise guy pals and their idiot wives, who pretended they didn't know what the hell was happening. As long as they went to church on Sunday, it was okay to look the other way." She shudders. "Hey, I'm no saint. I did the same thing–at first. Then, one day, Knuckles and I are running some errand– picking up a birthday cake for his mother. But he gets a call and the next thing I know he's got to make a detour. Do you know why?"

I shake my head.

"He had to put a bullet through the head of some guy who stiffed his bookie in order to pay his eight-year-old son's tuition to parochial school." Her voice trembles. "Knuckles drove right up to the front yard. The poor sap was playing catch with the kid. I'll never forget the look on the kid's face when his daddy's brains splattered onto the sidewalk."

"What did you do?"

"Do? I sat there like a zombie. When my heart started pumping again, I jumped out of the car and started running. Of course, he caught me–but only because I was wearing Jimmy Choos." She points down at her peep-toe pumps.

The shoes are hot blue, to match her body-hugging frock. They are locked onto her ankle with a T-strap. The five-inch heels make her almost as tall as me.

"Beautiful–but in the future, buy shoes with lower heels, and ones you can easily kick off. In other words, slingbacks," I caution her.

She frowns. "Wish I had that advice that night. Because of

these shoes, Knuckles cornered me in an alley. He slammed me up against the wall, held his gun to my head, and told me he loved me, but that if I breathed a word to anyone, no one would ever find my body. Not that anyone would come looking for me." She shrugged. "He was right about that. When I got involved with him, my family disowned me. And we never had kids because he shot blanks. Of course, those whore wives of his buddies could have cared less. The way they saw it, they're on a gravy train–at least, as long as none of their husbands gets knocked off. The night it happens, you never hear from those mooches again–a blessing in disguise, let me tell you." She holds up her drink. "To the last goombah standing. Thank God it wasn't Knuckles."

We belt back our libations, then Pucci puts down her glass and signals Bruiser for another round. "Hey, Donna, seriously–don't sweat it. If I'm passed over, I won't be throwing any pity party." She leans in and whispers, "I have a backup plan."

"What's that?"

"*The Real Housewives of New Jersey*. They need someone with talent, verve and real class, not to mention better hair. My talent agent is talking to them right now."

I choke on my wine. "You'd actually consider that?"

"Are you nuts? In a New York second!" She laughs as if it's the funniest question she's ever heard. "And you wouldn't, if they offered you a role? I don't mean New Jersey, but they do have the Beverly Hills housewives show, too. Of course, you'd have to move to a better zip code."

"Thanks, but no thanks."

"Seriously? With your backstory, I'd think you'd be a natural for a reality show."

"Yes, very seriously. And more to the point, I don't think Acme would appreciate it." I frown.

"That's a shame, because as far as I'm concerned, it's a deal breaker."

When she sees my frown, she giggles. "Lighten up, doll! I was pulling your leg," Pucci laughs. "The minute I cross the Jersey border, I'll be gunned down. We both know it."

I sigh with relief. "Pucci, I'm glad you realize it."

She holds up a palm and stares at it. "Considering my chance at longevity, right now Acme is the only game in town." It's the first time I've heard a tinge of desperation in her voice.

Thank goodness Bruiser slides our drinks in front of us. She lights up again.

"Salute!" She taps her glass to mine, then pauses. "You know, I've never had a girl's night out. Knuckles was too jealous to let me out of his sight, especially with those slut whore wives of his buddies. Even if it's just an excuse to get me drunk and poke a hole in my audition as the next Donna Stone, I appreciate a night doing anything other than watching reality television."

"So far, I like what I've seen."

As far as Pucci is concerned, this is reason enough for us to toast again.

Just as she takes a sip, some brawny guy with a glass eye and a nose flatter than a pancake accidentally jostles Pucci's arm as he makes his way to one of the restaurant's patio tables.

Her drink spills onto the front of her dress. Angrily, she turns to him. "Watch it, you clumsy ox!" Suddenly her eyes open wide.

She turns her head quickly so that he can't see her.

He cranes his head so that he can get a better look at her face. "Hey, don't I know you?"

"Are you from Atlanta, too?" Her question comes out in Southern drawl that is as thick as sorghum.

He squints, as if it will help his memory.

Ah, I get it—Pucci recognizes him, and is praying that he doesn't do the same.

It's time for a diversion.

I stand up and wave to two men who are standing at the hostess station. "Ooooh, Trixie honey, your adorable hubby just came in! And look! He brought one of his FBI friends with him. I swear! Y'all have to quit trying to set me up—but boy, this one is quite a hunk!"

The acronym FBI doesn't set well on Pucci's jostler. His first instinct is to look toward the front door. The two men standing there are smiling and nudging each other, as if they've won the lottery. To be honest, they look like traveling salesmen—one tall with a hawk nose, the other short and bald—but that doesn't register with Pucci's Problem Dude. All he knows is that if what I say is true and they're Federal agents, he wants out of there, and quick.

I wait until he ducks out the back, then I pull Pucci with me toward the front door.

We take the aisle between the restaurant's tables that is farthest away from the men who thought I was waving at them. Tall and Hawk-Nosed yells out to me, "Hey, where are you going?"

If he follows, he'll regret it. The last thing he'll want is to be caught in the crossfire should Pucci's old pal remember where he saw her last.

By the time we make our way to the sidewalk, there's a line out the front door of the restaurant. In Los Angeles, good eats bring out big crowds—all the better to hide from anyone who may be lying in wait for Pucci.

While I case the block, she loses herself in the crowd. It's dark outside, but from what I can tell, no one is hiding in any shadows, so I give her the high sign.

We parked near the front of the restaurant, on Melrose Place, just a half-block off Clinton Avenue. But if Problem Dude has a window seat, he can watch us get into our car. So, instead, we walk away from the restaurant and circle around to the alley behind it, where Ago has its own parking lot. This takes us a block out of our way before circling back to Melrose via Clinton Avenue.

It's a long block, giving me the time to ask Pucci, "Who is he?"

"Joey 'Toenails' Ponti. He's a lieutenant in the Carducci syndicate."

"What's he doing out here?"

"You got me on that one." She snorts. "Either he's out here running an errand for Carmine Carducci, or he's bullying his way onto some movie set. The son of a bitch used to brag that he helped De Niro with his wise guy patter for *Casino*. Now he fancies himself a movie consultant on all things Cosa Nostra. As if." She rolls her eyes, but there's a quiver in her voice.

"Do you think he recognized you?"

"Not necessarily. Back in Trenton, my eyes were brown, and I had long, dark hair." She pats her platinum bob. "If my cover is blown, does that knock me out of the running with Acme?"

"Not necessarily. But it sure as hell complicates matters." I truly like Pucci–all the more reason I'm somewhat disappointed that she's using Acme to run away from the life she has now.

Then again, at the time I joined, the same could have been said about me.

"Donna, I won't lie to you–I need this gig. I hate the fact that I'm always looking over my shoulder. If it ain't to see if the Carduccis are on my tail, I'm dealing with the Feds, who want to make sure I don't get whacked on their watch."

It looks as if Witness Protection is getting its wish–

And it's happening on my watch.

The car rounding the corner doesn't have its lights on, and it's going much too fast for this small alley.

I leap onto a debris box.

Pucci can't because her heel is stuck in a crack.

"Jump!" I scream.

"But…it's a Jimmy Choo!" She tugs at the ankle strap, but it's too late.

Pucci is low enough that he rolls right over her.

She disappears under the car's wheels, only to be dragged halfway down the block before her bloody, broken body breaks free from the chassis.

My first shot takes out a tire. The second one shatters the rear window. When the car rolls into a lamppost, I realize the second shot also found its mark: the back of Toenails' head.

My initial instinct is to go back and take care of Pucci, but a few people have already crowded around her, not to mention I hear the sirens, which means the place will soon be crawling with cops.

The last thing I need is to explain myself from a jail cell. Besides, there were enough witnesses around to get a handle on what went down. And once the cops run Pucci and Toenails' fingerprints through the Interpol database, they'll know why.

I hightail it out of the alley until I'm back on Melrose Place. Most of the shops are closed, so I crouch down in the darkened doorway of a closed lamp shop and call Ryan.

"Get out of there, and fast. I'll call my buddy at the L.A. Sheriff's Department to give him a heads up." From his tone, he's not too happy to hear that he's got to clean up this mess. "What the hell were you doing at Ago, anyway?"

"A little female bonding. Considering the circumstances, I know that sounds silly. But I really liked her, Ryan."

"Getting her killed is a hell of a way of showing it." He sighs. "Who's up next?"

This time, I'm playing it safe. "The Defense Department wonk."

"Line her up. And remember, she's not your buddy, she's your replacement." He hangs up before I can say anything else.

9

Creative Decorations

Decorations play a very important part in setting the theme of your party, and will have your guests talking about your event for the rest of their (hopefully not too short) lives!

Best tip: use authentic accessories. Now that you're an adult, crepe paper, cardboard and papier-mâché just won't do! If your theme is, say, "Oktoberfest," surround your outdoor event with bales of hay, and have your guests sit at long tables where they will swill Spaten and other German beers while listening to an authentic oompah band. And if one of your beer-sodden guests tips over a lit torch and the bales catch fire, don't worry, the fire truck's red color will blend well with your Bavarian green color scheme!

From what I can tell, Mary got my message and is behaving herself.

I don't take her word for it—not at this point, anyway. Believe me, I wish I could, but I need verified proof. It comes via the following:

1. Despite the mandate that she's not to do any social networking, I'm still monitoring her email, texts, and Facebook account. She uses the same password for all three, and it was easy enough to crack: *RinTinTin*

The bad news: she's broken my rule. The good news: I'm happy to see she's still such an innocent. She and her friends text about clothes, boys, movies, and music. I don't pick up any conversations with her mystery man, thank goodness.

2. Parental control software. This old standby is tried and true. There are numerous cell phone-tracking services available to parents. Right now, it shows me that Mary is right where she should be–in her world history class.

3. Acme's satellite surveillance. As long as I'm on the payroll, I have access to it. So what the hell, why not put it to some good use? Although she's not a terrorist or even close (I pray) I'm able to slide through the order to track. Can I help it if the SS surveillance manager, Clint Zuckerman, has a crush on me? I tune in just before every class break to make sure my hoody-headed eldest is on her way to her next class.

So far, so good.

And yes, I hate myself for doing this.

I pray she never finds out, or she'll hate me even more than she does now, if that's possible.

Now, for my next unsavory task of the day: negotiating a better event contract with the Savoy.

"YOU'RE POSITIVE THAT MRS. BING WON'T BE JOINING US?" HENRY Massey, the Savoy's buff, handsome hotel manager, looks nervously over my shoulder and through his office's glass wall, which overlooks the hotel's large, elegant lobby.

"You'll be dealing exclusively with me," I assure him.

He rewards my comment with a smirk. Worse yet, he walks around to the front of his desk and leans on it, right in front of me, which puts me at eye-level with his man candy.

Okay, yeah dude, I now know what Penelope saw in you. Or, I should say, about you.

I lean back to get a little air. "Mr. Massey, there are a few terms to our event contract which need altering."

His eyes narrow into tiny slits. "Such as?"

"I'm sure you're aware that the event is a children's dance. That being said, we'll have no use for liquor." Other than the few bottles of wine I'll have stashed in my suitcase to help me survive the night, but this is something that I need not divulge to him.

"It wasn't a deal breaker with Mrs. Bing. And, apparently, until now, it wasn't one with you either." He points to my John Hancock on the event contract.

I hate the fact that I allowed Penelope to trick me into signing it.

Seeing me wince, he shrugs nonchalantly. "Sorry, but at this late date, there is nothing we can do about the liquor order. However, I will have the beverages kept bottled and left in their cases, in one of the hotel's private storage rooms, adjacent to the kitchen. Your security key will be the only one that can access it. And to sweeten the deal"–he lets the word linger between us, as if it's a tantalizing fragrance, as opposed to a flagrant come-on–"I'll throw in the Savoy's Academy Awards Suite. It's only one of three suites on the penthouse level, along with the Emmys Suite and the Golden Globes Suite."

"Seriously, Henry, I'd much rather have the refund."

"*Shhhhh!*" He has the audacity to put a finger on my lips to silence me. He opens a drawer and pulls out a gold security card embossed with an A. "You don't know what you're saying. Follow me, and you'll understand why I'm doing you a favor."

He strolls out the door. I follow because I have no choice.

He doesn't head for the lobby's elevator bank. Instead, moves beyond it to a small alcove containing a wide double door.

He uses his security card to access it.

Within the alcove is a bank of four elevators: three on one side and one directly across from them. The bank of three are marked with letters over the door: "A," "E" and "G." The elevator on its own wall is marked "C."

He pushes the button beside the one marked A, for the Academy Awards Suite, I presume.

Maybe once we're up there, he'll realize I mean business and that there's no way he can change my mind.

HE'S CHANGED MY MIND.

It's not the one-hundred-eighty-degree view that runs from the Hollywood sign to the Pacific Ocean that does it for me. (Okay, maybe.) Or even the custom-made California King Bed, with its mattress made from Latin American curled horsetail and Mongolian cashmere, and costing almost two-hundred-thousand dollars. (Okay, yes, it might play a factor.)

As with the other penthouse suites, this one has a private roof-top terrace, with a staircase that accesses the hotel's helicopter pad. The football-field-sized living room is filled with antique furnishings, as well as a full-wall LED-LCD HDTV, and a Bang & Olufsen full-space integrated sound system. There's a white baby grand Steinway piano, and a private kitchen with an on-call chef.

This plush entertaining environment is flanked by two

bedrooms. Each has its own spa bathroom, with showers large enough for two.

Jack and I will share a bed and a bath.

The other will be blissfully empty.

Okay, yeah, I'm sold. Wait until Jack hears about this!

"Each of the penthouses has two stories. As you see, the bedrooms are located on the top floor for *complete privacy*." He purrs those last two words.

Ignoring the implication, I ask innocently, "I presume Mrs. Bing's room is on a much lower floor?"

"Yes, and unfortunately, her room is somewhat more modest–but no need to let her in on that secret."

"Agreed." I shrug nonchalantly.

I have more incentive than ever to hustle up a few more chaperones. But to play it safe, we will put webcams in all the kids' rooms. An even better idea: hire a battalion of armed security guards to put in front of every door, on every floor.

Try as I might, I can't tamp down my smile. It's all Henry needs to know he's won me over.

But he loses me all over again when he adds, "Of course, I will personally be on hand to turn down your sheets."

It'll be much more fun to see the look on his face when he finds Jack under the blanket.

He assumes the smile on my face is my pleasure regarding what's to come that night. Hardly.

I'm just about to pluck the security card from his hand when he slides it back into his pants pocket.

No, this isn't a game of Go Fish. It's straight out high stakes poker.

As if reading my thoughts, he says, "The card will be waiting for you at check-in, as soon as you sign the new event contract."

Fair enough.

THE NEXT CANDIDATE FOR MY JOB, JENNY McDOUGAL, IS NOT exactly a *femme fatale.*

Let me put it this way–calling her "homely" is being generous.

Gargoyle is a more apt description.

The former CIA analyst is tall and thin. Her nose is hooked, her skin is pockmarked, her teeth are bucked, her glasses are Coke-bottle thick, and her bright red hair is coiled so tightly that it looks like a rusted Brillo Pad.

It also doesn't help that she sports a 'stache that's thicker than Henry's.

Well, too bad. Jenny is a crack shot, knows several Chinese dialects, and she holds the highest belt in Judo, Chun Kuk Do, and Japanese fencing. Not to mention that her psychological profile came through with flying colors–

Okay, except for one little anomaly. Dr. Bellows gets straight to the point: "While under hypnosis, she divulged her fear of rejection, because of her looks. Or as she put it, 'No guy will mug me, let alone date me.'"

"Is it so bad that it'll be a deterrent to her role as a honeypot?"

"Afraid so." He grimaces. "Unless her target is a blind man."

I'm glad she's outside in the reception area and can't hear him.

I make it to her side just in time to witness the true test that she may not work out. Dominic has just entered the building. When he sees me, he asks in his typical stentorian decibel level, "Ah, Mrs. Stone, there you are! I presume your comely charge will be joining you any moment now?"

"As a matter of fact, she's right here." I grab hold of Jenny by her arm in order to pull her onto her feet.

It seems I've caught her off guard. Jiggling her arm while she freshened her lipstick created a larger lower lip than what's really there.

When she smiles, Dominic backs away, horrified.

To break Dominic's stare, I say, "Jenny and I were just about to go to lunch. Would you care to join us?"

He gives the lamest excuse possible–that he's needed on a conference call with POTUS–and scurries off in the opposite direction.

Totally bogus. I know for a fact that the last person Lee Chiffray would call at Acme is someone whom he refers to as, "that pompous pretty boy."

That's okay. Where I'm taking Jenny, we don't need him tagging along. "You've passed all your tests with flying colors," I tell her proudly. "What do you say we go out and celebrate? We'll have a spa day!"

Perplexed, her unibrow knits together like an Amazonian underbrush hit with a stiff wind. "Um…okay. If you think it's necessary. I'm a soap-and-water kind of girl, myself."

"All the more reason to reward yourself–on Acme's dime, too."

As we head out the door, I text the Sunset Tower Hotel to reserve two suites, as well as a deluxe spa package. Jenny will be given the works: a Turkish Hammam treatment, seaweed detox, milk bath, the premiere HydraFacial, and an hour-long massage. Afterward, she'll be treated to a haircut and high-lights, and a makeover by one of the Tower's celebrity salon stylists. By the time she gets back to her suite, she'll find it filled with designer duds and shoes in her size, courtesy of Beverly Hills' go-to personal shopper, Nicole Hopper.

Not only will Jenny feel like a million dollars, she'll look like it too. Tomorrow when she's good and relaxed, on the way back to the office I'll talk her into laser surgery to correct her vision.

Okay, yeah, and maybe just a smidge of rhinoplasty.

This job changes you in so many ways.

THE SUNSET TOWER HOTEL'S TERRACE BAR IS CROWDED. IT GOES without saying that all the chaises around the pool are taken. The only place left to stand was against one of the three-foot-tall glass guardrails that separate the terrace from a dead drop, some eleven stories above Sunset Boulevard.

Even before we turn back around from admiring the sunset view, a waiter hands us a couple of champagne flutes.

Jenny looks flustered. "We haven't ordered yet," she tells him.

He points toward a man lying on the chaise furthest from us. I recognize him as a lead actor in one of the latest and greatest Marvel blockbusters.

"Not too shabby," I murmur as I nod toward him.

Jenny follows my gaze. Her eyes grow large when she realizes who he is. She practically faints when she notices that her drink is accompanied by a written invitation to meet him tomorrow for dinner.

"He's smiling at you," I murmur.

She blushes at the thought. "Hot damn! I guess he's as blind as me."

At my suggestion, she took off her clunky old lady glasses for the evening. I figured, why muck up a work of art? In the past few hours, her 'stache was zapped with electrolysis, and the make-up artist did wonders in hiding the manly arch in her nose while accentuating her sky-high cheekbones.

Action Hero Hottie isn't the only one vying for her attention. Gawking is rampant. A five-foot eleven beauty with a long mane of red tendrils in an electric blue Alice + Olivia croc leather V-back mini-dress and five-inch heels is sure to cause a fuss, even in Hollywood's see-and-be-seen hotel.

Finally, Jenny honors Action Hero Hottie with an uncertain wave. "I feel like Cinderella," she murmurs.

"Good, because your new job is all about role playing," I remind her. "Being beautiful is all up here, anyway." I tap my forehead with a newly manicured finger.

Her smile fades. "So is being ugly. I was told that enough when I was a little girl."

"Your parents?"

"Singular–parent. My mother. But only when she was sober, which wasn't often."

I guess that's why it took me some convincing to have her order even a white wine spritzer. "The cut is always deepest from those we love most."

"Cut? Ha! It's the only thing she didn't threaten to do." She looks down into her drink. "I thought getting punched in the face was bad enough"–she points to the bridge of her nose–"until she put out her cigarette on my thigh." She lifts her skirt just high enough to show me a large dark blemish.

I shake my head. "How old were you?"

"Twelve. One of her asshole boyfriends had just made a play for me. He got a blowjob, and I got this."

"I'm sorry to hear that, Jenny." I glance around the terrace bar. "Well, I guess tonight is proof that Mommy Dearest was dead wrong about you. I mean, just look at you now! You could pass as a runway model. Most women would envy your figure."

She snickers. "Hey, let's give my new push-up bra credit

where it's due. It's the only reason I look even a tiny bit curvy. Let's face it, I'm way too skinny for my height."

To prove it, she turns sideways–only to trip on the low-lying ledge securing the glass wall that stands between us and oblivion.

Quickly, I grab her elbow and hold on until she catches her balance.

She sighs. "That proves I'll never be on a couture catwalk."

"It's okay. In our job, being built for designer couture is an asset. You fake a model's life only if the mission calls for it."

"Good to know. At least there's one advantage to starvation. Your stomach shrinks so much that you never develop an appetite."

"Didn't your mother qualify for food stamps?"

"You better believe it! And on good days, the cuisine was baloney-mayo-and-white-bread sandwiches. But Mama had a habit of washing down her sandwich with a fifth of cheap vodka."

"I thought you couldn't buy booze with food stamps."

"You can't. She earned her drinks the hard way: on her back, legs spread." Her eyes darken with sadness.

Time to change the topic. "How did you end up at Langley?"

Once again, her smile emerges. "All it takes is one great teacher to inspire you, right? Mine was my ninth grade French teacher. She was shocked at how easily I picked up the language. When Mama disappeared on a permanent binge, she talked my social worker into allowing me to be her ward. It paid off with a full scholarship to MIT in Asian Studies, with a minor in Geography. I was recruited right after earning my Masters in International Studies." She smiles sadly. "The rest, as they say, is history. No, make that salvation, because that's what it was. I became someone because of it." She looks down at her dress. "And now I'm reborn again. No longer an ugly duckling, but a swan."

I nudge her. "Your not-so-secret admirer is making his way over. It's a perfect opportunity to practice a little spycraft. Let's see what kind of false identity and cover you can come up with on the fly." I hold a finger to my lips. "Remember, Cinderella, this is a fantasy. Just keep it fun and games."

"Aye, aye, madam." She salutes me.

Our laughter must be infectious because the first question out of Action Hero's mouth is, "What's so funny?"

I step aside so that he can make his move. He comes in close—so close in fact that he and Jenny bump heads. He doesn't know that she can't see six inches in front of her nose.

So that she doesn't give this away, she smiles, nods, and laughs in all the right places while he chats her up: an anecdote about something that happened recently on the set of his latest movie.

Jenny plays her role well—that of the bemused princess. To prove that he's clever enough to win the keys to her kingdom, Action Hero goes into pantomime. But when he tries to illustrate that the story is getting even funnier, he makes a sudden move.

For someone who's practically blind, her instinct is natural: to take a step backward.

Only, in this case, there is no backward.

Her foot smacks into the security ledge of the glass handrail. She looks like a windmill with her hands flailing. But at almost six feet, gravity gets the better of her.

Proof that Hottie isn't really an action hero is that he's not quick enough, or strong enough, to break her fall.

For that matter, neither am I.

For the longest time, he and I stare down at her broken body on the pavement below.

When we turn around, we are faced with an army of cell phone cameras.

Like me, Action Hero Hottie knows enough to put his hands over his face. As he rushes out, he shouts, "I–I didn't touch her, I swear!"

The security cameras will validate his claim. Still, my guess is that it won't help his career.

Nor mine, for that matter. I have a lot of explaining to do.

I guess it's a good thing that I'll soon be retired–granted only seven days, five hours and three minutes, to be exact. But who's counting?

After this incident, Ryan more than likely.

I HIT THE SPEED-DIAL TO ACME AT LEAST SIX TIMES ON THE WAY home, each time leaving a message for Ryan to call.

I do the same on Jack's cell phone. Why the hell isn't he picking up?

If he won't, then neither will anyone else on my team. Something pertaining to the mission must be going down, right now.

I get home to find Aunt Phyllis cuddling with Trisha on the couch as they watch *Frozen*. Thank goodness, Jack must have asked her to pick up the kids and stay over until all of this stuff blows over.

"Where are Mary and Jeff?" I ask.

"Mary is upstairs, doing her homework," Aunt Phyllis assures me. "And before you ask–no, she hasn't used her cell phone, and yes, she isn't on her computer. In fact, I'm keeping an eye on it right now." She glances at the iPad beside her, where a security app indicates all live hot spots.

"What about Jeff?"

"He went around the corner to a friend's house. Don't worry, I checked his homework. His math went over my head, but he seemed to believe he knows what he's doing."

I roll my eyes. Hey, when it comes to sitters, beggars can't be choosers. "Okay, well, I'll be in the backyard if anyone needs me."

Phyllis and Trisha wave me off. *Frozen's* Elsa is in deep doo-doo.

Thankfully, the cartoon heroine is not in it as deep as me. In her case, two others haven't gotten killed.

So that no one sees me, I make my way to the tree house in the backyard, where no one can overhear my conversation, should either Jack or Ryan call in.

I've just climbed onto the top step of the tree house when I see them: Jeff, in a lip lock with some girl.

My son...is kissing some girl.

I'm mesmerized. Oh my God–is this my son's very first kiss?

How...awesome.

And now his hand is sneaking into her T-shirt–

Um...*no.* I'm certainly not going to just stand here and watch him cop his first feel!

My cough is akin to a gunshot, ricocheting through the tiny tree house.

Jeff and the girl leap away from each other. Their eyes are as big as saucers.

"Mom! ...Wow! I–I didn't expect you back so early," Jeff stutters. He's enough of a gentleman to help the girl up onto her feet.

"Obviously not," I press my lips together to keep from smiling. "Care to introduce me to your friend?"

"This is Gabrielle Mathews. We were studying…math." He points to the stack of schoolbooks tossed in a corner.

I cross my arms. "Oh? Aunt Phyllis informed me you'd completed your math homework."

"I asked Jeff to help me out, Mrs. Stone," Gabrielle exclaims. "I was stuck on a problem, and since I live just a few blocks over…I hope you don't mind."

"Not at all. I'm just surprised to find the two of you way up here."

Jeff's cheeks are flushed. Still, he insists, "We would have studied in the den, but Aunt Phyllis and Trisha were watching TV, and we're not allowed to have company in the living room. I thought it would be quieter in here."

"I'm glad to see you weren't disturbed. But I would imagine that Gabrielle's mother would feel as I do–that from now on, your study sessions should take place in the house."

Both children nod guiltily. Jeff let Gabrielle go down the ladder first. His gallantry doesn't stop there. He offers me the same privilege.

I take it so that he doesn't see me tearing up.

I give Jeff permission to walk Gabrielle home, if only to keep him out of earshot as I get lambasted by Ryan. His voice thunders, "I don't understand what you were doing there with her in the first place!"

"I told you–she was a little rough around the edges! I was smoothing them out for you."

"Don't do me any more favors," he mutters.

"Wait…does this mean you'd prefer I bow out of the vetting and training of my replacement?"

"Trust me, if I could, I would. But we're shorthanded right now, remember?"

How can I forget?

"And then there was one," Ryan grumbles. "Text Ms. Lloyd–the sooner the better. And, Donna, let me make a suggestion: *do not* leave the Acme campus with her, okay?"

"Your wish is my command," I declare airily.

"Good! Wonderful! Glad I have your word on it. Look, I've got to go now."

I wait for the click that indicates he's hung up, but none comes.

Finally, I ask, "Ryan? Are you still here?"

He doesn't answer. Instead, I hear someone else talking now. It's Arnie. Or, at least I can make out snippets of what he's saying: "–enough chatter to approximate a date–the week of the fourteenth."

"So, where is Tatyana?" Abu asks. "She couldn't have just disappeared into thin air."

"By jove, I think I've got it," Dominic exclaims.

"This isn't a tryout for *My Fair Lady*. Let's hear it," Ryan growls at him.

Dominic indicates his irritation with a loud sigh. "If you'll let me finish, I wish to point out that like the CIA, MI6 has also been tracking air traffic in and out of Middle Eastern hot spots. The day after Tatyana landed in Syria, MI6's surveillance feed tracked a Gulfstream 650ER private jet leaving Damascus and landing in a private airstrip in Caracas, Venezuela. Look here, as the sole passenger boards the plane."

I can't see what they're looking at, but I know it must be Tatyana when I hear Jack mutter, "That's her alright."

"Caracas was a refueling stop," Dominic adds. "From there, the plane went on to Mexico City."

"By now, she would have crossed the border into the United States," Abu points out.

In other words, we've lost her again.

"I can make out the plane's ID number to see who it's registered to," says Arnie. He must have zoomed in on the satellite feed. "I'll also hack into the Damascus Airport's manifest to validate ownership of the plane."

"If you hack into the air traffic control feed during takeoff, I'll do a translation of any conversation between the controllers and the pilot," Abu offers. "I may be able to pick up a clue or two that way."

Then I recognize Jack's voice: "What events are taking place on the week in question?"

"Let me check," says Emma, but the sound is tinny, as if she's on speaker. The soft moan of a baby confirms it. Everyone is quiet, waiting for what she digs up. It doesn't take her long. "The Clippers game, for one thing. And a town hall debate between Los Angeles' mayoral candidates."

"Neither of which can be it," Jack counters. "Granted, a terrorist attack at a sports game would make a statement, but if this is to be ISIL's first attack on U.S. soil, it'll go for an even bigger target."

"He's right," Ryan declares. "Emma, look for something very big and very public, with either national or international overtones."

"I'll keep searching," she assures him, "but right now, absolutely nothing fits that description."

"Maybe it's not within the Los Angeles metro area," Jack muses out loud. "Maybe it's within the region–"

"Oh, hell!" Ryan exclaims. "This new damn phone! I thought I hit the off button after my call with Donna–"

The click I hear next means we've been disconnected.

Half of me wants to laugh, but the other half wants to cry over the fact that Ryan–and Jack, for that matter–are actually concerned that I might have overheard them.

When Jack gets home, he'll drop hints to see if I give away what I know.

All the more reason to be in bed when he gets home, and fast asleep.

Between Pucci and Jenny's deaths, I hope I don't have nightmares.

10

Tot Party No-No's

Choosing the entertainment for a children's party isn't as easy as one might presume. Here are a few things to avoid:

- *No-No Number 1: Don't choose a theme previously chosen by those in his playgroup, or you'll look like a copycat—or worse yet, the parents of those in attendance will compare the successes and failures of both parties. The chances of you ending up with the fuzzy end of the lollipop? Fifty-fifty—lousy odds, both in and out of Las Vegas.*
- *No-No Number 2: Don't hire a clown. More than likely, at least one of the kids you'll invite is afraid of them. The moment the child cries, it sets off a domino effect, and pretty soon you'll have a sobfest on your hands—not to mention that years later, it'll be the first thing your own child will bring up when leaning back on his psychiatrist's couch.*
- *No-No Number 3: Stay away from stripper-grams, too. Both men and boys stare and giggle when they're around comely, young women with large breasts, no pants, and*

tiny tops. To top it off, those under the age of three will view them as their typical liquid lunch.

"So, what's on your agenda today?" Jack asks casually as he slathers his bagel with cream cheese.

"You mean, besides meeting with my replacement?" I pause what I'm doing: pounding chicken breasts for tonight's dinner, *cordon bleu.* "Well, let me see–I'm interviewing the entertainment vendors for the middle school prom. There's the photo booth guy, then there's the fortune-teller–"

"Wait…" He looks up, surprised. "By that, I take it she hasn't cancelled on you?"

"Who, the fortune-teller?"

He almost chokes on his coffee. "No, I meant the last replacement candidate for your job."

I frown. "No. Why should she?"

He winces at my tone. "Oh…I don't know. Just something I heard at the office."

I smack one of the filets–hard. "It's not my hang anymore, so perhaps you'll enlighten me."

"Only if you don't take it the wrong way." He can't take his eyes off the meat mallet in my hand.

I put it down. "Cross *my* heart," I promise.

"That's what I'm afraid of," he mutters. He smiles anyway. It's his way of making the best of this sticky wicket of a situation. "There may have been a betting pool in the office as to whether and when Tally Lloyd calls in and passes on the gig. I guess it's no surprise to anyone that word's gotten out about… well, about the series of unfortunate events that have taken place."

"Is that what they call it–'unfortunate events?' How very…

Lemony Snicket." Just the thought that my Acme colleagues are betting on my mistakes makes me pulverize another chicken breast.

Jack winces. "Frankly, I'm putting a light spin on it. Truth is, the spook loops are calling it 'Hotel California.' You know, like the song says"–and then he has the audacity to actually sing it–"*You can check out any time you like, but you can never leave*–"

I pound the chicken so hard and so fast that it practically disintegrates. "Yeah, okay, you Don Henley wannabe, I get the drift." I stop and take deep breaths. *One, two, three...*

No, I don't make it to ten. But I can control myself enough to place my hands on the counter with some semblance of calm. "Just out of curiosity, what time did you bet on?"

He lays down his bagel and cream cheese in order to look at his watch. "As long as she doesn't call between now and one-twenty, I'm still in the running."

"*Et tu, Brute?*" With a fork, I stab a sliver of smoked lox off the serving platter in front of him. When I jab it into his bagel, I barely miss his fingers.

He whips his hand away, and fast. "But, Donna honey–the pot is up to a thousand big ones!" Rubbing his knuckles, he mutters, "If I win, I have every intention of splitting it with you."

"How comforting."

He changes the subject to the weather. But there's only so long you can jabber on about the perpetual southern California sunshine.

Finally, when he can no longer take my stony silence, he changes tactics. "So, what's your guess as to where and when ISIL will strike?"

I stare up at him, innocently. "How should I know? Here's a shocker: I'm not on their mission team either, or even their need-to-know list, for that matter."

"Admit it, you were listening in on last night's conversation." He now feels it is safe to dig into his lox and bagel, and does so, with gusto. "I'm asking your opinion as one professional to another."

He's throwing me a bone. We both know it.

Then again, I'm so hungry to be kept in the loop, so yeah, I'll bite.

I frown, as if I'm contemplating my answer. In truth, I've been doing a lot of thinking about it.

He'd claim I'm obsessing over it. Okay, maybe I am, but he doesn't need to know it. "I agree with you that the event they're targeting has got to be something big, as opposed to past incidences, when ISIL's victims have been those who are in the wrong place at the wrong time. But my guess is that it's also something that is flying under the radar of the general public, which is why Emma isn't picking up on it. And whereas other countries have caved in to its ransom demands, the Americans and the British have refused to do so, on principle. But what if this time around, the captives have such high profiles that the countries have no choice but to pay the ransoms?"

Jack stops chewing as he contemplates this. "Interesting deduction."

"Was Arnie able to gather intel on the private jet that took Tatyana out of Damascus?"

Jack nods. "It belongs to something called Graffias International. It's an privately held corporation headquartered in Geneva. Its primary business is banking and investments, but it also has its hand in software development and transportation."

"In other words, it could be a front for the Quorum, or at the very least, laundering dirty money."

"We've come to the same conclusion. Emma is researching it now. Hopefully, we'll soon have a full list of Graffias' assets, investments and subsidiaries, not to mention its executive committee."

"Jack, have you asked the State Department for a list of any and all foreign dignitaries who may be slipping into town during the week in question–if not for a public appearance, then for fun and games?"

"We have. They claim there are none on the horizon. I'll push for them to verify it again."

"What about our highest-ranking officials?" I ask. He knows I mean POTUS and FLOTUS. But Jack despises Lee and Babette Chiffray so much that I avoid saying their names whenever possible.

"You mean, like President Chiffray?" Jack's smile flattens into a frown. "We've already checked his itinerary, as well as that of the Vice President, the Secretary of State, and the First Lady. None of them will be on this coast anytime soon."

He takes his empty plate to the sink. He doesn't look at me as he adds ever so nonchalantly, "By the way, have you heard from Lee lately?"

I frown. "You know I haven't. Why would you even ask?"

"Chill out. I only asked because he always makes it a point to call you when he's headed this way."

I shake my head. "Not anymore. Lee agreed with me that with Carl dead and my retirement from Acme, there was no need for further communication. You already know this, Jack."

He shrugs. "You haven't been exactly forthcoming these days. For all I know, things may have changed between you two."

Forthcoming? Ha! He's one to talk.

Noting the wary look on my face, he adds, "Trust me, it isn't my idea. For some reason, Ryan is convinced that POTUS will divulge anything to you–even state secrets. If, for any reason he's keeping a trip out here on the down-low, it would help Acme to know about it. In fact, it could be a game changer."

I smile sweetly. "Will it mean an upgrade in my status from its need-to-know basis?"

"You know as well as I do that it's standard Acme protocol to downgrade all retiring agents the minute they give their notice."

"In that case, I'll think about it, but no promises. Ha! I never thought that I'd have your approval to communicate with Lee Chiffray!"

"You have a nasty little habit of doing whatever you want, with or without my permission." He shrugs. "For some odd reason, you find him endearing. So, why not use every asset at your disposal–including Lee–to help Acme? Besides stroking your ego as you go on your merry way out the door, it may actually save innocent lives."

I'm so angry that the mallet slips out of my hand–a good thing for Jack, considering my aim. "Jack Craig, the way I see it, my relationship with Lee Chiffray has nothing to do with my ego, and everything to do with yours."

He nods grudgingly. "Yes, okay, I'll admit it. I hate that you find him so captivating." His eyes seek out mine. "Now it's your turn to be honest–if not with me, then with yourself, Donna. Do you really want to retire? Frankly, I get the feeling that you've had a change of heart."

"Even if I did–and I haven't, mind you–it's too late for that."

"Not as far as Ryan and I are concerned. The decision is yours to make–or not."

I wipe away a tear. "Have you forgotten that two women are dead on my watch–all because they wanted to take my place?"

Suddenly, he's at my side. "Jesus, Donna! Don't blame yourself for what happened to Jenny and Pucci."

"But I do, Jack! I'll admit it–Ryan is right. I wasn't supposed to be hosting them to a girls' night out. I was supposed to be training them to keep their eyes and ears open at all times! Instead, I encouraged them to let down their guard."

"You were only doing what all good handlers do: establishing mutual trust with your assets before sending them out into the field. You can't assess, let alone train them, if you don't first know their strengths and weaknesses."

I nod, but the truth is I don't feel any less guilty about it.

His arms go around me. "If it's any consolation, from what I've read in Tally's dossier, you won't have any issue gaining her trust–or for that matter, catching her off-guard. She's trained to be on high alert at all times." He kisses me tenderly. "And as soon as she's up to speed, you'll be free to focus on the kids–if that's what you really want."

"I do," I murmur.

I just never realized how hard it would be to give up something I'm good at, just because it's time to do so.

THE ADDRESS THAT THE PHOTO BOOTH DUDE TEXTED BACK TO ME IS located in a large warehouse in Culver City. Oddly, there isn't any signage on the roll-up door, just a number on the side of the building.

I knock several times before he finally answers. He's over six feet, a thin string bean of a guy with a scruffy goatee. Above and beyond that, he looks harried, as if I've interrupted something important.

"Enter," he says curtly.

The hallway is dark because every door is closed except for the one at the very end of the hall. As we pass the third door on the right, I hear a smack, then a grunt.

"Those are my models. You see, I'm in the middle of a photo shoot," he explains before I have a chance to ask. "This party booth stuff is just a way to make a quick buck. My true vocation is art house photography."

Intriguing. "What exactly does that mean?"

"I come up with scenarios that reflect some topic involving an unconventional human plight, then pose models with the right look around set pieces that demonstrate society's callousness."

"That's a mouthful."

He snorts at my joke. "You can say that again."

When we enter the open door, I turn around to face him and catch him scrutinizing me from top to bottom. "Fascinating! Hey, um, have you ever done any modeling?"

"Me? No. Why do you ask?"

"You've got a great look. I bet you photograph sublimely." He splays his thumbs and index fingers into right angles and holds up his hands so that I'm framed between them.

Sure, I'm flattered. I smile seductively. "How much does it pay?"

"Two hundred an hour." He rubs the lipstick off my front tooth.

Hopefully, that hasn't killed the moment for him. So that he knows I'm still game, I pluck his business card out of his hand. "Give me your card and I'll keep it in mind." Since I'm soon to be unemployed, maybe I can keep it in mind as a part-time income source.

Not to mention, I won't have to worry about blood splatters and bullet holes in my silk blouses.

His showroom contains three photo booths of varying sizes, as well as a rolling wardrobe rack containing a hodgepodge of costumes, hats, boas, wands and other toys. Some of the costumes are pretty risqué, as if he robbed a Halloween store.

The randy schoolgirl, the dominatrix, a baby doll peignoir, the stripper cop, you name it.

A basket beside the rack contains a few adult toys.

I pick up a dildo. "I'm hiring you for a middle school prom, so don't bother bringing these."

He giggles weakly. "Hey, you'd be surprised what kids play with nowadays."

I don't giggle back.

Hastily, he picks up a brochure and hands it to me. "Each booth takes four photos per sitting. You're charged by the hour, starting at seven hundred bucks for three hours, for the smallest booth. You end up with two four-shot photo cards per shoot." He points to the one on the right. "It's the cheapest because it holds just four people at a time, and you only get two four-shots. Usually, the kids like to pile in, and everyone wants a four-shot, so it probably isn't your best bet."

"And the prices on the other two?"

"Nine hundred and eleven hundred."

Yowzah.

All of a sudden, I hear sirens. They seem to be getting louder and coming this way.

He must hear them, too, because he quickly adds, "Look, tell you what–I'll give you the largest booth at a discount–"

There's banging on the door. Someone yells, "Open up! Police!"

Photo Booth Dude winces, but continues his spiel: "–say, the same cost as the middle booth! And I'll throw in four photo cards instead of two. Whattaya say to that?"

A loud crack can be heard as the door gives way. Photo Booth Dude takes a step back, better to see what's happening down the hall. "Wait here, okay?"

As if.

Instead, I head for the rear exit.

Too late. From what I can see just looking out the window, a line of cops are in the back too.

There's one other door in the room. I keep my fingers crossed that it's another exit, but it isn't. It's an office with rows and rows of file cabinets. Next to it is a small bathroom.

I open a drawer and pull out some files.

Surprise, surprise: Photo Booth Dude shoots porn stills.

Not only that, many of the pictures include underage teens, both male and female as well as couples and ménages of mixed and same genders, all in various states of undress, desire, nudity, and kids-gone-wild salaciousness.

In other words, the same sort of poses they'd probably text to their hotties' heart's desire.

Interestingly enough, most of the pictures are four-to-a-card, indicating that they were taken in his photo booths.

They kept their copies, and he keeps the negative. My guess is that he sells them online.

Darn it, I snag my skirt as I climb out the bathroom window, just as the police make it into the office.

By the time Photo Booth Dude and his two underage models are doing their perp walk, I'm safely back at my car.

This is one vendor I can tell Penelope we're crossing off our list.

When I call Penelope to tell her about Photo Booth Dude, she's livid. "I can't believe it! He came highly recommended!"

I snort. "By whom?"

"Why, by my husband, Peter…" Her voice trails off as the light finally goes on in that dim bulb she calls her mind. Then: "Never mind! In fact, you've got bigger fish to fry. Which band have you lined up?"

"Band? The kids would much prefer a deejay, so that they can dance to all the music they like–"

"Are you kidding? A deejay is déclassé. If this party is to be a hit–a sell-out–we need a headliner. Open your binder to page eighty-seven."

"I don't have it on me," I growl.

"Go get it, then. I'll wait."

She's got to be kidding. Okay, then, I am, too. I file my nails for a few minutes. When enough time has passed, I pick up the phone. "Yeah, okay, I'm on the right page now."

"Then you see who I'm talking about, don't you? You see how big this is don't you?"

"Um…yeah, sure." I feel as if I'm talking to a maniac off her meds.

"Donna, haven't you heard of her? We're talking Taylor Swift? Beyoncé…BIG! Katy Perry…BIG! Leonardo Cuthbert handles some of the top musical acts in the country!"

"What does this have to do with our prom?"

"Leonardo was my college sweetheart. I bumped into him a month ago, and…well, let's just say the flame was rekindled– not that I let him touch me or anything!"

"You? No, of course not." *Not.*

"He told me if I needed anything, to just call."

"So then, why don't you?"

"Because I'm not the Prom Committee Chair, or did you forget that?" she declares haughtily. "Must I do everything? My goodness, Donna, I've given you a golden opportunity to look good. Use it!"

Suddenly, I'm listening to a dial tone.

I'm sure it won't be the last one I hear today.

Now, I have to find the binder. Where the hell did I leave it?

Twenty minutes later, I find it in the garage. Jeff's been using it as part of his skateboard ramp.

I lug it into the house, and open it to page eighty-seven. Beside Leonardo's name is his telephone number.

A man's voice barks, "Yeah, who is it?"

A direct line? Maybe Penelope's right and the guy is still sweet on her. Only one way to find out.

"Mr. Cuthbert, my name is Donna Stone. I'm a friend of Penelope Bing–"

"Penny?" He laughs. "Jesus! She didn't waste any time. What does *she* want?"

"She mentioned you represented some musical acts. We were hoping that one might be available for our event."

"What's the date?"

"It a week from this Friday, at the Savoy. Sorry about the short notice–"

"Taylor's available. Would you want her?"

What…really? *Taylor Swift*!

"Of course! We'd love it!" Ouch! Forgot, I need to ask: "Um, how much are we talking about?"

"I've got to warn you, she doesn't come cheap." He hesitates. "She has backup singers–and the band, of course."

Hopes dashed. I should have known it was too good to be true.

"But because it's Penny…okay, tell you what: I'll let her go for, say, fifteen? I'll tell Taylor it's a charity gig. Gets her every time. She's working on some new dance numbers. She can try them out there. You know, impromptu, try it out in front of a small, hungry crowd. She loves doing it that way."

Yikes! Fifteen thousand is our prom budget for the next twenty years…

Then again, it *is* Taylor Swift.

And it was Penelope's idea.

"No problem, I'll send a check by courier, first thing tomorrow," I promise him.

He grunts before hanging up.

When I call Penelope with the good news, she practically crows. "I told you he'd come through," she declares smugly.

It's nice to have one thing work my way.

"And, don't forget, you've got a meeting with the palm reader in half an hour. The kids eat this kind of stuff up," Penelope assures me. She must guess I find her claim hard to swallow, because she then quickly adds, "And besides, a few diversions will keep their pea brains off more puerile activities."

The memory of Morton's chest-high handiwork is reason enough to keep the joint hopping with as many bells and whistles as possible.

A HALF-HOUR LATER, I'M KNOCKING ON THE DOOR OF SOMEONE who goes by the name of Madame Zenobia. I must have rung the doorbell a million times when, finally, she answers the door.

Madame Zenobia is a tall woman in her late fifties. Her stark-white widow's peak is in sharp contrast to the raven-hued hair falling loosely down her back.

In other words, she certainly looks the part of a gypsy hag.

I'm taken aback that she is hastily tying a black silk kimono at her waist. Is she just getting out of bed? In any case, obviously, she forgot we had an appointment. Even if she can read the future, her skills for remembering the present are sorely lacking.

"Mrs. Stone, is it? So sorry! I was communing."

"Ah! With spirits?"

"Nah! Mother Nature. Take a teaspoon a day of Metamucil, your bowels will work like clockwork." She stands aside to let me in. "Care to join me in the salon?" She ushers me out of the foyer.

When we enter the salon, she takes a turban from a hat rack and slaps it on her head before ushering me over to the circular table in the middle of the room. In front of it, two chairs sit side-by-side.

In the center of the table is a crystal ball. Madame Zenobia takes the chair directly in front of a deck of Tarot cards that sits on a silk kerchief. She sweeps an arm over both objects. "I presume you'll want a demonstration. By the way, I also read palms, and I'm a hypnotist. Which would you prefer first?"

I point to the cards. "Why don't we start here?"

"Yes, I presumed it would be your first choice!" She grins grandly. "And what question can I answer for you?"

Now, there's a question I wasn't expecting. "Hmmm. Okay…" I take a deep breath. The thing most worrisome to me is not the school dance, but Jack's mission–not that I'll say that to a psychic. "A major event is about to take place. I'd like to know how it may affect my life."

Madame Zenobia's eyes open wide. "Let's find out, shall we?" She takes the cards and shuffles them. When she's finished, she turns to me. "Please cut the cards with your left hand."

After I do as requested, she takes the right stack and lays it over the left one, then lays them out: the first in the center; the second one, to the first card's left; the third, centered beneath the first; the fourth, above the first card; then the fifth, sixth, and seventh to the first card's right side, in that order.

With my nod, she turns over the first card. "Ah! The two lovers–reversed! The event you mentioned has the potential to tear them apart."

Not good. However, I hold a poker face. "Go on."

She flips over the second card. It depicts a devil. "He represents captivity, or bondage. Just out of curiosity, is this event that concerns you an S&M party?"

"Hopefully it won't turn into one," I murmur.

"Should you think otherwise, keep my card handy. I excel at such gatherings. Go figure!"

She shrugs then turns over the third card. It shows a man in a chariot. "Some interaction during this time will force you to make an important decision."

"Can you be more specific?"

She snorts. "At the rate Mrs. Bing negotiated?" She knits her fingers over her eyes. "Sorry, things are too cloudy."

I sigh, but nonetheless I slap a twenty-dollar bill on the table.

"Clarity comes with the next card," she promises, as she pockets the cash.

Yeah right, we shall see.

As she turns over the lone card on the top row, her eyes grow big. "Ah, the Tower! With whatever decision you make, old allegiances will crumble, and new ones will be built in their place!"

"Your statement could mean anything," I point out to her.

Adamantly, she shakes her head. "Duh! You're not supposed to take it so literally. The point is to look *inward,* to draw the true meaning out of yourself!"

If I did that, then why would I need you?

When she flips over Card Number Five, she gasps.

I stare down at it. "What is that, a compass?"

"It's called the Wheel of Fortune. It portends that this event will change your destiny for good, one way or another."

My destiny will be decided on that night? *It's unmitigated malarkey! She doesn't know what she's saying…*

Then why the hell am I so scared?

Card Six depicts a king on a throne. In one hand, he holds a sword. In the other are the scales of justice. Madame Zenobia's caterpillar brows arch into bat's wings. "It's the card of judgment. Unfortunately, it's reversed."

"Why is that bad?"

She shrugs. "Depends. Let me put it this way. If you get stopped for speeding, don't expect to beat the ticket."

She doesn't know it, but much more is at stake. Will whoever commits the crime get away with murder?

The final card, Number Seven, is also reversed. It shows the World.

Madame Zenobia sighs mightily.

"What?" I implore her. "What do you see?"

"It ain't pretty. Whatever you're planning, don't expect it to be a cakewalk."

Noting that the color has left my face, she picks up my hand and turns it palm up. "Maybe we'll have better luck with this," she promises.

She spoke too soon. She winces as she looks at my lifeline, then asks, "Are you in charge of paying my fee?"

I nod.

"If you don't mind, I'd like to get paid in advance–you know, just in case."

Despite being insulted, I write out a check in her fee amount and hand it to her.

As she walks me out the door, she has one more word of advice: "Don't buy any green bananas. You may not be around long enough to enjoy them."

11

Last Minute Cancellations

It's inevitable that some of the invitees to your party will try to bow out at the very last minute. It's your party, but no need to cry, even when you wanna. Here's what you do instead:

1. *Lay on the guilt trip. Tell them that you've made their favorite dish. Remind them that you haven't seen them in too long. Lie about inviting someone who you know they're gaga to meet. Sure, they'll be disappointed when their crush is a no-show—even more so when they discover he was at the party they missed.*

2. *Invite your B-List: Yes, I know—the reason they're so far down the totem pole is that they aren't the scintillating conversationalists of those who have cancelled. Then again, maybe this time they'll surprise you by keeping their feet out of their mouths. Wishful thinking, I know. That being said, if the faux pas fly, send them on an emergency errand—one that takes them out of the house, and out of your hair until the party's over.*

3. *Beg your A-Listers to reconsider. If the reason for bowing*

out was the lack of a babysitter, hire one for them. (Just don't tell them that you picked the sitter up where all the local streetwalkers hang out. Oops!) If they're passing because they've gotten a better offer, guilt them with your tears. If that doesn't persuade them, perhaps it's time to go after the competition. It's hard to throw a party when your house has burned down. Molotov cocktail, anyone?

Tally Lloyd walks with purpose. Be it her ramrod straight posture, her take-no-prisoners poise, her long, lush mahogany brown hair or her honeyed Southern drawl, everything about her commands your attention.

Abu is more than impressed with the ease in which she converses with him in three of the Arabic dialects used commonly in Pakistan, Afghanistan and Iraq, as well as the languages of Urdu and Farsi. Arnie is happy that she's already up to date on all the Pentagon-approved tech programs, and can clue him in to what Acme can do to get a foothold into the DOD's various agencies based on our own tech gadgets and expertise. Her assault weapon marksmanship scores easily rival those of Acme's exterminators. To top it off, Dr. Bellows is pleased that Tally's psychological tests show no phobias, disorders or psychoses.

And everyone is having a blast hearing her and Acme's pilot, George Taylor, swap dogfight stories.

In fact, Dominic is so smitten with her that he offers to be her assaulter for the martial arts test.

"She'll whip your ass," I warn him. "It's not as if she's one of your fawning Dominic-imbos."

He winces at the reference to his Spooklandia fan club members, but his comeback has me smarting, too: "Perhaps you should stay away from this one, old girl–at least until tomorrow. Wouldn't it be nice to break the curse put upon you by whatever gypsy you've offended?"

He is the only one being offensive. To make this point, I poke him hard in the gut with my elbow. "I'm glad you lost your wager."

"If I take her home tonight, I'll be happy I did too," he gasps.

While Acme's martial arts instructor is putting Tally through her paces (or I should say, while she's putting Dominic through his), I head to Acme's rooftop deck–the one place I can make a call to Lee Chiffray without being overheard.

THE TEXT I SEND LEE SAYS SIMPLY:

I have a question for you.

I send via the only cell phone number I have for him, one set up to receive just my calls.

Oddly, I don't get a bounce-back, let alone a tone indicating that the number has been disconnected.

Now, all I can do is wait for him to text me back.

Acme's roof is not a bad place to hang out. Ryan has it tricked out like a beautiful garden, with grass, flowerbeds, benches, walkways, Japanese maple trees–even a six-foot-high box hedge on the highway side.

Best of all, it has a view of the ocean.

Despite Jack's jealousy, the truth of the matter is that there was only one thing that tied Lee and me together–our mutual desire to wipe Carl Stone off the face of the Earth. Now that he's gone, we have no reason to continue any sort of relationship.

I'm sure the first lady–Babette Breck Chiffray–was just as relieved about our final farewell as Jack was, despite the fact that she was Carl's eyes and ears, and possibly his friend-with-benefits too.

Well, now we'll never know. It's hard for me to fathom what Lee saw in someone as clueless, devious, and narcissistic as Babette. It wasn't as if he needed her billions, since he has just as much, if not more, in his own right.

The fact that he's a blond Adonis certainly helped ease any angst Americans had over the shock that their president-elect, Catherine Martin, put a hit on her husband, Robert.

By all rights, Catherine should get the electric chair. But she won't, because she did her political party the favor of stepping down before the actual inauguration.

And Jack actually thinks I'm crushing on someone who can pardon her? I think not.

And not just because she ruined my high school reputation, either.

I'm still so angry at Jack's bullshit that when I hear the buzz of the phone in my hand, my response is a cold and crisp, "What is it?"

Lee chuckles. "You called, so you tell me."

"Oh!" Thank goodness he can't see me right now, since I'm sure my face is the color of a Target dot. "Wow, thanks for calling back...Lee."

"Why wouldn't I? You were the one who wanted to call it off, remember?"

"We no longer have the same thing in common...remember?"

He laughs. "Despite your newly widowed status, I think we still have a hell of a lot in common."

I take a deep breath. "You're not making this call any easier."

"Good to hear! Unlike all the lobbyists who hang from the rafters of every building up and down K Street, I love it when you need something from me. Name it."

"I...I just wondered if you're coming to town anytime soon."

"It can be arranged." By the tone of his voice, I can tell he's intrigued.

"No–you don't get it. I'm asking if you've got a trip planned for Los Angeles. Already, I mean. You...and Babette? Or just you? Or just Babette?"

I can imagine I sound like a blithering idiot to him.

There's a long pause. Then: "Why would you ask?"

"Just...'cause."

"Oh, I see." Another long pause. Finally: "Officially, no. However, if you–"

"Good! Thanks, Lee! That's all I need to know." The neediness in his voice breaks my heart.

"But...Donna, I'd like to–"

I don't need to prolong the agony–his. "Don't worry, Lee. Everything is fine, just...fine! I–I look forward to when you're out here again, whenever. See you then."

Quickly, I hang up.

Now I can officially tell Ryan what he wants to know: POTUS is in the clear.

I'm sure it's something Jack will want to hear too. Well, he won't hear it from me. Ryan can, if he quote-unquote feels he needs to know.

That's what Jack gets for doubting me.

12

Dealing with Your Guests' Requests

Your vision of your party is that (a) it flows smoothly and without a hitch, (b) your guests enjoy every moment of it, and (c) your social set is buzzing for months that it was a raving success.

Despite your attempts to make all of your fantasies a reality, the typical swarm of metaphorical flies has the unsightly habit of plopping dead center in the ointment of your life. To ensure the day of your soirée isn't its next destination, here are a few do's and don'ts:

DO invite everyone you've ever wanted to host. Let this be your black-and white-ball (of which you are its one and only belle), your grand salon, your fête-accompli! (It's not spelled wrong; it's a pun. Just part of the fun…)

DON'T spare any expense. This is your time to shine! That said, pull out all the stops on food, drink, decorations, location, and most certainly the outfit you'll wear on your big night! (And if you're lucky, despite its great flavors and presentation, there will still be enough food left over so that you can live off of it until you pay off your credit cards.)

DO triple-check every little detail. If it's being catered, go over the menu and libations list with the caterer at least three times.

Remind her that there are no second chances, no makeovers, and no make-goods. Take her to the shooting range with you and she'll hear you loud and clear.

DON'T forget to ask your guests if they have any odd predilections you will need to accommodate. But once you do so, be prepared to be bombarded with a list of food allergies–and don't be surprised if you get a couple of odd sexual requests as well. Some people want you to be their fantasy as well as their host!

"You're sure?"

For the life of me, I don't know why Ryan doesn't believe me when I relay the conversation between Lee and me.

I make the letter X over my chest. "Cross my heart, hope to die."

He shows his relief with the ghost of a smile. And yet, there are dark rings around his eyes, and his forehead seems even more lined than I remember it.

If I try to hug him, he'll shrug me off.

Too bad. I do it anyway.

Glad to see I'm wrong, and he hugs back.

And thank goodness the blinds are drawn, so that the rest of the office can't see that he's such a softie.

Jack bounds in without even knocking–nothing new there. Seeing our clinch, he does a double-take. "What the hell is going on here?"

Like me, Ryan couldn't care less and stays put. He lifts his hand off my back in order to give Jack the finger.

Jack shrugs and eases down on Ryan's couch, as if he doesn't have a care in the world. "So, what's the verdict?"

"It's not POTUS or FLOTUS," Ryan assures him.

"What a relief." Jack's sarcasm indicates he feels that it's anything but.

Tally's head pops in next. "Mistress Stone, I want you to be the first to know–I aced it!"

"I'm not surprised," I assure her.

"Well, someone is–the infamous Mr. Fleming." She delivers this with a proud smile. "Sorry, but he may be on the disabled list for a couple of days."

"Serves him right," I mutter under my breath. "What happened?"

"Let's just say he put his hand somewhere it shouldn't have been. But a sprain is better than a break, am I right?"

Ryan buries his head in his hands.

Tally holds out her hand. In it is a note. "It's from Dominic."

My perplexed look prompts her to add, "He made me promise not to read it."

I take it gingerly, and open it:

My dear Donna,

I beg you to stay clear of Madam Lloyd. Doing so will allow the obvious attraction between this luscious lady and myself to continue toward its inevitable course. At the same time, it will go far in fading the blemish on your growing reputation as a black widow trainer.

Heed my words,

Dominic

I crumple it up and make a three-point shot into Ryan's wastepaper basket.

Tally tilts her head in my direction. "Boss man, I've got to run an errand. It's not far, but it should take me out of the office for the rest of the afternoon. Mind if my keeper goes with me?"

Ryan nods solemnly.

As I walk past him, he growls under his breath, "Don't make me regret this."

Once again, I cross my heart.

When I'm out the door and I'm sure no one is watching, I make the sign of the cross.

TALLY LIED TO RYAN AND JACK. WE'RE IN HER RENTAL–A SLICK black Tesla Roadster–headed to Van Nuys Airport where she left her Learjet 45XR.

With me, she's more honest–make that direct. But, as she puts it: "Considering my perfect test scores and the luck of the other candidates, I presume the gig is mine for the asking."

I show my agreement with a nod. "You're right. At this point, beggars can't be choosers."

She laughs. "Thanks for your honesty. However, before I formally sign on, I need to ask you a few questions, and I felt it would be easier for you to let your hair down if we talked outside the office, just the two of us."

"Under normal circumstances, I'd agree with you. But lately, I haven't had good luck with the candidates outside the confines of Acme's offices."

"I'm willing to take my chances. The whole purpose of my taking this gig was to leave a desk job behind for good."

"I can assure you, Tally, a desk is the last place you'll find yourself." I chuckle. "Although, admittedly, I have found myself on *top* of a few desks."

"I can imagine." She looks away for a moment. When she's ready to face me, there is a new resolve in her eyes. "I hear you. It comes with the territory."

"On a positive note, not every mission is a seduction. You'll learn, very quickly, that each one will vary. In the first, you may be a carrier. Another may call for an extermination. A third might entail breaking and entering in order to secure vital intel. The next may mean the exfiltration of an asset." I hesitate. "I don't need to tell you that there are no guarantees for your safety."

Her grin dissolves into hardened grit. "I made it through three tours in the Middle East. I'll take my chances."

"It's probably why you turned out to be the best person for the job after all."

"No. You were the best hard woman. You were the best honeypot." She takes her eyes off the road just for a moment to make her point. "Donna Stone, you're a legend."

I'm truly humbled that she thinks so. "It's flattering to hear, Tally. But it's come at a very high price."

Like heartbreak. And trust.

And innocence.

She pulls into the airport's parking lot. "Save it. In a couple of hours, we'll be watching the sun go down on a Baja coast beach. It'll make for great girl talk."

She's right about that.

Something tells me this is the start of a beautiful relationship.

"YOU'LL MISS IT, WON'T YOU?" TALLY AND I ARE SITTING ON chaise lounges on a sliver of beach caught between a placid Pacific and a hardened lava ridge. Her plane landed only a few yards away, on the hard-packed sand.

From what I can tell, we're in the middle of nowhere–certainly south of Lázaro Cárdenas, but certainly north of ticky-tacky Guerrero Negro. The owner of the beach's sole food truck speaks only Spanish. Since Tally doesn't know the language, when I grabbed our piña coladas, I ordered dinner for us, too: soft tacos filled with thin-sliced marinated steak.

To keep our hunger at bay while we wait for our order, the cook hands me homemade tortilla chips, along with a bowl of yummy salsa.

"*Delicioso!*" I exclaim. "What's in it?"

He beckons me forward. "*Un ingrediente secreto,*" he whispers. "*Crema de anacardo.*"

Ah! Cashew cream. I'll remember that for when I make it at home.

But right now, I'm a million miles from there, at least emotionally. Maybe that's why Tally's question doesn't seem so hard to answer. "The fact that it'll be over by next week is hitting me just now. But I've got my children to think of."

Tally shrugs. "It's why I chose not to have kids. You can't be a kamikaze and worry about getting home in time to make dinner."

"At some point, you'll want to get out of the game," I point out.

She snorts. "You know the odds. They'll take me out feet first." Her gaze never wavers. "Look, Donna, if you hadn't met the ambiguous Mr. Stone, who's to say you wouldn't have stumbled into the armed services, or some government job, or Acme, or with some other cowboy organization that handles the bad guys for the rest of the world? Don't fool yourself! You always had it in you. It's just that he provided the detour."

"Yes–and, eventually, the on-ramp, too." I shrug.

"Hey, trust me, I get it." All the fun has gone out of her voice. "I made a choice, too–and I don't regret it in the least. I came into this world alone, and I'll go out the same way." She shrugs. "Despite what you think, you will too. Remember: kids grow up, and move out. They get lives of their own. So, you see? The odds are you'll end up just like me anyway–alone."

I shake my head adamantly. "Not exactly. I'll have Jack."

She laughs. "Who ever knew Wild Card Jack Craig would end up being someone's Mr. Right!" Tally feigns ignorance. "How did you meet him again? Ah, yes, through Acme! And now, you have your happily ever after story–or do you? Don't tell me you don't worry about him with each mission. And don't tell me you don't already regret that you won't be by his side every step of the way."

I can't because she's right–I do.

But I no longer have the privilege. She does.

I'm okay with that, because I know she can hold her own in any dogfight.

I smile and tip my glass to her. "He's in good hands with you. Tally Lloyd, you're invincible–a veritable Super Woman."

"Trust me, I too have my Kryptonite." She digs into the salsa with a chip and takes a big bite.

I laugh. "Oh? What's that?"

She waits until she swallows before answering. "I'm severely allergic to nuts."

Oh hell, now she tells me.

The fact that I've quit laughing gets her attention. She follows my gaze. When she realizes I'm staring at the dip, her eyes open wide with fear.

Just as she pulls out the epi-pen from her jacket pocket, I reach out to calm her. Our hands collide and the one thing that will save her life falls onto the sand bar. As she gasps for air, I reach down for the epi-pen, but a wave washes over it, and it tumbles just out of reach.

By the time I grab the epi-pen, it's too late. She is convulsing.

The bartender informs me that the nearest clinic is twenty miles away by rough road, and tosses me the keys to his jeep. I practically carry her to it because anaphylactic shock has over-taken her.

By the time we get to the hospital, all they can do is pronounce her dead on arrival.

THE CALL TO RYAN IS NOT ONE I LOOK FORWARD TO MAKING. HE must not like seeing my telephone number on his Caller ID because he growls hello into the phone.

My message is the last one he needs to hear. After a litany of curses, he shouts, "This is crazy! It's true what they're saying! You're a black widow trainer!"

"Well, my esteemed colleagues are wrong!" I retort indignantly.

"I say it is! Three strikes, Donna!" He hyperventilates another few moments. When he calms down, he growls, "Tell the truth. Are you doing it on purpose?"

"What do you mean by that?"

"You know what I mean–*killing off the competition.*"

"How dare you! I won't even dignify that with an answer! Listen, if you prefer that I bow out of training a replacement–"

"Prefer it? Hell yeah, I prefer it! And so would anyone who wants to apply–if there's anyone left. Once the word gets out, I doubt that very much indeed. Oh, and Ms. Stone, one last thing."

"What is it, Ryan?" I wince because I'm afraid to hear his response.

"If you expect to collect any of your exit package–or for that matter, whatever bonus you've accumulated this year to date–you'll first have to attend a minimum of three SA meetings."

"What? Now, that's not fair, Ryan!" I sputter. "Just what the hell is SA?"

"Spooks Anonymous. It's a non-profit organization that was set up by the covert-ops community as a way to help with the emotional decompression of exterminators and other highly stressed assets, so that they may better re-assimilate into society."

"You're kidding, right? Granted, our jobs may be abusive at times–your harassment now is a good case in point–but it's not as if we're strung out on some drug!"

"No, I'm very serious. There's an active chapter in Los Angeles. I know someone who may actually consent to be your sponsor. You'll get a call from Bosworth Hobart within a day or two."

"Sounds peachy." I slam down the phone.

When I pick it up again, it's not to call SA, but to get George down here with a helicopter, as soon as possible. I request that he pick me up in equipment that can handle Tally's body as well.

Tally was wrong about one thing. She didn't die alone.

But she shouldn't have died at all.

By the time I get home, it's after midnight.

The house is dark. Jack's car is not in the garage, so I assume he's still at Acme.

I'm quiet as I walk upstairs because I don't want to wake Aunt Phyllis or the children.

I pause when I pass Mary's door. The urge to hold her in my arms is overwhelming. No matter how briefly you've known them, watching helplessly as the last seconds of someone's life flows out of them makes the relationships you care about most even more precious. I don't like that the estrangement with my daughter has gone on this long. I want to talk to her, and to laugh with her again.

I open the door, just a crack. Her body is just faintly outlined through the moonlit night coming in through her window.

Her body, and someone else's.

Their bodies are so close that if I didn't know my own daughter's size and shape so well, they could pass as one, despite the fact that he is taller.

Not to mention blond.

Oh…

Fuck.

No way.

She's sleeping with her Mystery Date.

Instinctively, I draw my gun with one hand, and yank the covers off with the other.

Thank goodness, the boy is sleeping over the sheet, and Mary is under it. Both of them are fully clothed.

As Mary and her friend-hopefully-not-yet-benefitted scramble out of bed, my daughter exclaims, "Mom…Please, don't shoot him! It's not what you think!"

I waver from doing so. Finally, I drop my arm and flip on the overhead light.

Even when my eyes adjust to the brightness, I still can't believe who's standing in front of me:

It's Evan Martin–Bobby and Catherine's son.

Okay, yeah, this I have to hear.

13

Party Crashers

Inevitably, word will get out that you're throwing the social event of the year, if not the decade. (I'd say century, but I haven't seen your guest list, so I reserve judgment on that for now.) I might as well warn you now that some starry eyed wannabes will do their utmost to crash your party. The best way to handle unexpected guests is to:

1. *Scan your party periodically with hidden webcams. You can't be everywhere at once, so why not plant digital video cameras in every room? Not only will you catch interlopers, you may also see those who sneak off into your bathroom to make out. (Bonus! You'll get to listen in as your besties gossip on what they really think of you.)*
2. *Hire bouncers. Raid this week's trendiest hot spot for a couple of brawny guys who won't take any guff from an insistent party crasher. (Tip: make sure they have at least a fifth grade education, so that they can read the guest list you hand them.)*
3. *Release the hounds. Yes, I know. You're worried that despite the incomparable training received by your pack of*

Tibetan mastiffs, one of them may tear into the wrong guest. Not to worry! Upon arrival, spray skunk essence on those who belong.

Should this cause a mass exodus, you've still accomplished your goal: getting rid of undesirables.

I USED TO THINK THAT EVEN ON THE WORST DAY OF YOUR LIFE, HOT cocoa had a way of making the world right again.

Not today. Not if half of what Evan is telling us is true.

"So, Evan is the boy you've been sneaking around to see?" I ask Mary.

She nods defiantly. "We've stayed in contact since–well, since his father's funeral. He's dropped out of school. He's been living in cheap hotels. I convinced him to come out here because he's got nowhere else to go, Mom! When he got here, he found one off the 405, but now he's run out of money."

I shift my gaze to Evan then back to her. "Why didn't you tell me before now?"

"I would have, but Evan was being stupid about it."

Evan turns red. "I've been making a lot of dumb decisions lately. I felt that with all the bad blood between you and my mom, you'd figure out a reason to say no, and that would make Mary even madder with you than she already is."

I don't want to tell him that her anger is already at fever pitch.

He has a point about one thing. Under normal circumstances, the fact that Catherine tried to stab me to death should have put a damper on any goodwill I have toward her family, but it did just the opposite: I truly feel sorry for Evan.

Even more so since the parent he needs most is the one he no longer has in his life.

"Mother, when Evan finally agreed to come here, you'd just gotten back from a trip," Mary says. "But by then, you'd heard I'd been slipping out during lunch to meet with him, and you went ballistic and accused me of…of…" She glances over at Evan, too embarrassed to go on.

I turn to Evan. "Tell me everything, from the beginning."

His tale is not pretty. "After Dad died and Mom went to prison, I was left on my own. As you know, I was in the middle of my junior year at Overton Prep, in Massachusetts. My parents had already paid my tuition through my senior year. You get a bit of a break if you do it, or you can earmark the difference to the school's scholarship fund. Dad opted to do that instead."

Of course, he would. He was always generous to those less fortunate. I knew this firsthand.

"I was a straight-A student. I was also a co-captain of the lacrosse team, and of the JV basketball team. But when news came out about Mom's role in Dad's death, suddenly it was like I couldn't do anything right at Overton." Shamed, he drops his head. "I couldn't sleep at night. I was distracted by all that was going on. My grades dropped, and I wasn't holding my own on either team."

"Surely your counselor at Overton acted as your advocate to your teachers and the head of school," I point out.

He snorts. "Hardly! Like all the counselors on staff, Mr. Shackleton is a psychiatrist. His way of helping was to give me 'something to sleep.' The dosage he gave me was so high that I missed many of my morning classes, not to mention a practice or two. When I asked him to lower the dose, he refused. When I took it upon myself to cut the dosage in half, it was used as part of the reason for my permanent suspension, along with my falling grade point average."

"Between grieving the loss of a parent, and the anguish of learning that your mother, the president-elect, was going to prison, of course there was a chance your grades would suffer," I murmur. "I can't believe anyone could blame you for your mother's deeds–"

"Oh, I can," Mary exclaims. She blushes and looks down. Her father may be dead, but she's left to shoulder the infamy of his shame.

As am I, Jeff, and Trisha.

"She deserved to go to jail." He looks me straight in the eye as he states it as a fact, nothing more or less. "Frankly, she deserves–well, worse. But I'm paying for it, too. You know what they say: 'The sins of the father...'" He looks sideways at Mary. "Or, in this case, it's the mother."

"Did you check into other schools?"

"When I applied to other private preps, the drop in my GPA was the excuse they gave to turn me down." He shrugs. "We had the farm in Massachusetts, but because Mom was in Congress, I grew up in Georgetown. I applied there, to the local public schools. It turned out to be a very big mistake. This is what happens when you're a wealthy white kid who won't hand over his ATM card to the school's bad-ass gangsta." He pulls up his T-shirt to show me cigarette burn marks.

Seeing me flinch, he tucks his shirt back into his jeans. "I'm not that rich anymore, anyway. Without my dad at the helm, his company is in a free fall. My mother's legal fees are humongous, and our personal financial manager has made some bad calls too." Just speaking of the problems weighing him down makes the tiny lines on his forehead seem to grow deeper. "Mrs. Stone, I didn't know where else to go. The trusts are bleeding cash at such a fast rate that I'll be broke before I reach my twenty-first birthday. The D.C. townhouse is in foreclosure. As for the farmhouse, it was paid off years ago, but I'll never go back there. I've already put it on the market. The only lookers are those who want to see where 'the killer congresswoman' lived."

I don't blame him in the least for not wanting to go back there. It's where his mother gave a hit man the order to kill his father.

Carl was the hit man.

It's something I can never tell Evan. Or Mary either, for that matter. Not after seeing the deep sadness in her eyes as she listens to her dear friend's plight.

Not after watching her as she lays her hand over his and squeezes it tightly, in solidarity.

And certainly not after agreeing with her when she implores, "Mom, it's okay if Evan stays here with us, isn't it? He can finish high school here, at Hilldale High."

"It's fine with me. He can take the bonus room over the garage. However"–I pause and take a deep breath–"despite your feelings for your mother, I think you should tell her your plans, Evan. She has a right to know."

He shakes his head. "She has no say in my life anymore."

"You may think that's the case, but until you're an emancipated minor, she still has some authority over you."

He shrugs. "I'll file as soon as possible. But I'm through with her. Feel free to tell her yourself."

Great. It'll be the cherry on the cake of my day.

Seeing my face, Mary says, "Mom, I promise–no more playing hooky." She holds her head high as she adds, "And no more fights with the other kids when they say cruel things about–about my father."

Evan murmurs, "Mary, I'll be there for you. No, really, we'll be there for each other."

As I make Evan a second cup of cocoa, I hold in my tears to the point where I can't talk, because I know I'll choke on them.

When I finally pull myself together, I say good night and go upstairs to bed. First thing tomorrow, I'll call the Federal Prison Camp in Alderson, West Virginia to ask if they can accommodate a visit to Inmate Number 27955-101, known to the outside world as former President-Elect Catherine Martin.

EMMA PURSES HER MOUTH INTO A SOUR FROWN. "UM…ARE YOU sure they'll be okay? I mean, Nicky's been so fussy lately. I can't seem to get him to sleep. Not to mention, Phyllis seems pretty busy this morning."

She has reluctantly agreed to allow Phyllis to watch her newborn while we go on a run. Ironically, Emma's limited exposure to my aunt has never really caught her in the best light.

Noting her frown as Phyllis puts Nicky's bassinet on top of the dryer while she sorted the laundry, I pull her out the door with me before she changes her mind. "I'll admit it, Aunt Phyllis can be absentminded, but trust me, Emma–Nicky won't end up in the dryer or something."

I conveniently neglect to mention the time Aunt Phyllis once took then four-year old Jeff with her to her senior poker night. Because it was the first time she won every hand, one of the other ladies (I use the term lightly) claimed my son was counting cards for her.

He was, but the point I'm making is that they got out of there in one piece.

Okay, granted. Phyllis lost her upper bridge somehow, but as long as Jeff held on to all of his fingers and toes, I chalked up the evening as a success.

The jogging trail I've suggested takes us out of Hilldale, through nearby headlands overlooking the Pacific Ocean. On purpose, I haven't mentioned the Acme mission at all. Instead, I've kept the topic on the shenanigans involving the prom. Emma shakes her head when she hears about the pedophile photographer. When I get to the part about the Tarot card reading, she's laughing so hard that she has to stop.

We're at the very top of the hill, so it's as good a place to catch our breath as any. As we gaze out over the Pacific Ocean, Emma exclaims, "Wow! Beautiful!" She sighs deeply. "Thanks for talking me into doing this."

I squeeze her bicep. "Hey, you were the one complaining that you're no longer the lean, mean fighting machine you once were."

She smiles. "I guess getting out again in the middle of the day for fresh air and sunshine is one of the perks of being a lady of leisure, even if it's only temporary–I mean, in my case, anyway."

I open my mouth to say something, but nothing comes out. What is there to say, anyway? She's right. I, on the other hand, have a permanently out-to-lunch status.

In the wake of three deaths, make that *persona non grata* status.

Emma takes my silence as tacit approval. "Boy, I'll bet you're ecstatic that the whole 'replacement' situation is finally over."

What does she mean by that? Has Ryan come to his senses and realized that no one can follow in my footsteps? *Well, about damn time.*

"It was inevitable, right?" I lift my head, better to bask in the glory of it all.

"I can't believe it happened so quickly! And to get Mara Portnoy, of all people!"

And just like that, my fantasy of being irreplaceable dissipates in the stark bright light of reality. "What do you mean?"

Realizing that she's once again the bearer of unexpected news, Emma grits her teeth. "I thought Jack would have mentioned it to you. After all, it was his idea. She was the Acme sparrow based in Istanbul. Before that, she was based in Paris, around the same time as Jack. She retired, too. It's been at least five years by now. No one knew why. The typical rumors went around–you know, burn out. But Ryan left the door open for her to return if she changed her mind. Jack had the bright idea of reaching out to her. We were all surprised she said yes."

"Oh." I nod and twist my lips into something I hope resembles a grin. "Well, at least it's someone I won't have to vet."

"Considering Jack's previous experience with her? I'd say not. I guess when you're partners as long as they were, every wink and nudge is shorthand."

"This Mara woman was Jack's partner? He's never even mentioned her name to me!"

Emma takes a step back, as if once again she's put her foot in the proverbial *merde*. "It was before my time, but from what gossip Dominic told Arnie, apparently they had a falling out over...well, someone."

Was it Jack's now-deceased wife, Valentina?

If so, Mara would find it ironic that he is now living with the woman who was married to the person Valentina left Jack for: Carl.

I shake off Emma's concern with a tap on the shoulder. "Last one home is a rotten egg."

"Why bother?" she mutters. "You've always been faster than me–not to mention I already feel like a rotten friend."

Still, she must be game because she takes off down the hill, leaving me in her dust.

She's seen me angry. I guess she feels the bigger her head start, the better.

WE GET HOME TO FIND NICKY SOUND ASLEEP, ALBEIT STILL ON TOP of the dryer, which rocks as the clothes within it tumble around furiously.

"I can't believe it," Emma murmurs. "He's out like a light–finally!"

She gives Phyllis a hug, but my aunt waves her off. "A little trick every mother should know. They miss the motion in the ocean." She moves her hands back and forth in unison as her eyes drop to Emma's wasp waist. "You're just a little thing! I'll bet he was, too, when he finally came out of you."

Emma nods. "He was barely six pounds. Came early, in fact. The stress of the job, I guess." She nods toward me. "This one has her priorities straight. I may follow her out of the racket."

Dear sweet Emma, can we ever really leave it behind? Be careful what you wish for…

Emma looks at her watch. "Crikey! I'm late for…" She looks over at me and winces.

Ah, so she's got to jump on a phone conference for an update on the mission's status. "You don't want to miss the call," I say evenly.

Before Aunt Phyllis can object or pshaw, Emma smacks her with a kiss and grabs Nicky's carrier. "Grab the diaper bag and walk me out," she suggests to me.

The tone of her voice promises so much more than goodbye.

As she positions Nicky in his car seat, she says, "I've got some big news."

Guilt. I love it. Always delivers.

"Arnie and I have set the big date–finally."

"Oh!" Not what I expected, but hey, I'll run with it. "Great. For what?"

"Our wedding!" She is totally exasperated with me. "Ironically, for next Sunday. I say ironically because, A, we'd hoped for a longer lead time and, B, it was the only date available in the place where we want to hold it. We got so lucky that there was a cancellation, apparently a groom with cold feet."

"Lucky–for you and Arnie, anyway. Where is it?"

"Griffith Observatory, during a full moon."

I laugh. "You aren't werewolves, you know!"

"Please don't tease me." Her cheeks pink up. "It's just something I told Arnie I wanted to do, a very long time ago. Like an elephant, he never forgets anything. He made all the arrangements–except for the most important one."

"Let me guess. He forgot to order the invitations."

She sighs. "You got it. So now I'm asking people face to face. It's a small wedding party–just our closest and dearest friends, so I don't mind."

"We'll be there, of course. But it's...so soon, Emma. Are you sure you don't want to give yourself more time–I mean, with all that's going on at work?"

"I know, I know–we've put it off this long, so why the rush?" She pushes her bangs off her forehead–a true indication that she's anxious about it. "But I'd rather do it before Nicky is old enough to ask why we aren't married. My parents never tied the knot. I feel it made all our lives seem–oh, I don't know, inconsequential, I guess."

Emma has never talked much about her parents or siblings. In fact, just accepting Arnie's proposal of marriage was a big step for her, if only because she never felt worthy of his love, despite her nonchalant attitude toward his outright adulation. But I take her word for it that it means a lot to have those who love her most there with her.

I'm honored to be included as one of her friends.

"Donna, will you be my Maid of Honor? In fact, Arnie is asking Jack to be his Best Man."

It's my turn to blush. "I'm honored. But don't you mean Matron of Honor? I'm married, remember?"

"No, you were divorced. Or widowed." Reminding me of Carl's recent demise makes her uncomfortable enough to pretend that it's more important to fidget with Nicky's cap as opposed to looking me in the eye.

"Yes of course. Old habits die hard." So do old husbands. Mine especially. "I'm happy to accept."

"Wow! Thanks!" She bumps her head as she shifts away from the car in order to envelop me in a bear hug. "Hey, do you think Trisha would agree to be the flower girl?"

I chuckle. "No problem there. Anything that gets her into a fairy princess dress with flowers in her hair is an instant yes."

She jumps into the front seat of her car, and starts the engine. "Wonderful! Now, let's all say prayers that whatever happens regarding the mission comes down either before, or after, next Sunday."

As she drives off, it hits me that if Acme's mission fails, it may not be the joyous event she envisions.

I pray for all our sakes that this is not the case. That we can all pretend to lead normal lives for yet one more day.

By the time Jack gets home, we've already sat down to dinner. He does a double-take when he realizes we have a guest: Evan. With Aunt Phyllis, it's a full house.

"Evan–here? When did this happen?" he asks, as he bends down to kiss me.

"Last night. You got home so late and left so early this

morning..." My voice trails off. The last thing he needs is a guilt trip.

"Things have heated up. I'll tell you about it after dinner." He reaches across Trisha's head to shake Evan's hand, but noting Evan's relief at his acceptance, it turns into a bear hug instead.

Trisha won't be left out. She throws her arms around both of them. "Group hug!" she shouts.

As Mary watches this, the tension goes out of her face. It's replaced by a calmness I haven't seen in quite some time.

Not since before she knew of Carl's existence, and his role in her life.

I love Jack for so many reasons. His care and concern for my family is one of them. His adoration by them is another. And no man has ever made me feel so alive.

There was a time he could tell me anything. But now that I'm on a need-to-know basis with Acme, the emotional intimacy between us has lessened.

It all feels familiar to me. Why is that?

Oh, yes, now I remember. It's how I felt, that one day long ago when I picked up Carl's cell phone by mistake. I would have assumed it was merely a wrong number if Carl hadn't angrily snatched the phone out of my hand. Instead, at that moment I realized that the husband whom I thought I knew so well was, in fact, hiding something from me. It made me sad to think I'd never feel close to him again because he felt there were things he had to hide from me.

My situation with Jack is different. I know he loves me, and that I can trust him with my life–and have, on numerous occasions.

And yet, I'm just as sad now.

But I set my mouth into a placid smile and keep it that way throughout dinner.

It should be interesting to see what Jack has to tell me.

It's a great night for a stroll. Without any clouds to block its glow, the three-quarter moon gives off enough light so that we don't need the flashlights we've taken on our way to Hilldale Park.

Lassie and Rin Tin Tin romp ahead of us. They're up for a walk any hour of the day or night. Our path takes us right by Gabrielle Mathews' house. I spot her in one of the top windows. She's on her cell phone.

I wonder if she's talking to Jeff.

Jack follows my sight line. "What are you staring at?"

"She's a friend of Jeff's. I found the two of them up in the tree house–*smooching*."

"Jesus, I'm gone for a few hours and the place goes to hell in a hand basket," he murmurs.

"You've had more important things on your mind."

To show he appreciates my understanding, he swings me around so that he can kiss me.

Sweet.

We walk the rest of the way in silence. When we get to the park, Jack tosses the florescent tennis ball he brought for the dogs. For the next half-hour, they chase it as well as each other. Still, he doesn't say what's on his mind.

When the dogs go off in search of other critters, we sit there for what seems like an eternity, but it's not really. Finally, he says, "Because of the timetable of this mission, Ryan and I spent the last twenty-four hours combing through the personnel files of Acme operatives and agents who we could pull in from another office, if only temporarily."

"Any luck?"

He contemplates my question for a moment. Finally he nods. "In a way, yes. A currently inactive agent came to mind. You might have heard about her–Mara Portnoy."

"Nope, can't say I have. Our paths have never crossed, as I remember."

"She was my idea. I'd worked with her years ago, when we both were based in Paris. Eventually, she transferred to our office in Sofia, Hungary. The last I'd heard, she had retired. But she's ready to come back. Mara is a nice person. You'll see, when you meet her."

My snort scares a robin out of its nest. "Do you seriously think Ryan will let me within a hundred feet of her?"

"Don't be silly. Let's not forget that your perspective is the most relative one, given her position. If anyone knows that, it's Ryan."

"She's a known quantity, and therefore ready for active duty," I counter. "Jack, seriously–she doesn't need my blessing."

"She's been out of the game for too many years. A lot has changed. Even if she's a good fit, she won't go out into the field until she's ready." He turns my head so that our eyes meet. "Besides, I've already told Ryan that she has to get 'your blessing,' as you call it, if she's to work on my team."

He's right. It's his team. Not ours. Not mine. Not anymore.

And if she's the right woman for the job, I can live with that.

Jack has handed me a gift. He's allowing me the chance to ensure that whoever takes my place is the best person to have his back. I hope he's right about Mara and that I like her too, so that he will have someone else by his side, maybe when it matters most to him: when he's in danger.

It's all I can ask for. "I'll look forward to meeting her."

"Good. Why not drop by the office during lunch then, the day after tomorrow?" His kiss is one of gratitude.

No, it's more than that. It is filled with sweetness and promise.

It tells me what I long to know: he already misses me when I'm not at his side.

He will always be happy to come home to me.

He will always come home.

$$\_\_\_\_\_\_\_\_\_\_\_\_\_\_\_\_\_\_\_\_\_\_$$

14

Make Your Invitations Special!

During any busy party season, all invitations begin to look alike. To assure that the invitation to your bodacious shindig gets read, considered, and answered (hopefully, positively), follow these fail-proof tips:

- *Tip #1: Make sure that the invitation is elegant. Use a font that is subtle, but stands out. (In other words, stay away from any font used by car dealers, porn sites, or traveling circuses.)*
- *Tip #2: Have the invitation delivered in a noteworthy manner. Perhaps the packaging should be three-dimensional! Your missive can come in an elegant box, or attached to a champagne bottle (write the details on the label).*

One way your invitation will get the attention it deserves is to have it hand-delivered, perhaps by a hooker. Better yet, send it via the party's bouncer. Make sure he brings a bat with him, so that he gets the point across that you're serious about their saying yes.

- *Tip #3: As a last resort, send it with a bribe. Checks are déclassé. Consider cash instead. Last one accessing the Swiss bank account is a rotten egg!*

BY MOST STANDARDS, THE FEDERAL PRISON CAMP IN ALDERSON, West Virginia, is considered a country club. Or, because it houses only women, more like a girl's reform school.

Before Catherine arrived, Martha Stewart was considered its most notable alumnus. Her few months of incarceration were spent knitting a couple of sweaters, teaching a few cooking classes, and doing macramé. If she had any stock tips, she kept them to herself.

From what I can tell by how toned and tanned she is, Catherine is viewing her time there as a fitness spa.

When she realizes that "Jane Smith," the Federal agent who requested the meeting, is really me, her cackle roars through the visitor room. "Well, well, if it isn't my old high school bestie!"

"You're looking good, Catherine."

She coils her right arm into a muscle pose. "What were you expecting–a straightjacket and a Hannibal Lecter mask?" Her middle finger rises from her fist. "Sorry to disappoint you! If you must know, I'm the belle of the ball."

She taps the guard on the shoulder. "Get me out of here."

I call out, "Catherine, wait! It's about Evan."

She stops and turns back around. "What about him?" she growls.

"He's safe–for now. But it hasn't been easy for him."

"Join the club," she mutters. Despite her attempt to freeze me out, I see that her eyes are glazed with tears.

I don't say anything. I wait until she can't stand it anymore and blurts out, "Why won't he write me?"

"He…he's ashamed. And scared, and emotionally depressed, and lost, and…well, he's no longer at Overton."

"Why not? His tuition is paid up–"

"They used the drop in his grade point average to terminate his studies there. When he wasn't accepted at any of the other private schools, he tried public in Washington D.C., but it didn't work out."

"Ha! I can imagine." Her frown curls into a grimace. "He's soft, like his father. All he had to do was hire the biggest bullies, and his problems would have been solved. Survival of the fittest."

It was a strategy she'd used all of her life. I know firsthand. As a child, I was one of her casualties.

But it was her husband, Robert, who paid the ultimate price when she hooked up with the Quorum.

In the meantime, she ends up at an eight-year weight-loss camp, as she waits for the inevitable pardon from the vice-presidential candidate who took her place: Lee Chiffray.

I must not be doing a great job of hiding my disgust for her because suddenly her eyes narrow. "How do you know what's happened to him?"

"Since your incarceration, he's kept in touch with my daughter."

"Your daughter?" she chortles. "I presume she's turned into a boyfriend-robbing slut, just like her mother."

Keep your cool.

"None of his other friends have stood by him. It's why he showed up on my doorstep." I take a deep breath. "Catherine, despite all we've been through together, I'm willing to give him what he needs–a place where he can breathe again, to find his footing and move forward from his grief over Robert and…and over you too."

"And you're here to get my permission?"

"No. He won't need it. He's started the process of becoming an emancipated minor. Considering what you've put him through, I don't think he'll have any problem getting it."

She leans back in her chair. "Then why are you here, Donna?"

"Because you're a mother. Because you're *his* mother. Despite how he feels about you now, if he hears you care, it may make all the difference for you both."

She doesn't say anything. She just stares at me. Finally: "Bullshit! You're here to rub my nose in it! Not only did I lose Robert to you, but now you've got Evan wrapped around your little finger too!"

"Get a grip, Catherine! Robert loved you, not me."

"You clueless bitch. You may be blind, but I'm not. He pined for you all through college!" Seeing my stare, she mutters, "What? You didn't know about it? Figures! Then again, there's a lot you don't know." A single brow lifts in unison with the ominous smile on her lips. "I'll bet you didn't know that your husband, Carl, was the one who–"

Before she has a chance to spit it out, she's tapped on the shoulder by the guard. "Time is up, Catherine."

As she rises, I reach out my hand to stop her. "Wait! Finish what you were saying! Are you talking about his role in Robert's death?"

She shakes it off. "Sorry, pet. I've got another engagement. You know how it is here at the spa–quite the social whirl!" Noting my grimace, she curls her finger at me, as if we're girlfriends and she has a secret to share.

I hesitate, but my curiosity gets the better of me: yes, I want to know what Carl did. When my ear is close enough, she whispers, "No, Donna dearest. He had something bigger planned. Use what little imagination you have–and know that it's *much, much* worse."

Before I can move my head away, she snaps at my ear. Her teeth catch just a bit of the upper rim. She yelps as my elbow slams into her nose.

The guard drags her away, but she cackles as if the last joke is on me.

Maybe it is, who knows?

When I pull my hand away from my ear, it's smeared with blood.

I don't need this.

Carl is long gone. Evan needs me. My children need me.

And Jack loves me.

I've got to get some hydrogen peroxide on my wound, before it becomes infected. She's a politician. Who knows where her mouth has been?

Just as importantly: I've got to move on from Acme.

I've dodged the last two calls from Bosworth Hobart, the Spooks Anonymous sponsor. It's time that I man up.

That is, show up at a meeting.

He picks up on the first ring. He doesn't say hello, or even my name. Instead, he mutters, "What took you so long?"

"I want to–"

"Yeah, yeah I know–you want to come to a meeting. Tonight, nine o'clock, Trinity Church, downtown." He hangs up without waiting for my reply, whether it is an excuse, or a confirmation.

Yes, I will go. It's time I figure out if I'm addicted to government-sanctioned killing.

Probably not. But, if so, I hope it's like Weight Watchers, where I can still have my sugar-free cupcake and eat it, too.

"HI, MY NAME IS FRANK, AND I'M A...A RECOVERING SPOOK. I'VE

been retired for nine years, six months and twenty-two days." The bald, portly gentleman confessing at the podium speaks hesitantly. He is sweating profusely, and has a slight Slavic accent.

In unison, the crowd murmurs, "Hello, Frank."

Except for me. I'm too busy thinking that this is just my eleventh day (ninth hour and forty-two minutes) and I can't imagine I may still be counting the days nine friggin' years from now!

Realizing that I'm dumbstruck, my sponsor, Bosworth, nudges me into the customary greeting. What the hell–in for a dime, in for a dollar.

All night long, I've been listening to sob stories from folks like me: those who, for one reason or another burned out–or for that matter, got out before receiving their burn notice or a bullet to the head.

There's Jasper, the hard man who plays Russian Roulette to keep from going on a killing spree, and Ursula, the swallow who became a nun. There's Lionel, the access agent who is visited by the ghosts of those he recruited and outlived, and Lydia, the Betty Bureau who spent her whole life playing Moneypenny and never married. Now that she's retired, she feels useless. She may have been a mere pawn in the game of Spy versus Spy, but no bridge club, knitting circle, or garden can ever give her the same thrill as knowing what deadly pawns are being moved around on the international chess board.

I am not one of them.

I am still capable. I am still needed.

I am still wanted.

Lydia, who sits behind me, mutters to the man beside her, "Bullshit! His real name is Ivan Balázs. He headed up North American ops for Hungary's secret service–the TEK. Three of our best agents were deported from his country when he defected. Another two disappeared."

Bosworth taps her on the shoulder. "Shut up and let him speak."

She hawks a loogie in disgust.

Frank-slash-Ivan is undeterred. "It's been six-hundred-and-eighteen days since I've acted on my tendencies toward covert ops." He winces. "But old habits die hard."

Several people nod in appreciation of this revelation.

Encouraged by the support, he continues, "I see shadowy figures everywhere. I circle the block and double back to make sure I'm not being followed. Once, I punched out a waiter because I thought he was Micah the Exterminator."

"Micah has been dead for three years. Drowned, in Cuba," Jasper yells from the back of the room.

Frank–a.k.a. Ivan shakes his head. "I don't believe you!"

Insulted, Jasper stands up. "I should know! I killed him myself."

A woman on the other side of the room snorts loudly. "You say that about everyone." Her accent pegs her as a Castilian.

He shakes his fist angrily at her. "Can I help it if I was good at what I did?"

"We were all good–until we couldn't live with ourselves anymore. That is why we're here, *idiota*!"

"It's not your turn, Viola," Lionel hisses. "Sit down!"

She pulls out a stiletto. With lightning speed, it flies through the air toward him.

The intended victim ducks just in time.

The person behind him isn't so lucky.

Take it from me, when it comes to a roomful of spooks who may or may not have diplomatic immunity, nothing clears it out more quickly than a dead body.

"What will happen to the victim?" I ask Bosworth as we shuffle out the door with the others.

He looks around. "Not to worry! There are at least six expert cleaners in the crowd tonight. It happens about once every couple of months."

Why am I not surprised?

Ursula nudges Lydia. "Have you heard the rumor? Mara is back in play!"

My ears perk up at my replacement's name. Maybe they know something Jack doesn't, and should.

Lydia sighs longingly. "So, there's hope for the rest of us."

Ursula shakes her head. "Speak for yourself. I've found what I was looking for: redemption."

Is that what I'm seeking, too?

If so, I doubt I'll find it here.

However, there is an Alcoholics Anonymous meeting after ours. I wonder how much of the crowd hangs around for it. My guess is at least half.

Not me. There's a Lodi Zin at home with my name on it.

15

Meeting and Greeting

The manner in which you greet your guests sets the tone for your event. With that in mind, here are a few considerations:

1. *Form a receiving line. Despite the fact that your family consists of your pit bull, a cockatiel, and your deaf aunt, it's a great way to have your guests show their respect. (Hint: DO NOT place the pit bull beside the cockatiel unless you want your family to shrink by one. "Cockfight" is an exciting theme, but one you may want to save for a time when your aunt is occupied elsewhere.)*
2. *Hire a trumpeter and an announcer. You've seen it at royal functions and coming out parties: as each guest enters, his or her name is announced. The horn blowing adds a flourish of fanfare. Granted, your guests will leave with headaches and a few may claim that their hearing aids are shot to hell, but it'll be one party they'll never forget!*
3. *Know everyone by sight, and by name. If it takes testing yourself with a photo chart, just do it! Even more endearing is to greet your guest with a shared memory that*

reminds him or her why their attendance means so much to you. Remember, however, there is no need to pronounce to the wife of an old boyfriend that you too appreciated how well he's endowed, or to remind your old college roomie of the night you spent together in jail.

When in doubt exercise discretion.

ÉDOUARD ARCHAMBAULT, THE HEAD CHEF AT THE SAVOY, APPEARS unclear as to what constitutes a square meal for a bunch of 'tweenagers.

He winces when I cross certain items off the menu–say, smoked white sturgeon caviar layered with Dungeness crab on ember-roasted yams, or for that matter, duck liver toffee infused with olive oil, smothered with raw milk jelly, nesting on a bed of seaweed.

"But–but..." he sputters, "The delicacies have already been approved by Madam Bing! In fact, the caviar has already arrived and cannot be returned!" He points to several large wooden boxes against the kitchen wall.

Our prom's profit has been spent on fish eggs.

I've heard Penelope's name so often today that I want to scream. Despite her insistence that I'm in charge, she seems to be micro-managing the event behind my back.

I just don't get it! Tickets were selling briskly even before the announcement of Taylor Swift as the party's entertainment. Of course, now the dance is a sell-out. And because we went over our income goal, I hired Margot Sutcliff, one of Los Angeles's premier event planners, so that I wouldn't have to deal with Henry's salacious remarks.

Penelope's abuse of her is far worse. For example,

Margot and I agreed on eight-person round tables, but Penelope changed the order to ten-person rounds. I also asked Margot to order pale blue and silver linens and balloons in the school colors. Penelope canceled my order, asking for gold and black instead, insisting it was "far more elegant."

The good news: Not only did we sell out the dance, we got rid of all the hotel rooms, too! Thirty rooms, ten each on three floors. Two chaperones are in one of the rooms on each floor, while four children of the same gender share the other nine rooms, for a total of one-hundred-and eight young'uns.

And, of course, I'll have the Academy Awards Suite.

And, luckily for Jack and me, it shares the penthouse level and an exclusive elevator with just two other suites—neither of which are Penelope's, thank goodness.

I pat Édouard gently on the shoulder. "I'm sure that the dishes are quite delicious. It's just that I don't think they'll be appreciated by the guests. Trust me on this, Monsieur Archambault. I'd hate for you to hear your masterpieces be compared to 'boogers and snot.'"

He sighs loudly. "Madam, the culinary ignorance of *enfants américains* is a national disgrace."

"I couldn't agree more, Édouard. Still, I feel that chicken breasts, mashed potatoes, and perhaps something green as opposed to puce is more appropriate." Even I'm at a loss as to what vegetable will be universally acceptable to middle-schoolers. "Any suggestions?"

He winces. "Bacon-wrapped string beans?"

"Nice!" I honor him with a thumbs-up.

Heartened, he pronounces, "And for dessert, perhaps a sweet tart with Meyer lemon curd!"

I smile appreciatively, but shake my head no. "Why don't we just let them eat cake?"

He slams his menu book shut. Clearly, our meeting is at an end.

However, as he walks away, he holds his head high. When it comes to cuisine, he's a king among chefs. But sadly, he serves at the pleasure of the bourgeoisie with their uninformed appetites.

I DON'T KNOW WHAT I WAS EXPECTING ABOUT MARA PORTNOY, BUT it wasn't a lithe, statuesque blonde with sky-high cheekbones and startling cornflower blue eyes.

And, considering she retired over a year or two before I started with Acme, the last thing I was expecting was that she was actually a year younger than me.

I can't count the number of men's heads that turned as she passed them following the hostess to the three-seat by the window overlooking the crashing surf of the Pacific Ocean. It was as if she glided above the restaurant's hustle and bustle–above life in general–floating on a cloud.

Is such serenity the result of an eight-year sabbatical? What kind of distress caused her to take a leave in the first place? Was the issue truly behind her?

So many lives depended on the answer being a resounding yes.

She put out her hand to Jack first. He stood to take it. In fact, he augments his shake with a kiss on the cheek.

Her greeting to me is a bit more awkward. Shyly, she holds out her hand.

When I grab hold, it's to pull her in close, for a hug.

Her clinch comes with a sigh of relief.

Like me, she's glad that we're off to a great start.

JACK AND MARA'S ATTEMPT TO PLAY CATCH-UP IS SHORT AND sweet. He asks her where she lives now, and she answers, "Spain. Beautiful country. Slow moving. The people are simple, and I love the life there."

As far as Mara is concerned, I'm dying to know why she quit. Like me, perhaps Jack is too polite to ask. Or else he already knows the reason, which means I'll have to prod it out of him instead.

I don't care to find out if she knew Carl. My guess is yes, since his reputation–both within Acme and the Quorum– preceded him. Thank goodness, she's too polite to ask about him.

Instead, she asks me the ages of my children. "Seven, twelve, and fourteen," I say proudly. "The boy is in the middle."

"Ah, wonderful!" Her eyes shift to Jack. "You always said you wanted a large family," she reminds him.

I never knew that about him. If I ever get her alone–something I'm sure Ryan will never allow–I'll seek out other little tidbits about the life he had before he shared mine.

She graces me with a smile. "It's so nice to finally meet you, Donna. From everything I've heard, I can see why Jack married you."

Awkward.

I can hold a poker face as long as Jack. Still, I'd like to know if her remark was deliberate. "I, too, am glad that Jack arranged this meeting, Mara. But you've been misinformed. We're not married."

"Interesting." Her eyes leave my face in order to search out Jack's. True to form, he's looking at the menu.

When her eyes meet mine again, I am put off by her sly smile. "Then Jack did the right thing in calling me."

What the hell does that mean?

I signal our waitress. "A martini, please. Dirty and dry."

Jack looks up sharply in order to stare at me. He knows I only order martinis when I want to get good and drunk.

I'm only surprised that he doesn't want to join me.

THE CONVERSATION STAYS ON SAFE TERRITORY: THE GOOD OLD DAYS.

If you work together long enough, business colleagues develop a verbal shorthand. And just like a bicycle, once you get the hang of it, it stays with you for life.

I see it in action when Mara says, "Hey, remember the incident in Prague?"

Jack shakes his head with a laugh. "How could I forget? All that damn rain!"

Then, in unison, they say: "And all that damn blood!" before breaking out in shared chuckles.

How adorable. They could be a vaudeville act.

I'm quite aware that Jack had a life before me. I also know he's got a long history in covert ops. The sixty-four-thousand-dollar question is about his history with Mara Portnoy. Who was she to him, and why is he reaching out to her now?

A CALL FROM RYAN COMES JUST AS DESSERT IS SERVED.

Knowing I'm here, I'm sure one of his questions is if whether Mara has survived our lunch.

"If you'll excuse me, I have to take this," Jack murmurs.

The way he strolled out of the restaurant with a benign

smile on his face, you'd presume it was a call from a golfing buddy to set up their next tee time.

After a few moments of silence, Mara realizes the ball is in her court. "You're wondering about our connection, aren't you?" she asks.

Duh. Ya think?

I nod hesitantly. "Jack has been less than forthcoming."

"I gathered that."

I shrug. "That's the name of the game we're in, isn't it?"

"In this case, no." She puts down her fork, which holds just a tiny bite of a slice of hula pie. "Jack did so out of respect for our friendship. You see, Jack blames himself for the death of someone very near and dear to me: Kiril Dragonov. He headed Acme's Hungarian Bureau."

"I've seen his name on the Wall." The Wall, located in Acme's rooftop garden, is a memorial to the company's agents who have been killed in the line of duty.

"Jack has always blamed himself for Kiril's death."

I look up sharply.

She bows her head. "Sadly, he was doubly pained to discover I had a relationship with Kiril."

"Why?" I ask.

"He was sent to identify Kiril's body. Had he known about us, he would not have allowed it to be buried in an unmarked grave." She shrugs. "These things happen. Spies die alone. We know this going in. But Kiril and I were to be married. We'd planned to leave Acme together, to start a family. Needless to say, when I learned about his death and his subsequent burial, who knows where, I fell to pieces. I was too despondent to show up for work. I thought, what's the point? Our business—never ends."

She's right. Our successes are small. We may move the game

in one direction, but in time, our enemies move it back in the other.

"Knowing this, why would Jack have thought to ask you to come back?" I wonder out loud.

"When he called me, he said it was his experience–and yours–that the opportunity to avenge those we lost provides us with a new purpose. He has a point, but it doesn't apply to me. You see, I don't expect any form of satisfaction. I expect nothing because I feel nothing. What better mission partner to have by your side than one who doesn't give a damn?"

"Let me toss this out there," I counter. "Say, one who does?"

As she holds up her fork, the melted ice cream pie drips languidly onto her plate. "Donna, you never asked why Jack blamed himself for Kiril's death."

"You're right, I didn't. And yes, I'd like to know, if you don't mind telling me."

"Gladly. You see, Jack presumed that Kiril's killers were long dead and buried." Once again, she carves a bite-sized mound of pie with her fork. "Kiril's killers were Jack's wife, Valentina–and your husband, Carl."

She takes a bite of her pie.

At this point, I feel as if I need to throw up.

"No need to come in," Jack tells me as I drive him up to the entrance of Acme's offices. He reaches over for a kiss.

I have no problem accommodating him–with the smooch, anyway. As for his request that I stay in the car, I shrug it off, all the while smiling sweetly. "I'm going inside, too. I want to congratulate Arnie on his upcoming marriage."

"Ah! So Emma talked to you."

I nod. "And of course, I said yes, about being her matron–I

mean maid of honor." I look out the window. We've broached the topic of marriage ourselves, but never really honed in on a date. So many terrorists, so little time.

Granted, for me, that situation has changed. Still, it takes two to marry. "How about you?" I ask. "Did you say yes to Arnie?"

"By all means, I told him he could count on me. I only wish it weren't happening so close to when all of this is coming down."

"So now you know when?" I sit up straight. "Oh, my God! Did Acme's cryptographers break the microdot's cipher?"

Jack lets loose with a sound that's half groan, half laugh. "Damn it, Donna, you know I can't tell you, one way or another."

"Yeah, yeah, I know–I'm on a need-to-know basis." I reach for the passenger door handle.

"Wait! I wanted to ask…I mean, you haven't said what you think of Mara."

Really? Are you sure you want to know what I think?

Okay, Jack, if I'm to be honest, let me say right upfront: she scares the hell out of me. I think she's here for the wrong reason. I think she blames you for how her life has gone…

But no, I can't go there. He's a man, which means I have to let him come to his own conclusion–

No harm, however, in pointing him in the right direction.

I purse my lips, as if I'm seriously contemplating his question. "I like her…a *lot*…" *Not.*

He takes my pause as a bad sign. (As he should. That's Pavlovian. Well-trained men know to do this every time.)

"What?" Noting my pause, he braces himself against the back of the passenger seat.

"There is no 'what,'" I assure him. "Frankly, I think she'll fit right in." I smile demurely. "To be honest, I think you're right to let her ease back into things. You know, to make sure she's not put into a situation in which she may sink as oppose to swim." (And take the rest of you down with her, in Titanic proportions. *Iceberg! Iceberg!*)

His brows move closer together as he contemplates my assessment. Before he has a chance to speak, I add, "I presume her skills are a tad rusty?"

"We'll know tomorrow after her shooting range and MA test."

I pat his hand. "Good! And I presume she'll be meeting with Dr. Bellows too."

Jack shrugs. "He saw her before she joined us for lunch."

He doesn't sound too enthusiastic.

Of course, I want to know why. Arnie can wait. I've got to see if the good doctor is in.

Hopefully, he's not.

DR. BELLOWS MUST STILL BE OUT TO LUNCH, BECAUSE HIS DOOR IS closed. Make that locked.

No problem. As a former Camp Scout Girl, I'm always prepared. Sadly, there is no scout badge for breaking and entering. When I'm done doing so, I peek in for visual confirmation: he's not sitting at his desk.

All of Acme's files are digital. I can only access his computer with a password–his, not mine, although mine is still active for now.

He should know better, but I try the usual stuff that most idiots use: 123456, QWERTY, PASSWORD, and his name (Bellows).

I'm getting nowhere, and it's ten 'til the top of the hour. I may not have much more time.

I glance behind the desk at his credenza, to see if I can get some hint as to what his password might be. There are books on Freud and Jung. A picture of his dog (Freud) and his cat (Jung).

I can take a hint.

First I try FreudJung. Dead end.

Then I try JungFreud. Again, nothing.

Then it hits me: Phallus12

He wishes.

Bingo, I'm in. As luck would have it, her file is on his computer screen. Quickly, I skim it. I don't like what I read.

Fear…Repression…Depression…

Risk for violence…Homicidal ideation…Possible suicidal tendencies…

More extensive evaluation strongly recommended.

Well, there it is, in black and white.

I'm sure Jack will be disappointed, but hey, better safe than sorry.

I hear snoring. I look around, only to realize Dr. Bellows is napping on his couch. Making that whimpering sound of a fearful dog. I guess he's having a bad dream.

I'm not surprised, considering all he hears and sees.

I tiptoe out the door.

JACK COMES HOME GRUMPY.

In anticipation of this, I have his favorite meal waiting for him: rare filet mignon, my famous garlic mashed potatoes, and braised Brussels sprouts. For dessert, I also try out a new recipe for angel food cake with an orange glaze.

Oh, and yes: a big tumbler of his favorite scotch.

I've dolled myself up. All through dinner, I smile. I flirt. I flutter my fingers against his skin to remind him who appreciates him.

He smiles, but it's an effort. His eyes are weary. He's got a lot on his mind. My guess is that after Dr. Bellows' beauty rest, he buttonholed Jack and read him the riot act.

I guess the search for my replacement begins again.

In a way, I'm not disappointed when Jack heads up to the bedroom earlier than usual. I follow him up. While he undresses, I head for the bathroom. In the linen closet is a pretty pink box that holds just the right thing for making him forget his troubles and get happy: a new silk peignoir. It's sheer white, short, and with a single silk ribbon to untie it, so that he may ravish me.

Or, considering his mood, I may be the one doing the ravishing.

When I'm through with him, he'll call me his angel of mercy. He'll feel invincible again. The error he made in considering Mara will still be an annoyance, but it won't be the end of the world.

I am his world. And my goal? To make sure our world never ends.

By the time I get out of the bathroom, he's asleep.

Hmmm.

I nudge him, but he's out like a grizzly bear in winter.

I roll into bed beside him and wedge myself under his broad beam of an arm. I stare up at his face. Only while sleeping is his brow smooth and the corners of his mouth relaxed. I don't remember a mission in which he was this tense. He is always the calm eye in the middle of every storm.

Then again, in the missions we've shared, he's had me as his sounding board, his backup, his touchstone.

His gentle snoring lulls me to sleep too.

WHEN I WAKE UP, I'M SHIVERING. THE SUN HAS YET TO RISE, BUT Jack is gone.

There is a note on my bedside table that reads:

Next time. I promise. —Jack

It's nice to know he misses me as much as I miss him.

16

Buffets

When faced with a large hungry crowd, forego the sit-down meal for a buffet! Here are a few tips on how to keep everyone happily fed and feted:

- *Tip #1: If the head count is over twenty, center your table in order to have two lines instead of one. That way, the line moves quickly—always a good idea if you expect a knock on the door from the local SWAT team.*
- *Tip #2: Separate the silverware. Put all spoons in one easy-to-pluck-form preferably in a container, heads down; forks in another container, prongs down; and knives in a third one, blade down. Why? Because the last thing you need is for someone to reach in and cut their hand. However, if someone does and his blood splatters on the rare roast beef, fear not! You had the good sense to serve it rare, so just insist it's "au jus"—anything to keep the line moving!*
- *Tip #3: Inevitably, there is someone who has decided that chatting to the person behind them is more important than*

filling their plate and moving forward. For this person, a poke with a cattle prod is not at all inappropriate.

- *Bonus Advantage: Others watching him writhe in pain won't dilly-dally either.*
- *Bonus Disadvantage: They may actually run right out the door, so only use the cattle prod as a last resort.*

As suggested in the Spooks Anonymous handbook, I must now work hard to fill my time with things that keep my mind off my old life, and focused on my new.

With that in mind, after school drop-off, I sign up for a class at Serenity Now, Hilldale's yoga studio.

The woman at the reception desk–make that sitting upright on it, with her legs spread-eagled–introduces herself as Harmony. "Welcome! We look forward to having you live long and prosper!"

She's certainly agile. Perhaps she's Vulcan, as well. My eyes shift to her ears. I'm a tad dismayed to discover that they don't have pointed tips. "Thank you, I'd like to sign up for your next class."

"It starts in fifteen minutes," she assures me. "But the true benefit of yoga isn't a mere fifty-minutes of serenity, but a life-long commitment to its virtues." She grasps a class brochure with the toes on her right foot and holds it out to me.

Impressive. Of course, I've seen the same trick done by pole dancers, only in their case they're reaching for a double sawbuck out of some guy's jacket pocket.

The desk practically levitates as she goes over all the various plans, which when you cut the bullshit, boil down to this: minimally, a fifteen-class commitment for three hundred bucks.

Apparently, serenity does not come cheap.

But since it's the price I need to pay to keep my mind off the life I left behind, I sign on the dotted line.

It'll be worth it when I see the look on Jack's face as I assume Harmony's oh-so-bendy position.

OUR INSTRUCTOR IS A WOMAN WHO IS SLIM BUT MUSCULAR. SHE introduces herself as Amity. "Blessings, all! It is an honor to have you join me." She bows slightly. The rest of the class follows her lead, and I follow theirs.

"And we are all honored to have Yogi Rothchild with us today. He is observing me, and therefore you too, as part of my ascension as an instructor." She bows at him.

The class turns and does the same.

I don't because I've never seen a yogi with a potbelly and wearing a tracksuit.

The lights go low. Gentle music wafts over us. Amity moves us through a warm up of various positions that stretch our muscles and free our minds. Amity insists that once we take a new position, we pause and close our eyes as she counts slowly to ten, "The better to reach inner peace."

Try as I might, it's still hard for me to break free of my survival training, so I compromise and keep only one eye open.

As the positions get more complex, I notice that Yogi Rothchild is roaming the room. Every now and then, he squats so that he's eye level with someone's comely ass.

In one position—the downward dog—mine rates his attention. He's not expecting my eyes to be open. That's okay. I'm not expecting him to be wearing smart glasses that take pictures, which I presume will soon find their way onto the Internet.

And he's certainly not expecting me to hook his leg with

mine so that he falls backward. Then I yank his glasses off his face and crush them under my heel.

At least I didn't smash his face, too.

His howl brings Harmony into the room. "What the hell are you doing?" she screams at me, somewhat inharmoniously.

"He's taking pictures of us!" I pick up his glasses. "See? These are smart glasses."

"No, they're not!" Harmony points to the lenses.

I'll be darned, she's right. "Oh...um, sorry," I stammer. "I guess the fact that they're super ugly threw me off."

"They're tri-focals!" Yogi Rothchild shouts, not very serenely. "They cost me six hundred bucks!"

Harmony grabs my arm and pulls me out of the studio.

I hand her my credit card again, to pay for my mistake.

"Since you're a bit too tense for our normal classes, I suggest private lessons," she says coldly.

As I walk out the door, I show her that at least one part of my body is quite supple: my middle finger.

FOR THE MOST PART, HILLDALE IS A HAPPY PLACE. IT ISN'T ALL that old, but its homes and buildings are reminiscent of those you've seen a million times in Norman Rockwell paintings. The trees lining Hilldale's wide avenues are tall, broad and lush. The birds that make their nests in them chirp happily, as if they're escapees from a Disney cartoon.

The illusion that this is the perfect place to forget your troubles and be happy is reinforced by the placid smiles on the faces of those I pass as I walk down the sidewalk to my car. They exchange niceties with the town librarian. They nod to neighbors. While waiting for a Popsicle from the roving ice cream truck, they chuck the plump cheeks of their children and they trade harmless gossip with their friends.

But we who walk in the deep dark shadows of those who harm the innocent know better: all is not as it seems.

For example, the clueless don't see the ice cream vendor's sleight of hand as he passes encrypted messages. The unaware don't realize that when the librarian reminds a patron of an overdue book, she may be relaying a coded message that could save lives.

The innocent will never know that the neighbor who makes the best cherry pie in town is a hitwoman who anonymously defends them from bad guys.

As I walk down the street, it dawns on me: I should be happy too, but I'm not.

For those I love, I can't afford to be clueless. With all I know, I can't pretend to be ignorant.

Try as I might, your friendly neighborhood hitwoman will never be innocent again.

I've got to face facts: I may not be cut out for retirement.

Thank God it's only taken me thirteen days, eleven hours and three minutes to figure that out.

And now that Jack needs me more than ever, I should discuss re-entry with Ryan and him.

I head over to Acme.

"HAVE YOU SEEN JACK?" I ASK RYAN'S ASSISTANT, NATASHA.

"Great question. Half an hour ago, he and Ryan were heading toward Martial Arts." Her brow furrows into two tense lines. "Everyone is running around like chickens with their heads cut off."

She need not say more. I get it. The mission is going down, maybe even tonight.

Yikes. Yes, they need me now, more than ever.

I run downstairs to the MA studio.

Mara is in there, warming up.

Mara? ...But...

Jack kept her on his mission team?

I'm too stunned to do anything but stare at her.

"I dare say, she's quite flexible!" Dominic can't seem to keep his eyes off her.

When her lunges elicit a sigh from him, I can't stand it anymore. "Don't you have anything better to do than stalk the poor woman?" I growl.

To indicate that he's miffed at my jibe, he juts out his dimpled, square jaw and he pushes his broad shoulders back, the better for me to be awed by all six-feet-two-inches of him.

Well, one of us is, anyway, if the satisfied grin he gives himself in the room's mirrored wall is any indication. "My dear Mrs. Stone, if you must know, my presence here is sanctioned by our fearless leader. More to the point, Jack specifically asked me to audit Mademoiselle Portnoy's physical readiness as it pertains to the mission at hand–something I plan to do quite thoroughly."

As Mara folds at the waist in order to touch her toes, Dominic tilts his head sideways in the hope that doing so gives him a better view of her pert backside.

I move forward, so that I block his view. "You're lying. She won't have time to get up to snuff for a mission this important!"

A half-turn gives Dominic the view he covets, albeit through the mirror. As mesmerized as he seems to be, he has enough wherewithal to retort, "Then the dolly will have to wing it. *'Better three hours too soon than a minute too late.'*"

"What the hell does that mean? You mean, this mission goes off in three hours?"

"From what you've just said, it means your education in Shakespeare leaves a lot to be desired." He shrugs. "To be expected. The American academic system–"

"Spare me the lecture, you Oxfordian snob!"

Without turning his head, he mutters, "How dare you! I'm a *Cambrian* snob."

I'm wasting my time here. I run back upstairs.

I've tried to be subtle about Mara, but it's time Jack knows what I really think. I feel guilty that I wasn't more forthcoming before now. It was the one thing he asked of me and I almost failed him.

I can't let him make a stupid mistake just because he can't have me at his side.

I FIND JACK HUDDLING WITH RYAN, ABU AND ARNIE IN ACME'S largest conference room, the one ironically referred to as "the Cone of Silence" because of its lack of recording devices and steel construction, which deters anyone who may want to hear what goes on in there.

I walk in just in time to hear Emma, who is speaking via speakerphone. "–facial recognition has in fact verified that she is now in the vicinity of–"

Seeing me enter, Jack immediately disconnects Emma. He nods to Arnie. "Text her, and tell her we had an unexpected breach. We'll resume in a few moments."

So, that's what I am now–an *unexpected breach*?

By the time I've counted to five in my head, he's wearing his poker face and I've quelled the urge to tell him how much I hate him–

Let alone knee him in the nuts, which would be the unexpected breach he'd least expect.

Instead, I smile pretty and ask sweetly, "Might I speak to Ryan and Jack– alone?"

There is not an inch of my being that Jack doesn't know intimately. Be it the look in my eye, the gait of my walk, the turn of my head, or the tone of my voice; he reads me quicker than the latest James Patterson bestseller in the hands of a devoted fan.

In other words, there are no surprises.

Yes, I am that obvious to him.

Jack nods toward the door. Abu and Arnie have been around us too long to argue.

Ryan looks as if he wishes he could follow. Well, that's just too bad. We'll need a referee, and he's elected.

Should shouting commence, I can only thank my lucky stars that this confrontation is taking place in the Cone of Silence.

Jack bides his time until I begin.

Fine. I won't show any emotions, either. It's unladylike, not to mention it's unbecoming of a covert operative–

Fuck it. I'm pissed, and I deserve answers.

I flop down into the conference chair directly across the table from him. "I don't get it. When I asked, you assured me that Mara wasn't going to be part of this mission!"

At first, Jack frowns, but then realizing that I've gotten under his skin, he takes a deep breath and starts again. "I changed my mind." He gives me an exasperated look. "Why should it matter all of a sudden?"

"Because…well, because if something should go wrong–if she loses her life because she wasn't ready for the challenge, or if any one of you should lose your lives because she isn't up to snuff, I'd…" I throw up my hands in frustration. "I'd never forgive myself. In fact, I–"

"Wait!" He grimaces. "For once, this isn't about you. It's

about me. It's *my* decision, based on the time constraints and our infiltration plan."

"Yes, it is about me," I insist. "You see, I want to–"

Before I can finish my sentence, before I can explain that I'd like to come back, he growls, "No, Donna! For once, what you want doesn't count. It's my prerogative as this mission's leader"–he takes a deep breath–"and I want Mara."

Mara, who feels nothing.

Mara, who has a death wish, and seeks revenge.

Mara, who still blames Jack for Kiril being lost to her.

The warmth of the single tear rolling down my cheek awakens my urgency to make him understand all of this. "But, Jack–"

"Donna, I've no doubt that Mara will live up to the highest standards there are"–Jack's grimace softens–"*yours.*"

But that's the problem: *no other woman is like me.*

She'll never have my history with Acme.

She won't know the nuances of my mission team.

And she certainly will never know Jack as well as me.

I walk over to him, so that we're eye to eye. "I want to go on record that I think you're making a terrible mistake."

He nods nonchalantly. "Duly noted. Now, if you don't mind, my team has to get back to our briefing."

He turns his back on me and clicks on his iPad–his way of showing me I'm being dismissed.

I look to Ryan, the fearless leader.

Oops, spoke too soon. The best he can do is shrug and nod toward Jack.

Coward. Thanks for nothing.

I slam the door on my way out.

As I'm driving home, I get a text from Hilldale Middle School's principal, Mr. Belding:

Can you join me at my office today, around 1 pm?

Finally, someone is thanking me for all my hard work!
I text back: *Look forward to seeing you then.*

I go home and change before driving to the school. I choose a yellow and white polka-dot blouse over a slim white pencil skirt; and I wear my best pearl necklace and matching earrings, and put my hair up in a demure French twist. The shoes that are perfect for this ensemble–five-inch yellow stilettos–are taller than I like for daywear, but Belding is tall, so I'll make an exception. I'm willing to bet he wants a photograph taken with me, for the school newspaper. I can see the headline now:

Jeff Stone's Mother Throws Party of the Century

Or something like that.
Yes, I know–I'm grasping at straws.

When I get to Principal Belding's office, Miss Bliss, his secretary, hustles me through his door immediately.

Seeing me, he rises from the chair behind his desk. I smile as I step forward–

Until I see the woman sitting on the couch in the far corner of the room:

Penelope.

Jeff is beside her. He's trying hard not to cry.

My double-take puts a smug smile on her lips.

I look from her to Principal Belding and ask coldly, "Why exactly was this meeting called?"

Before he has a chance to answer, Penelope declares, "Because your son is a terrorist!"

"Now, now, Mrs. Bing! 'Terrorist' is such a harsh word." Principal Belding clicks his tongue. "However, ruffian would fit the bill."

I ask him, "And why do you feel this is the case?"

"Because my son is currently at Hilldale Emergency Clinic getting his nose bandaged," Penelope sniffs.

I fold my arms across my chest. "What did he do to provoke Jeff into hitting him?"

"He called my father a terrorist, and then he called me 'Mohammed Stone!'" Jeff shouts.

I look at Belding. "I'd say my son had a right to be angry."

"I disagree. A misunderstanding is no reason for fisticuffs," Belding admonishes me. "As you know, in some cultures Mohammed is a very noble name."

"By calling my son's father a terrorist, we all know that Cheever's intentions weren't by any means noble."

"Nonetheless, Hilldale Middle School has a very strict 'first punch' rule–immediate suspension, for one week. No exceptions for any school activities."

Jeff looks up, shocked. "But–but that means I can't go to the dance tomorrow night!"

Ah, so, that's what this is all about: Penelope wants Jeff out of the picture so that Gabrielle will accept Cheever's invitation to the dance.

She's willing to break my son's heart.

Ain't gonna happen.

"Did Jeff apologize?" I ask.

"Yes!" Jeff is adamant about this. Penelope smiles supremely at the memory.

"Then I think we can all agree that enough punishment has been administered," I say sweetly.

"Excuse me?" Belding growls.

Frankly, there is no reason to excuse me. Goodness, it's not as if I've pistol-whipped either of them–but that's because I would never carry a gun into a school.

Secondly, they'd both enjoy it too much.

I know this because during carpool one afternoon last year, Cheever let it slip that he'd never be suspended from school because of his mother's quote-unquote special relationship with Principal Belding.

He then had the audacity to ask if Mr. Stone and I had a quote-unquote safe word, too.

"Like what?" I asked.

"Like, say, 'poppin' fresh dough,'" he explained. "That's theirs."

At that point, Morton asked, "What's a safe word?"

I zigged and zagged on the road, as if I had to avoid a dog or something, but really it was because I didn't want to explain S&M protocol to a sixth-grader.

No chance like the present to see if what Cheever said was true, or if it was his imagination working overtime after breaking into his father's porn stash.

I walk up to Belding and lean in so that only he can hear what I have to say: "Poppin' fresh dough."

He blanches. His lower lip quivers. His eyes ask, *How do you know?*

I don't say another word. All it takes is a raised brow.

"What's going on?" Penelope growls suspiciously.

Belding busies himself straightening the only file on his

already clean desk. "The boy apologized. He's free to go to the dance–with a warning."

Jeff practically runs out the door.

I walk slowly, and make sure to close the door behind me.

Miss Bliss and I exchange winces when we hear Penelope's unintelligible roar. A moment later, there's a loud smack and a groan.

"I guess somebody's been a very, very bad boy," Miss Bliss murmurs.

Something tells me this isn't the first time she's heard such goings-on, and it won't be the last.

17

Last Minute Prep

As with everything else in life, success is achieved in the tiniest of details! With that in mind, here are a few things to remember before opening your door to your eager guests:

First, at least eight hours before your event, call together everyone who plays an integral part in its success—the event planner, the valet, the caterer, the florist, and the entertainers—to go over the floor plan, the timetable, and their specific roles. Answer their questions, and ask any you have as well.

In fact, tying them to chairs and shining a spotlight directly into their eyes will have them answering you in a fine, forthright fashion. However, should you feel someone is fudging an answer, don't hesitate to whip out your Taser. (Hint: It can also be used in such party games as Truth or Dare. However, expect more dares than truths.)

Next, distribute cell phones to your party team! Having them at your beck and call with the push of a button goes far toward easing your stress. In fact, don't stop there! GPS tracking should also be considered. And, for the ultimate control, keep them on leashes.

Finally, have an ambulance service on speed dial. If your guests aren't scared of you, your party team certainly is, and someone is sure to have a heart attack.

"You're lying," Mary declares to Jeff.

"Mom!" he yells down the stairwell. "Tell her that I'm telling the truth!"

"Inside voices!" I yell back. Tomorrow night is the prom, and with everything going on, I've got the start of a vicious headache.

Three glasses of wine will do that to you.

So will three chaperone cancellations. I've been hitting the phones all day, trying to drum up replacements, but no luck. Seems that when the kids are away, the parents will play.

Evan has convinced me that watching a replay of John Oliver's *Last Week Tonight* will make it better. Not that I'm paying attention, but Evan finds him a hoot. Anything that makes Evan laugh these days is okay by me.

I'm not so happy, either. I haven't heard from Jack.

And yes, I'm somewhat miffed that his declaration that my opinion counted in Mara's hiring was bogus.

Great. Good luck to them all.

I hadn't planned to be widowed once, let alone three times.

If you were divorced, are you still widowed? I'm not sure I can figure that out without a team of attorneys. If you were never married, but still living together, what does that make you?

An idiot, I guess.

And certainly unlucky in love.

Mary storms down the stairs and into the great room, followed closely by Jeff and Trisha. "Mom, Jeff says that Taylor Swift is singing at his dance! Is that true?"

"Yes." My affirmation echoes within the jumbo-sized goblet raised to my lips.

"Told you," Jeff jeers.

"Shut up, I'm talking to Mom." Her eyes grow big. "Mom, why didn't you tell me?"

"I'm sorry…I guess I thought you'd heard." No, my eldest mostly tunes me out. From now on, if I want her attention, I'm adding the name Taylor Swift to every other sentence.

Mary looks up at me, pleading. "Can you score a ticket for me?"

"Aren't you a little old for her?" Evan teases.

"I…yes, I guess," Mary stammers.

He shakes his head. "Well, I'm not. I think she's hot."

"I'll let you both see the concert, under one condition–that you act as chaperones at the dance."

They slap high-fives.

Jeff turns white. "No! Mom, no way!"

Has he lost his mind? "Excuse me? May I ask your line of reasoning?"

"Because…because…" His face goes from white to bright red. "I have a date."

Mary makes a kissy face.

I pinch her arm to make her stop. Biting my lip so that I don't laugh, I turn to Jeff. "Did you ask Gabrielle?"

He nods nonchalantly. "Yeah. But now I have to learn how to slow dance."

"It's easy, dude," Evan assures him. "They've even taught chimpanzees how to do it."

"That's about Jeff's speed," Mary mutters. "Maybe we can take one from the zoo, and he can practice with it."

Jeff throws one of my nice couch pillows at her.

I grab the rest of them before Mary can retaliate.

"Taylor Swift," Aunt Phyllis's brow furrows in the hope it

prods her memory. "Is she the one that did the duet album with Tony Bennett?"

"Lady Gaga," Mary and Evan say in unison.

"Too bad. Still, it beats bingo, so count me in too," Aunt Phyllis declares.

I toast her with my glass. "Sure, why not? The more the merrier."

Trisha's lower lip quivers. "Does this mean I have to stay home alone?"

I bundle my youngest onto my lap. "No, of course not! You can share Aunt Phyllis's room with her"–I look over at Mary–"and you, too. Evan, you luck out with a room for yourself."

He raises a brow. "Only if I'm not lucky enough for Taylor to want to serenade me all night."

Mary's eyes narrow. "Like that will ever happen." She pauses and then adds, "Although, you do resemble Justin Bieber–around the time she dumped him."

"Not Jake Gyllenhaal?"

She snickers. "You wish!"

"No, you do," Jeff guffaws.

Mary doesn't need my pillows. Her sandal does just as well. It clips her brother on his forehead.

"That's it!" I holler. "Teach your brother to dance."

I take my bottle and head upstairs. Something tells me Jack will be having another late night.

PROM DAY MORNING IS TYPICAL OF SO MANY DAYS IN SOCAL: warm, with clear blue skies.

Jack never came home. Did the mission go down last night?

I'll know by one of two ways. The first is if he shows up in time to escort the rest of the family to the prom.

Or, Ryan will show up at my doorstep, to give me the news in person that Jack didn't survive the mission.

I'd much prefer the former, having already gone through the latter.

By the time I get to the Savoy, for a rundown on any outstanding details, Margot, the party planner, is already there–with Édouard and Henry. Margot is frowning, which is not a good sign.

My first inclination is to wince, but until this party is over and I'm safely ensconced in my palatial suite, I have to plaster a smile on my face and play nice, so I declare, "A beautiful morning, everyone! And I'm sure tonight will be just as wonderful."

"That depends," Margot warns, "on whether you're willing to accept some last-minute changes Mrs. Bing called into Édouard late yesterday."

"Madam was so insistent that our chef prepped the kitchen all night in order to accommodate her," Henry sniffs.

I brace myself. "Okay then, what items did she choose?"

"To start, there is the smoked white sturgeon caviar layered with Dungeness crab on yams–"

I purse my lips to keep from groaning. Penelope was fit to be tied when I deleted the caviar before. It makes me wonder if she ordered it to resell on the black market.

"–followed by turnip, radish, dried fish, and seaweed bouillon," Édouard says proudly. "The next course is live scallops on the half shell, followed by roasted pigeon wrapped in cherry leaves and aged for thirty-two days, which is served with a beet soufflé and bone marrow fritters. And for dessert, Cherries Jubilee!"

On this last item, he whips his hand out with a flurry, practically knocking Henry off his feet.

I can't believe it! Penelope is so upset about Cheever being tossed over for Jeff that she's willing to sabotage the dance.

I look at it this way: if I insist on the more kid-friendly menu, the chef will no doubt commit hari-kari with the full set of Henckles knives hanging on the wall in the kitchen, so I must defer.

That's okay. The success of the event doesn't hang on the students' opinion of the food, anyway. They aren't going to remember anything about it–only what they wore, and who danced with whom, and who kissed whom.

Oh yes, and that Taylor Swift sang at their prom.

Ignoring Édouard, I smile at Margot. "It sounds wonderful! I appreciate your hard work–all of you." I squeeze Margot's hand.

She gets it: *let's just get through this in one piece.*

Jeff and I may have won Round One, but Round Two goes to Penelope.

She keeps it up, she'll feel my knockout punch, and I'm not speaking metaphorically.

HENRY NOTICES THAT I'VE GOT A ROLL-CASE WITH ME, AND guesses rightly that I'm dropping my stuff in my suite.

My security card is already in my hand when I reach the doors hiding the penthouse elevator banks. I slide it open, then rush to the elevator for Suite A, and insert my card.

Just as the elevator opens, Henry grabs me around the waist and shoves me against the wall.

Bad move. I knee him in the groin.

He yelps.

When he's able to pull himself upright again, he mutters,

"I—was saving you from breaking your neck," I look to where he's pointing—into the elevator shaft.

He's right. It's empty. Had I stepped into it, I would have broken my neck. I didn't see the sign beside the door, which announces OUT OF ORDER.

"What...how..."

"As you know, the hotel did its soft opening last week," he reminds me. "To be honest, we're still working out a few bugs." He looks down the shaft—at least a twenty-foot drop and shakes his head. "Your next stop would have been the private garage for the penthouse and concierge suites."

I look up into the dark abyss, which rises another twenty stories above us. A shiver goes up my spine. "Henry, please forgive me! I'm so sorry!"

He nods stoically, then points to the elevator marked C. "Shall we?"

I follow him in. He pushes a button, and up we go.

WHEN THE ELEVATOR DOOR OPENS AGAIN, WE ARE ON THE concierge level.

"Now, put your card into the slot, here." He points to a card slot at eye level.

I do as he asks, and the elevator rises again. This time when it opens, we're inside the Academy Awards suite.

I look around, confused. "How did this happen?"

"This is also an express elevator," he explains. "Its first stop is the concierge level, which is right below the penthouse suites. However, it is the only elevator in the center core between all three floors, which also allows it to open into the three penthouses."

"I don't get it. How is that possible?"

"Take a look around this elevator. Do you notice something different about it?"

I look closely at its three walls. Suddenly it hits me. "There are no walls to this elevator!"

"Exactly. The elevator's four-sided metal frame holds just floor and ceiling platforms. That way, when a security card is inserted, the right doors swing open into the desired suite. Otherwise, in case of an emergency, the hotel staff would have no other access into the penthouse suites."

"Couldn't you have just moved me to another penthouse suite?"

He shakes his head. "I'm happy to say we've booked all of them tonight, as well as the whole concierge level–very last-minute, for a small gathering. In fact, I was offered money for this one as well, but it would have been wrong to renege on my promise to you, especially since you've followed through on yours." He leans in, much too close–

I slam my fist into his nose.

"Ouch!" he screams.

Too bad. I'm taking the offensive. "How dare you!"

Hesitantly, he reaches over slowly–

To brush lint off the shoulder of my dress.

"Oh! I'm…so sorry! I thought you were being…you know, inappropriate."

He raises a brow. "My husband wouldn't like it. For that matter, neither would I."

"Oh!" As it dawns on me what he's implying, I blush. "When you said you'd be turning down my sheets personally, I presumed–"

"I meant it, as a courtesy of the hotel. As manager, I want to make sure everything is done right, especially during opening week. Our maid staff is still too new to be trusted with our VIP guests."

I wince. "I guess I got the wrong impression…from…"

"Let me guess–Mrs. Bing." He sighs. "The woman has an active imagination, not to mention roaming hands."

"I'm so sorry you've had to put up with her."

"You've been a wonderful buffer, not to mention a joy to work with."

"Well, thank you, Henry." His compliment brings a smile to my face.

Seeing it, he smiles too. "Mrs. Stone, rest assured, despite Mrs. Bing's meddling, everything is under control. By the way, just to give you a heads-up, she had several bottles of your vodka order delivered to her room. Otherwise, as I promised, the rest of the wine and spirits has been boxed, and is in a closet next to the ballroom."

I join him in a chuckle, but only because it beats crying.

AT HENRY'S SUGGESTION, I SPEND THE REST OF THE AFTERNOON relaxing.

First, I run a nice soothing bath with the hotel's signature orange rosemary bath salts. They do their magic. I almost fall asleep in the tub.

After my bath, I wrap the hotel's sheer chiffon kimono around me and I move to the bed in order to take a nap. The mattress feels like a cloud. Still, I toss and turn whenever my mind wanders to thoughts about Jack.

When I awaken, it's to the sound of my own voice, praying for his safety.

I look at the clock. Aunt Phyllis and the children aren't due to arrive for another hour, so I go out on the balcony to catch the last rays of the sun. It's warm enough to sunbathe, so why not? I open the robe as I lay down on one of the terrace's many chaises.

Except for the traffic noises wafting up from the Avenue of the Stars some thirty floors below me, I hear nothing. But for some reason, I don't feel alone. I look around. The hotel towers over every other building in Beverly Hills. And as Henry pointed out, I can't look into the penthouse immediately adjacent to mine.

Sighing, I adjust the back of the chaise so that it reclines. When I lay back, I see him: a man, on the balcony of Penthouse G, which also faces the ocean.

His terrace juts out far enough that when he looks back, he can look down onto me.

He smiles at what he sees.

He's gray-haired and over fifty. His face is tan, but his eyes are light.

"Walther, darling! Hurry, dearest, we don't have much time." The woman's purr is loud enough for me to hear.

My new friend, Walther, shrugs. Our staring contest is over. Still, he shows his appreciation with a bow and a tilt of the hand before sauntering back inside.

Thanks for the mammaries? I think not.

So much for quote-unquote affording your guests complete privacy.

Angrily, I whip my kimono around me and walk back inside. I barely push the sliding glass door and still, it slams behind me.

I guess I don't know my own strength.

He may not want to, either.

18

Keeping out the Riff-Raff

Realizing the importance of your upcoming fete in the hierarchy of your social set's must-attend events, it is wise that you devise a plan to keep out the riff-raff while your celebrated guests trod the red carpet to your abode. To ensure their security, consider the following:

1. *Electric Fencing. Ideally, it will go all the way around the perimeter of your estate. That being said, anyone whose hair is standing on end, glows when the lights dim, or shocks you when shaking your hand is a possible interloper and should be shown the door immediately.*

2. *Retinal Scan: Installing a retinal scanning device at your front doorstep will not be as off-putting as it may sound! In fact, those who like to feel exclusive at all times will love it, I promise! That is, unless you install the wrong machine—say, an excimer laser, which is used for refractive eye surgery. In that case, expect a malpractice suit.*

3. *Code Words. Much simpler than a retinal scan! By embedding a code word in each invitation with strict*

instructions to use it upon entry to the party, you'll be able to determine if someone is a legitimate guest.

Important Tip: Do not–I repeat, do not–make it the same as your S&M safety word, because not all of your guests will appreciate a lash across the back with a cat-o-nine-tails. (That being said, you'll be surprised at those who do.)

MY PARTY ATTIRE–A FITTED BLACK RAW SILK TUXEDO ENSEMBLE, worn over a blouse of sheer black illusion–earns a wolf whistle from Evan. "Looking good, Mrs. Stone!"

I honor him with a smile. Evan and Mary have met me in the lobby, along with the other brave souls who have offered to chaperone.

Everyone except Aunt Phyllis.

Oh, well. We don't have a lot of time, so I dole out the security cards for their rooms, and those of their young charges, and then I explain the rules to everyone:

The children will be here in an hour. Once those students staying on their floors have arrived, the chaperones are to walk them into their assigned rooms, and to read them the rules and regulations for staying out of trouble. At six-o'clock, the children are to go into the ballroom, but the chaperones hold on to the room keys during the dance. At midnight, everyone turns back into a pumpkin and goes back to their rooms. If a child gets ill or tired, one of the chaperones is to accompany him or her back to a room, and stay there with them. If others feel the same way, they can join the first child for some quiet time activities, such as reading, listening to music, or watching television.

I'm happy to see that the chaperones are excited. They'll be taking lots of pictures to capture the moments.

I hand Evan my second security card. "When you see Jeff, give this to him. I've got a suite on the nineteenth floor, and it has a second bedroom. We'll be roomies." It's now obvious to me that Jack won't be joining me. That's okay. This evening was supposed to be about Jeff. I look forward to listening to my son's thoughts about his very first dance.

I look around. "Where are Aunt Phyllis and Trisha?"

"She's watching the band set up." Mary rolls her eyes. "She's asked two of the guys for their telephone numbers. She wants to see if they'll play for her on Bingo night."

I smother a laugh. "Is Trisha with her?"

Mary shakes her head. "Janie flew into town. She called to see if Trisha could sleep over at Lion's Lair–"

I grab Mary's arm. "Did she say whether the president was with her?"

"There was a large Secret Service detail there," Evan pipes up. "But it must have left right after us because it passed us on the 405."

Oh, hell–Lee is in town after all! And wherever he's headed will be Ground Zero for the terrorists.

I have to let Jack know–*now*.

"Do you know which exit they took off the freeway?"

Mary and Evan shake their heads.

"I've got to call Jack. You two are my eyes and ears. If you need anything, text me."

I run off to find a quiet spot in which to have a life-or-death conversation.

THE CLOSEST PLACE IN THE LOBBY THAT AFFORDS ANY PRIVACY FOR my conversation is the VIP elevator bank, so I slip into the alcove with my security card.

A housekeeper is standing in front of the concierge floor elevator. Beside her is a cart loaded with caviar and other delicacies from chef Édouard's kitchen.

The alcove may be getting busier, so I make the decision to go up, too, in order to call from my room.

Try as she might, her security card won't work.

Not out of politeness, but because I want my privacy, I say, "Here, let's try mine." I swipe it, and the door opens.

"Gracias," she says, but she is so shy that she keeps her eyes firmly on her cart.

When she rolls her it into the elevator, I notice her limp.

Suddenly, I feel guilty for having been so rude. It's a long ride up. So that we don't have to make it in silence, I say, "Beautiful day, isn't it?"

She nods and looks over for just a second, but I can't see her eyes through the thick-framed glasses that sit high on the bridge of a nose bent to one side. She forces herself to grin, but it only makes me feel sorrier for her. Several of her teeth are missing. She's around my age, but the deep scar on her cheek makes her look older.

It's obvious that she's been abused, poor thing. It was good of Henry to give her a job. Even with one of the highest minimum wages in the country, Los Angeles' cost of living far outstrips that difference. I can't even imagine what it would cost to get her teeth fixed, let alone to have a doctor see about her leg.

We ride up in silence. Before the doors open, I put a twenty-dollar bill in her palm. She purses her lips as she stares down at it. "Gracias! Gracias!" she whispers, but she is still too shy to look at me.

The doors open on the concierge level, which is bustling, to say the least. Not a party, but some sort of business reception. Lots of suits: mostly men, but at least one woman too. They come and go from their private rooms toward the large reception room at the far end of the hall. Through the babble of voices, I make out snippets of French, German, Japanese, and Chinese.

The maid waits for me to get off first, but I shake my head. "No, I'm going up to the penthouse," I explain. When she gives me an uncomprehending look, I demonstrate by pointing up, then slipping my card into the elevator's card slot.

"Ah!" she says, impressed.

"Adios," I say as the doors close.

Once in my room, I call Jack. When he doesn't pick up his phone, I call Ryan's cell phone. He's not picking up either.

I text both of them LION IN TOWN.

That should get their attention. It's our code name for Lee.

My next text is to Lee. It simply says, URGENT.

Where the hell are they?

I spend the next hour pacing the floor, but when it's five-thirty, I realize that there is nothing I can do except to go down and play hostess to a ballroom full of middle-schoolers.

Thank God they won't know what's happening.

Innocence is fleeting.

So far, the prom is a raging success.

The children squeal and hug at the awesomeness of it all: at how well they've scrubbed up, at their own preciousness in their dresses and tuxedoes, and at the wonderful setting for their first big prom.

Margot and her decorating team have done a fantastic job of creating a wonderland out of balloons and tiny starry lights. After the children are done eating, one of the ballroom walls will break away to reveal the bandstand and dance floor.

In the meantime, they are swaying to the deejay's mixes, going in and out of the fortune-teller's glass gazebo, and lining up for the photo booths. (I picked them up at a police auction. Gee, I wonder where they were seized from?)

I seek Margot out to thank her. She laughs. "Thank you. Mrs. Bing's response was less appreciative. She was livid that you changed the color scheme again."

"That's just too bad. If she gives you any more grief, find me. I'll take care of her. Where is she, anyway?"

Margot nods toward the buffet line.

Penelope, in a formal red one-shouldered gown lined with gold piping, is arguing with some boy who refuses to take the plate in her hand. When our eyes meet, Penelope glowers at me.

I curtsey in return. Giving her the finger would be more appropriate, but considering our surroundings, it would be déclassé, and it certainly wouldn't set a good example.

Margot mutters, "The food is the only fly in the ointment. All you hear about it is 'Oooh, yuck', and 'disgusting.'"

I shrug. "Still, a good time will be had by all."

The shrill scream proves me wrong.

Margot and I turn to find that a ruckus has broken out at the far end of the room. It seems that Cheever figured out what to do with the oysters: shove them down the bodice of the dress of the girl who spurned him: Jeff's date, Gabrielle.

When she screams, her knight in shining armor, Jeff, takes a handful of caviar and shoves it in Cheever's face.

In no time, an all-out food fight ensues. Caviar is the weapon of choice.

"Stop it! Stop it! This stuff is fifty bucks a pound!" Penelope shouts, but she's outnumbered.

Margot is about to walk into the fray when a waiter walks up to her. He points toward the breakaway wall. She thanks him. Turning to me, she sighs with relief. "Oh, thank goodness! Taylor is here, and has already set up on stage! That should calm the children down."

She gives Penelope the high sign. Penelope tries her best to shout commands that the children stop, but they can't hear her.

My taxi whistle stops everyone cold.

With as much dignity as she can muster, Penelope wipes the caviar off her face and proclaims, "The dinner portion of our dance is now over. As your hostess, I'd like to introduce you to tonight's special guest–Miss Taylor Swift!"

The walls fold away, to reveal an elaborate raised proscenium stage. Over it hangs a banner that reads TAELOR SWIFF.

Henry's staff misspelled the name of one of the world's top entertainers. Yikes!

Seeing it, Penelope turns bright red. Her head whips around so that she can glare at the likely culprit: me.

Suddenly, the lights go dim, and the first rifts of Taylor's song, *Shake it Off*, can be heard throughout the ballroom. The children rush toward the stage, clapping, and swaying to the music.

When the stage curtains slowly open, they let loose with a frenzied squeal. You hear the singer's voice before you actually see her:

I stay up too late
    Got nothing in my brain
    That's what people say
    That's what people say...

Did I say her? Make that, him.

The giveaway is the bobbing Adam's apple.

Hmm. Well. That explains the difference in the spelling of her name, and the rock-bottom price for the booking.

Taelor's back-up singers aren't all as petite as she. At least the ones with the more prominent five-o'clock shadows are all the way in the back.

Margot must notice too, because she grabs my arm. Her eyes are open wide, but she keeps her mouth shut because Penelope is within scratching distance.

In unison, we shift our gaze to Penelope for the inevitable moment in which this unexpected surprise dawns on her, as well.

We don't have to wait too long.

Penelope's shock is revealed in how wide her eyes get, and how she clutches her throat. She takes a step forward because she can't believe what she sees. When, finally, she can move, she practically runs backward–

Into one of the buffet tables.

If the food doesn't make it to the floor, it's only because it lands on her first.

Margot runs over to help her up.

Not me. My phone is buzzing. I look down at the Caller ID: Lee.

Finally, some answers. I head out of the ballroom, toward the VIP elevator room.

∼

"WHERE ARE YOU?" I ASK.

"I love you, too," Lee mutters.

The call has too much static. I can barely hear him. "I'm not playing games! Look, I know you're in town."

"Oh, yes? How is that?"

"Janie called Trisha and invited her over."

"Damn it!" he mutters. "Babette begged to come west with me. When I told her it was to be a quick trip–in and out in

226

twenty-four hours–she used 'mommy-daughter' time as her excuse. You'd think she could spend a full day with her own daughter without getting bored."

I wince at his bluntness. "Lee, I think you're in terrible danger. Please tell me where you are."

He sighs, but says nothing. Finally, he murmurs, "The Savoy, in Beverly Hills. In a few moments I'll be meeting with some international delegates to have a serious discussion about ISIL–"

"I'll be right up!"

"It'll take you too long to get here. Even with my police escort, The 405 was a God-awful mess–"

"No, I mean I'm already here, in the Savoy! For my son's prom!"

"Oh! …Well, in that case–aw hell, our connection is awful! Call me on the house line. Ask for Lee Lyon's room." He hangs up.

There is a house phone on a side table in the alcove. I ask the operator to connect me with Lee's pseudonym.

Even before I'm able to say something, Lee answers. "I'll send someone from my Secret Service detail down to the lobby to get you."

He must have put his hand over the phone for a moment, because the sound is muffled. When he finally gets back on, he says, "Ed is on his way. Head over to the elevator room for the penthouses. It's hidden behind–"

"I know where it is," I interrupt tersely. "In fact, I'm in the alcove outside of it as we speak. I have a penthouse here too."

"That's…convenient," he murmurs.

The only thing I can think of is to say, "Jack thinks so."

"What do I think?" Jack's voice says behind me.

I turn to see him standing behind me–

With Mara, Ryan, and Arnie. They're dressed formally, in

suits, although Arnie's is a size too small in the gut and the arms. Everyone looks shocked to see me.

"And what the hell are you doing here, Donna?" Jack mutters.

"Hello to you, too," I say coldly. "Excuse me? Have you forgotten that Jeff's prom is being held here, right now–and that I'm in charge of it?"

Before I have time to respond to him, the door opens. A burly man sticks his head out. I recognize him as one of the Secret Service agents I've seen before, who's always trailing Lee.

Jack frowns. "Lee is here, too–and you conveniently forgot to mention it?"

Ed looks suspiciously at Jack. "If you're ready, Mrs. Stone, the president will see you now."

I follow him toward the elevator.

And Jack, Ryan, Mara, and Arnie follow me.

The man puts his hand on Jack's chest. Nodding in my direction, he says, "Just her."

Jack knocks it away.

I wedge myself between them. "Ed, POTUS is expecting them too."

My eyes don't waver. Finally, he steps aside to let us enter.

I go to the back of the elevator. Jack makes it a point to stand beside me. Like everyone else, we stare straight ahead. "By the way, I did leave you a message," I mutter to him. "Several, in fact, from the moment I learned Lee was in Los Angeles. You should check your cell every now and then." I look him up and down. "For that matter, where have you been for the past twenty-four hours?"

"Here," he hisses back. "We broke the cipher. One of the conference delegates is a plant. I've been leaving messages for you, too, asking you where you are!"

"He's right," Arnie pipes in. "Cell phone service around the hotel is crappy. Something's wrong. My guess is there is some sort of transmission jammer in the building."

When the elevator bell rings to announce us, Jack holds me back for a moment. "I'm sorry I forgot where the prom was being held. The hotel's name sounded familiar, but I couldn't remember why."

It's understandable, considering you have a lot on your mind, I want to say, but I hold my tongue because, just then, the elevator doors open.

Lee is standing there. He has a smile on his face, and anticipation in his eyes–

Until he sees Jack, at which point he murmurs, "Hail, hail, the gang's all here."

Apparently, he considers the man who was staring at me from the balcony as part of the gang, because he's here too.

Walther grins when he sees me.

I do my best to keep from scowling at him.

19

Making Introductions

A party only gets started when your guests have been introduced to each other. These tips will get the ball rolling at a breakneck pace:

- *A: Make intriguing introductions. "Dolores, do you know Sylvia? No? Surprising! I could have sworn she was 'the other woman' for whom your husband left you. Isn't that so, Syl? Can I get anyone a drink?"*
- *B: Don't be afraid to introduce controversy. For example: "Lydia, I'd like you to meet Horace. He just got out of prison after serving time for manslaughter. Horace, Lydia believes in the death penalty for all kinds of felonies. Can I freshen anyone's drink?"*
- *C: Be sure to point out commonalities. "Joe, do you know Elvira? No? Odd! I'd have guessed you would, since you attend many of the same orgies. Elvira, show him that little tattoo on your inner thigh. It may jog his memory. In the meantime, does anyone want a cocktail wienie? Oh! ...No offense, Joe..."*

Lee introduces us to his other guests. Walther's last name is Achterberg. He is a state secretary in Germany's Ministry of Foreign Affairs, and recently assigned the additional position of chairman of the UN Middle East Peace Consortium.

It's why he rates the penthouse suite overlooking mine.

Besides him, the United States Secretary of State, James Worthington, is here, as is Walther's assistant, a young and beautiful woman named Gretta Kruger; and Luther Fried, the Consortium's Chief of Security.

Gretta doesn't speak, so I can't compare her voice to that of the woman I heard earlier today while I was sunbathing on the terrace. But by the casual way in which Walther touches her hand as he passes her a note, I presume she is one and the same.

I recognize Luther's name, if not his face. He is retired from Mossad, the Israeli intelligence agency, where he headed up the Political Action and Liaison Department, the unit charged with interfacing with other intel agencies from around the world.

Everyone listens quietly as Jack spells out everything Acme now knows about the meeting that is to take place downstairs:

That ISIL has been tracking their moves for quite some time; that there will be an attempt to sabotage the meeting–perhaps use it as a hostage situation; and that this intel is coming from the inside.

When Jack is finished, all eyes turn to Lee. He, in turn, glances over at Walther.

"Does your intelligence indicate how this attack is to happen?" Walther asks Jack.

"No," Jack concedes. "But if it is an inside job, the saboteur could do so by letting in the assassins once the meeting is underway, or he or she could release some sort of harmful agent that incapacitates the attendees."

"But we've taken every precaution! Our security detail has been well-vetted, as have the committee members," Luther Fried insists. "If what you say is true, the source must have identified the saboteur in some manner."

"Only by a code name–*Sin*," Ryan declares.

Walther shrugs. "Even his name has an element of foreboding. Are we to presume it indicates the level of chaos to be expected?"

"Our organization is leaning toward its Sumarian interpretation," Ryan explains. "In that case, *Sin* is the mythological name of a deity–the Moon god. Even in that capacity, it represents darkness as opposed to light, war as opposed to peace. This god is symbolized by a crescent moon."

"This is an insightful history lesson, but sadly, we are already a quarter-hour behind schedule." Walther looks at his watch. "I can assure you that each of the committee's members and its support staff have gone through extensive security checks–and not just by our own country, but yours as well."

Lee nods. "If that weren't the case, I would not be here to participate."

"Mr. President, if what Acme suspects is correct, at the very least, our operatives–or for that matter, your Secret Service detail–should do one more security check before you go into that meeting room," I counter.

He stares at me before conceding with a nod. He turns to Worthington. "It is presumed no one else knows I'm to attend. Is that correct?"

Worthington nods, as does Walther.

Walther turns to Gretta. "Escort the president's men."

Lee turns to his Secret Service detail. "Ed, you and Charlie from Secretary Worthington's detail will go with Ms. Kruger,

Mr. Fried, and Secretary Worthington. So that the delegates aren't alarmed, let me suggest that Gretta introduce them as hotel security, as opposed to White House personnel. If you feel the coast is clear, send up a white smoke signal."

"I'd like Mara to accompany them, too," Jack suggests.

"Good idea," Lee agrees.

If Mara hadn't been here, it would have been me. Instead, I must get back downstairs to see what other havoc has taken place in the ballroom since I left it.

As I follow them to the Emmy Suite's elevator, Jack grabs my hand. "Where are you going?"

"To deal with more mundane issues. There are two hundred children downstairs, having a food fight while a chorus line of trannies lip syncing through a pop star's greatest hits. Do me a favor and send me a text if it turns out we need to evacuate."

"Trust me, Donna–cancel the party." From the look in his eyes, I know he's worried about collateral damage.

I nod to let him know I hear him, and run after the group going into the elevator.

SINCE EVERYONE ELSE IS GETTING OFF FIRST, I POSITION MYSELF near the back of the elevator. Mara notices this, and finds her way back there with me.

The ride is a short one. No one speaks. Instead, everyone looks forward.

When the elevator door opens, the others bolt down the hall toward the meeting room. The door is open, but no one can be seen, except the four security guards. They allow the newcomers to enter, then close ranks behind them.

Before I can push the button for the lobby, Mara places her

hand over my wrist to get my attention. "Donna, don't worry. Everything will be okay."

I nod, but I have nothing to say. I get it: she's fearless. But that's because she has nothing to lose: whereas I have everything.

She's about to walk out of the elevator when we hear it–the whiz of bullets and the screams.

Mara and I duck back on opposite sides of the elevator. We're shielded by the part of the elevator platform not exposed to the open doors, but we look out just the same. She's already pulled her gun from her back holster.

Having presumed that the only fights I'd be breaking up are between two girls crying over the same pimply-faced guy, I have no weapon. Then I remember that the stilettos I'm wearing really do have stilettos as heels, so I yank off the heels and pocket the blades so that my shoes are now flats.

We look out just in time to see Charlie and Luther flailing backward as they are riddled with bullets.

Ed runs back down the hall toward us.

Just as he enters the elevator, someone appears in the hallway with a semi-automatic.

The maid.

Oh…*shit*.

When Ed sees our faces, instinctively he turns back around.

The bullets from her gun slam into his chest.

I slide my hand up in order to push my security card into the slot above the elevator buttons.

Just then, the maid realizes Ed wasn't alone in the elevator. She points her gun–

The bullets pierce the doors just as they slide shut.

When the doors open again, we are in my penthouse.

Mara looks around. "But…this isn't POTUS's suite!"

"It's mine," I say.

She and I grab Ed's body and lug it into the foyer. I take Ed's security card from his pocket. Lee's other men may need it.

Mara follows me to the closet holding the C Elevator. "Behind these doors is the elevator that goes exclusively to the concierge level," I explain. "But each penthouse security card can summon it as well. It's a security measure." I tap the doors. "Help me pry open these doors. Afterward, we'll call Jack and Lee on the house phone to tell them what happened downstairs. They need to pry open the doors to this elevator shaft on Lee's side as well. That way we'll be able to leap through the shaft."

Try as we might, the doors refuse to open unless the elevator is summoned–something I'm not willing to do.

Time to call Jack.

A Secret Service agent picks up Lee's house phone. A moment later, Jack is on the line. "What happened? Where are you?"

"In my penthouse, which is on the same level as POTUS's. Mara is with me, but Ed and Charlie are dead, as is Luther."

I hear Walther's voice in the background. He's asking about Gretta.

Before Jack can relay the message, I say, "Tell him we don't know if Gretta was shot. She was one of the first to go into the room, so we lost sight of her."

I explain how the penthouses share the elevator bank with the concierge elevator. "Mara and I have to pry open the door on my side. Otherwise, I'll have to summon the elevator, and it may contain a terrorist or two."

"Which means that we can't summon it here, either," Jack points out.

"Okay, let's play this out," Mara says. "Donna and I push the button. The elevator comes up. The door opens. Donna doesn't have a gun but I do, which I'll use to take out the assailant. Then at least we've secured the elevator, leaving the rest of the terrorists on the concierge level."

"But if we piss them off, they may retaliate with more hostage executions," I counter.

She shakes her head. "Donna, we have a fifty-fifty chance that no one is in there now, and we can secure it before they figure out we can summon it."

She's got a point.

I nod. "Jack, we're hanging up. Listen for our knock. Shave and a haircut."

"This is no time to joke, but I love you anyway." He clicks off.

Already, I miss his voice.

Together, Mara and I move a solid wooden side table from a wall, and turn it on its side, facing the elevator.

I summon the elevator, then I position myself behind the table, while Mara flattens herself on one side of the elevator with her gun raised.

The elevator bell rings. The door opens—

From what we can tell, it's empty.

Mara swings in, to check it out.

A man who has been hiding behind the wall to the left of the open door moves forward. He rams her in the gut with his semi-automatic rifle. As she doubles over, he swings the gun into position to fire it—

And I throw one of my knives.

The stiletto finds its mark: his jugular. Blood gushes out of him so fast that his body jerks and twitches. He grunts as he falls backward, dropping his gun before slumping to the floor.

I kick the gun away, and put the elevator on emergency hold so that I can drag Mara out onto the hallway floor.

I sit with her until she can sit up. "Are you okay?" I ask.

She nods. "Yes…thank you."

I help her to her feet. "Let's knock on the sides of the elevator shaft. One of them opens up into POTUS's penthouse."

She follows me back onto the elevator platform. We tap hard on the right side for a few minutes, yelling Jack's name. Nothing.

We tap the backside, also calling his name.

A moment later, he answers, "Donna! Mara! I'm here."

"Great!" A wave of relief washes over me. "Jack, you need to try POTUS's security card in the exterior slot, to see if the door opens. If we can get it to crack just a little, we can wedge it open and pass through. But we have to keep the elevator on this level. Otherwise, the terrorists can get out, or come up."

"Got it," he says.

The next thing we hear is banging and the groan of the doors coming open, at least enough for us to slip through.

With Jack and Arnie's help, Mara and I do just that.

"How many are there?" Jack asks.

"You mean, besides the maid?" Mara asks. "The security detail was flanking the meeting doorway. There were five of them. They waited until the Secretary of State, Gretta, Charlie, Ed and Luther were in the room before the action took place."

"So, the hard men are the committee's security team." Jack turns to Walther for answers.

"Impossible! Luther handpicked those men," he insists.

The penthouse phone rings. Everyone stares at it. Jack walks over and picks it up. "Yes?"

He listens for a moment, then covers the receiver with his hand. "It's Gretta! She's alive, and asks to be put on speaker."

Walther's face floods with relief, but a minute later, his relief turns to anxiety as he listens along with the rest of us.

The fear is evident in her voice. Like him, she speaks English with a slight German accent. "Our captors are ISIL terrorists. They have purposely jammed cell phone transmissions going in and out of the building, and have cut all outside phone lines as well. All exits have been electronically sealed off." She pauses before adding: "President Chiffray, I apologize, but I was…was beaten to confirm you are here."

Her sobs choke her. There is a slap.

Walther winces when he hears it.

When she collects herself, she continues: "Mr. President, you are to surrender to them. If not, they will begin beheading the delegates–one every twenty minutes. They have a live video feed and will be transmitting this event to news outlets all over the world, including CNN, here in America. Should you not accede to their demands, as soon as the delegates are dead, they will seize other guests in the hotel as hostages and keep beheading until you do. However, your life for the others will stop the beheadings. Are you brave enough to sacrifice yourself for those who are innocent of deeds as heinous as yours?"

Lee sits there, stunned. Finally, he murmurs, "I will give them my answer in…in twenty minutes."

"As an incentive, they will kill an infidel–China's Minister of State Security. It is being broadcasted now."

Jack clicks on the television and searches channels until he finds CNN. Anderson Cooper reports: "–exclusive footage. Let me repeat, this is a live feed, taking place here, on American soil; however, it has yet to be determined where. The international delegates had arrived, in secret, to meet with President Chiffray on the topic of a joint coalition to combat the well-funded terrorist organization known as Islamic State of Iraq and the Levant, also known as ISIL. The United States and

Britain are the only countries that do not–I repeat–do not pay ransoms for hostages. In this case, the terrorists are not asking for a cash ransom. Instead, they are asking for the United States president to present himself in exchange for all the other hostages."

Cooper stops cold. His eyes grow large. "Excuse me, breaking news! We've just been told that one of the delegates is to be executed now! We have a live feed, and viewer discretion is advised."

The newsroom dissolves to grainy footage of a man kneeling against the seat of a wooden chair. His hands are tied behind his back. His shaking is visible, despite the graininess of the camera feed.

Another man stands over him with a large curved sword. He is wearing a hood, but in perfect English, he declares, "Our demand is simple–your American president for those he has turned against us and who now deny our sovereignty. The world will then decide if his ransom is worth paying–seventy trillion dollars." He pauses, as if knowing this amount is eliciting gasps from around the world. "One by one, our hostages will be slaughtered if the coward does not come in their stead. The first beheading is *now*."

The sword swings downward.

The man's head falls from view, leaving his lifeless body.

The video feed cuts away. Anderson Cooper shakes his head sadly as he murmurs, "Again, what you saw was a live beheading." The journalist turns to his co-anchor, Wolf Blitzer. "Wolf, you've been talking to intelligence experts on United State's policy regarding hostages and ransoms. What is the consensus? Should President Chiffray agree to the terms? And, if not, will our allies still stand with us as their own security ministers are being sacrificed?"

"A bigger question, Anderson, is if the president acquiesces to their demand, will the United States pay a ransom, which no doubt will be larger than some of our allies' annual budgets? Or is he the exception to the rule?"

Jack turns off the television.

I look at Lee. He has lost all color in his face. His hand shakes as he reaches for a glass of water.

A rustling can be heard on the cell phone speaker. When Gretta gets back on the phone, she says, "You have twenty minutes before the next beheading."

The line goes dead.

"How many delegates are left?" Ryan asks.

"Four," Walther answers. "The United Kingdom's chairman of the Joint Intelligence Committee, as well as France's Minister of Defense, and Secretary of State Worthington. And of course my colleague who heads *da Bundesnachrichtendienst*–Franz Heller, who is Federal Minister of Special Affairs."

Ryan nods. "I imagine at least one security officer came with each of them?"

"Yes. But I presume they have already been killed," Walther points out.

From the looks on the faces in the room, no one else doubts this.

"Okay, first things first," Ryan says. "We'll need to break the cell transmission block. Find Abu and Dominic in the lobby and fill them in as well."

I'm relieved to know we've got some backup elsewhere in the building.

Arnie nods. "It's doable, but it won't be easy."

"Try your damnedest," Ryan growls. "We also need you to cut the video transmission feed they've set up. We can't let the world see beheadings taking place on U.S. soil."

"My guess is that the antenna for its transmission feed is

coming from somewhere outside the building. If so, it can't be jammed," Arnie explains.

"Then we need to find it and kill it. At the same time, we need to get the rest of the guests out as soon as possible."

"I can take my elevator to the ground floor," I offer. "The hotel's manager, Henry, can tell us what we need to know."

"Arnie and I will go with you," Jack says. "Mr. President, if the terrorists' patience wears thin, the concierge elevator is how they'll come looking for you."

Lee nods at the two members of his security team left standing. They position themselves beside it.

Jack and Arnie follow us through the elevator door and into my penthouse, where we access my suite's private elevator.

The ride down feels like an eternity.

20

Mixing and Mingling

The key to any party's success is getting your guests to interact. This is easily accomplished, if you:

1. *Introduce party games. They can be something as simple as Mail Call ("Everyone who's a bottom, raise your hand...") or as complex as a scavenger hunt. (Word of caution on the latter: Don't send the guests into your dungeon, or they may pass on your future soirées.)*

2. *Break up couples at the dinner table. Make the seating boy-girl-boy-girl. (This assures that the men will talk about something other than sports.) Doing so not only gives you an opportunity to use your new place cards and themed cardholders, it allows new friendships to emerge. (Note of caution: in the odd chance you're called as a witness in a divorce trial, blame it on your wonderful hosting skills.)*

3. *Introduce a scintillating conversation topic. Should you know that someone's wife is having an affair with another guest's husband, by all means announce it. There's nothing*

more exciting than accusations, recriminations, and admissions of guilt!

∼

"MRS. STONE, IF YOU'RE HERE TO COMPLAIN ABOUT THE DOORS and phone reception, I'm already apprised of the situation, and my staff and I are working diligently to correct it." To say that Henry is frazzled is putting it mildly.

I grab his arm. "Henry, we have a bigger problem. This is Jack Craig and Arnie Locklear. They work with a private security company associated with the National Security Agency."

He shakes the other men's hands.

"We have a hostage crisis taking place on the concierge level," Jack explains. "An international terrorist group has it in lockdown. The hotel's penthouse guests are also threatened. For now, we've blocked the joint elevator between the floors, so it is contained to those areas. However, the clock is ticking. People's lives are at stake."

Henry's face loses all color. He eases into his chair as the realization that his hotel's successful launch is anything but.

"Is there a way to track everyone in the building?" I ask.

Henry nods, still stunned.

Jack commands, "Please allow Arnie to man your computer."

Henry moves out of the way for Acme's tech-op. "You'll need my access code."

"Nah, got it covered, guy." Arnie plops down into Henry's desk chair. He cracks his fingers before putting his hand on the computer keyboard like a concert pianist before launching into Rachmaninoff's Prelude in C Sharp Minor and starts clicking away.

A moment later, the screen changes to a three-dimensional diagram of the building.

"The glowing dots you see are guests and staff, generated by their body heat," Henry explains.

Arnie whistles. "Very cool security feature for a hotel."

The largest mass of dots is congregated in the ballroom–around two hundred–and another twenty or so in the restrooms adjacent to it, and another fifteen in the hotel's kitchen.

There are also twenty-three in the lobby. How many of them are terrorists, waiting for the word to take more hostages?

I thank God the hotel is fairly new and still relatively empty. Lee's penthouse shows six more dots.

There are only one or two dots on each floor until the Concierge Level, in which we count ten dots. Five must belong to Gretta and the delegates who are still alive, and the other five are their captors.

Including the killer maid. I wince at the thought. "Henry, one of the maids is the terrorists' accomplice. She's brunette, perhaps Latina. She has an odd nose, and a deep scar on her face."

His brow furrows as he tries to summon a name to match the description. "That would be Carmelita. She was only hired four days ago. She is on shift now."

"Arnie, hack into Human Resources and pull up her employee photo," Jack says. "Send it to Emma so that she can do an Interpol search. Maybe she'll come up with a match."

The maid's face appears on the computer screen. Jack's eyes open wide. "Tatyana!"

I gasp, "*That* is Tatyana?"

He grimaces. "Yes–when I was done with her."

And I let her up onto the concierge level. By doing so, she was able to let the other terrorists up too. After killing the committee's bodyguards and security detail, they took their places, prior to what they'd hoped was the president's appearance.

Jack says, "Arnie, use the hotel's security cameras to give us eyes on the concierge level."

"The hallway and the meeting room have cameras," Henry offers.

Jack nods. "Thanks for that. Arnie, once you've got eyes, capture pictures of the terrorists and relay them to Emma, so that she can start an Interpol search or set up a file on them."

Arnie nods, but keeps his fingers clicking on the keyboard.

"Henry, you say that there are intercoms in every room?" Jack asks.

"Yes, in every bedroom, bathroom, and living room," Henry answers. "The ballroom has several of them, too, as well as the concierge level meeting room. It's a feature that differentiates us from all other hotels. With a push of a button, a guest has direct access to me, without having to go through the hotel switchboard. Also, if a housekeeper needs to contact manage-ment, it's the quickest way to do so."

"Is there a way to turn one on and listen, and at the same time be mute to the guest?"

Henry's cheeks turn pink. "Well...yes. But let me assure you, eavesdropping was not the intent of management. The feature you mention is built into the system. For that reason alone, only I can be contacted."

"We'll keep it between us," Jack says dryly. "We'll need to evacuate the hotel as soon as possible. You say that you've been trying to override the locked doors?"

"Yes!" His voice cracks with desperation. "But it's not work-ing! At this point, only an act of God–or a fire–will open those doors." He shudders at the thought.

Suddenly, an idea comes to me. "Jack, I know how to start a fire quickly. Of course, before I do, we have to make sure everyone is ready to exit the building." I turn back to Henry and Arnie, "Look for the heat from the blaze near the ballroom's kitchen."

"But…the dance!" Henry protests.

"I'll contain it as much as possible, I promise." I cross my heart. "When you see it, hit the intercom to tell those in the ballroom, the kitchen, the lobby, and *only* rooms below the concierge level to evacuate the hotel immediately–all staff included–to the back side of the hotel. It can't be seen from the concierge-level meeting room. If we're lucky, they won't know about the evacuation."

"I'm staying. I go down with the ship," Henry declares stoically.

It may not be the *Titanic*, but if my little diversion gets out of hand, it could turn into the *Towering Inferno*–not that I want to point that out to Henry.

Jack taps my shoulder. "I'll be in the lobby with Abu and Dominic. Something tells me a few of the terrorists' accomplices are waiting there for a high sign from above. If anyone looks suspicious, or tries to impede the egress of the guests, we'll take care of them." He looks at Arnie. "If, after the alarm is sounded, you still see body heat in any of the hotel rooms below the concierge level, let Abu know so that he can check it out."

Arnie waves him off. "Will do, boss."

I wait until Jack and I have left Henry's office to come clean. "Jack, I can never forgive myself. I'm the one who let Tatyana onto the concierge floor."

My remark stops him cold. He's silent for so long that I'm almost afraid to look at him.

When I do, the look on his face stops me. It's not anger, but regret. "Donna, I'm sorry. I should have followed my instincts and kept you in the loop all this time, protocol be damned. You've always been the best sounding board for me."

I hold a palm to his mouth to hush him. "At the time, you did what you thought was correct. Still, a woman always loves to hear her man say, 'you were right.'"

He doesn't just say it, he shows me by pressing my palm to his lips and kissing it.

I'd love to stay by his side, but I can't. It's time to set this place on fire.

It's hard to believe I've been gone from the ballroom only a half hour.

Thank goodness, the children are rocking out to the entertainment. However, Penelope doesn't appreciate it at all, and she's giving Margot an earful.

I steer clear of them as I make my way into the kitchen, where I can access the closet storing the liquor.

Édouard and his assistants are so busy prepping the Cherries Jubilee that they barely notice me slip by them. They certainly don't see me pull an apron off a hook on my way to the storage locker.

As Henry promised, my security card slides effortlessly into the door's lock.

All of the cases are stacked against one wall. I open a box holding a case of gin, which is the cheapest of all the liquor in our stash. The kitchen's floor is concrete. If I'm right, it should contain the fire to the one thing I'll soak in the gin: the apron.

I've just opened it when I hear Penelope screech, "There you are! Where have you been?"

Lovely, she saw me and followed me in.

I hide the bottle behind my back before turning to face her. "Putting out fires," I retort. Really, I'm still figuring out how to start one without turning Henry's hotel into a towering inferno.

"I can't believe you hired a female impersonator to entertain our children!" she screeches.

"If you remember, the referral was yours," I remind her.

She looks at me as if I'm crazy. Then it dawns on her. "But... Lenny Cuthbert would never lie!"

"He didn't. He represents a Taelor Swiff, not *Taylor Swift*," I point out to her.

Her lower lip trembles. "And to think I introduced that... that *person*! You knew all along, and you let me take the credit for hiring her!"

"You're crazy, Penelope! I discovered it at the exact moment you did–when the curtain opened!"

Suddenly, it dawns on her to look around. "Aha! So this is where you've hidden our liquor. What did you plan to do, resell it behind my back and pocket the profits?" She walks around me so that she can see what I'm hiding. "Ha! You've been tippling! I'll just bet you're drunk!"

As she yanks my arm around, the open bottle spills onto her floor-length gown, soaking it.

She glares at me. "This is Dior! And now, it's ruined!"

She raises her hand to slap my face.

That's it–I've had enough of her shenanigans.

I grab her wrist and twist her arm behind her back in such a way that should she move it at all, it's broken. She squawks from the pain. "How dare you! Let me go!"

Instead, I goose-step her out the door.

We're passing Édouard just as he lights one of the Cherries Jubilee. The heat from the dessert finds a new fuel source: Penelope's dress.

It catches fire.

In an instant, Édouard grabs ahold of her dress. In one swipe, he rips the filmy material off her body.

Thank goodness for all of us that the gold corset and thong

she wears beneath don't go up in flames too. I'd attribute it to all the boning and gut-gripping spandex, but I'd prefer to think that she somehow got ahold of flame-retardant unmentionables–a wise move considering her previous experience with fire at school dances.

The flaming dress flies through the air and lands in the humongous serving bowl of Cherries Jubilee. A loud whoosh can be heard as the roaring blaze leaps skyward.

As it turns out, the smoke alarm works perfectly. The kitchen's exit door opens immediately. The chef and his crew hustle out with Penelope in tow.

Over the intercom, Henry announces, "There is a fire in the building. Please make your way to the nearest exit! Repeat, there is a fire in the building…"

I RUN OUT THE KITCHEN DOOR, INTO THE BALLROOM AND SCAN THE room for Evan, Mary, Jeff, and Phyllis.

Mary and Evan are hustling the children out a side exit door. The other chaperones, including Aunt Phyllis, are doing the same.

I pull Aunt Phyllis aside. "I've just texted you a check list of the prom attendees. Please do a headcount. I've also sent a text message to their parents to tell them that their children are fine, but that due to the fire, the dance is over and that they should pick up the children via the hotel's back parking lot. For those who were supposed to stay over, the hotel will hold on to their belongings, which can be collected tomorrow. After all the kids are picked up, take Mary, Evan and Jeff home, okay?"

"Will do!" Phyllis sighs. "I have to tell you, that Taelor Swiff is some awesome singer! What a cute little girl! I don't know what you were doing, but you missed quite a show!"

"That's what you think," I mutter. "This is just the opening act." I want to laugh, but I can't. There are still too many lives at stake.

Including Lee's.

~

THE HOTEL'S ATRIUM LOBBY IS EMPTY, EXCEPT FOR FIVE MEN WHO appear to be sleeping on the luggage cart being guarded by Abu. Their hands and ankles are cuffed, and there is tape over their mouths and bands over their eyes.

Two were in suits, another two in khakis and golf shirts, and the last one is dressed as a bellman. The items found in their pockets lay in a heap on the lobby reservation desk. Dominic wears white gloves as he rummages through the booty for anything that might identify the suspects.

Jack and Henry walk up. With his security card, Henry opens an empty luggage closet, which will be the captured terrorists' home until the NSA can make it here to take them in for interrogation.

"That was a fast takedown," I declare.

"It's easy with this." Dominic pulls a pen from his inside jacket pocket, which he then clicks open and shut. "Contains Propofol. One prick, and they're out like a light."

"Sounds like being on a date with you," I mutter.

He raises his head, miffed. But before he has a chance to retort, Abu points out, "The bellman spoke English, but with a Soranian accent."

"Could you tell what tribe or region?" Jack asks.

Abu shrugs. "Sunni. Perhaps from Erbil."

"He also had this walkie-talkie on him, which I guess is the terrorists' way of getting around the cell phone jamming." Jack tosses the communications device to Abu. "If someone calls him, fake it. You know, tell them everything is fine down here. We've got to buy some time."

Arnie pokes his head out of Henry's office. "The phone lines were pulled from underground, but Emma figured out where the cell phone block is coming from." He points to a limousine parked in the hotel's entry turnabout.

"Super! And she's not even onsite," I exclaim. "How did she do that?"

"She triangulated the coordinates based on where cell phone service was dead. From there, it was a matter of deduction." He beams as he explains it. He's always in awe of her, and it's not just infatuation.

"I'll take care of the damnable thing," Dominic says. He picks up a car key fob from the terrorists' booty and makes his way out the door and to the limousine. He finds what we're looking for in the trunk and brings it in with him, handing it to Arnie.

Jack stops Arnie before he turns off the signal. "Once the jammer is deactivated, everyone's cell gets activated, including those on the concierge level. There's got to be something we can do so that they don't know we're in the clear."

I snap my fingers. "I have an idea! Let's move it to a spot directly over the concierge meeting room and recalculate its blocking coordinates so that its reach goes in only one direction—down—and blocks that portion of the concierge level."

Jack breaks out into a smile. "Brilliant! Arnie and Dominic, come with us. Arnie, after you've set up the jammer, head back over to Henry's office, so that you can keep watch on the concierge level security cameras—"

He stops talking when he sees someone coming our way: Aunt Phyllis, with Evan and Mary.

I run to them. "What's wrong?" It dawns on me that Jeff isn't with them. "Mary, where is your brother?"

She shakes her head. "He never made it to the parking lot. We've looked all over the ballroom and the hotel's lower level, and we can't find him."

"Could he have hitched a ride with one of his friends?" I ask.

"I don't think so," says Evan. "When we got here, he was so excited to find Gabrielle that he left her corsage in your room. I saw him leave the ballroom before the fire alarm went off. I think he left to retrieve it."

Noting my worried look, Arnie says, "I'll check to see if there are any hot dots in your room." He trots off.

I pace the floor until he comes back. He also looks worried.

"What is it?" I ask.

He looks down at his feet. "There are now nine hot dots in the concierge meeting room, and two hot dots standing near the concierge elevator. I rolled back the footage and noticed a hot dot in the fire escape stairwell. The security feed of the concierge floor confirms what I suspect. It shows him coming out of the stairwell. Tatyana let him onto the floor, and led him into the hostage room."

I turn to Jack because I don't want Mary to see the fear in my eyes.

"Phyllis, why don't you take Mary and Evan home?" Jack suggests. I'm glad he's able to keep his voice calm, almost nonchalant.

"No," Mary says adamantly. "I want to stay here, in case… in case Jeff or Mom need me."

Evan puts his hand on her shoulder. "I do too," he says.

Phyllis puts her hand on his. "Three Musketeers."

I swallow hard. "Okay, then, follow me. But once we're there, you must stay put–no matter what happens."

To Jack. To me.

To Jeff.

ARNIE AND DOMINIC JOIN THE FAMILY STONE ON THE ELEVATOR ride to the penthouse suites.

Lee's Secret Service man indicates that he is in his bedroom. The door is closed.

Walther is nervously pacing the floor. When we walk in, he looks up anxiously. Seeing us, he shrugs, but says nothing. I'm glad. If he proclaimed the suite off limits to my family, I'd break his nose.

For their safety, I place Mary, Evan, and Aunt Phyllis in the other bedroom with strict instructions: "Stay here. Lock this door. No unnecessary sounds! Talk in whispers. Unless it's Jack, me, Jeff, or President Chiffray, don't open it to anyone. There's a bathroom and a mini-bar, so you should be fine."

"And no television," Jack warns them.

Aunt Phyllis looks over at him, puzzled. "Why not, in heaven's name?"

Jack doesn't break his direct gaze with her. "You have to trust us on this."

She must because she doesn't say another word. Mary and Evan exchange concerned glances.

We luck out that one of my penthouse's bedrooms is exactly on top of the concierge meeting room. Arnie makes the necessary settings to the cell phone jammer to reduce and pinpoint the coverage. Afterward, he takes the elevator back to Henry's office so that he can keep up his reconnaissance.

When Jack, Dominic, and I walk back through the concierge elevator platform, Lee's Secret Service man says, "The president would like a word with you."

When we open Lee's bedroom door, we are met with sad, sad eyes.

Lee is sitting on the edge of his bed. His face is drawn. His eyes are glazed. He takes both my hands in his. "Donna, please sit down."

No…

Oh, no…

God, no.

21

How to Get Rid of the Guest Who Won't Leave

No matter how many broad hints are given, inevitably, one of your guests will overstay his or her welcome. Here's how to lose the guest, but at the same time, keep the friendship:

- *Tip #1: Excuse yourself to put on your pajamas. Nothing says, "Get the hell out of my house" like a woman in a flannel granny gown. (In other words, save the black silk baby doll peignoir for another night.)*
- *Tip #2: Glance at your watch. Often. Exclaiming, "My, my, it's getting late" or "I have such an early morning" should also give the guest a clue that he has overstayed his welcome. (So will the command, "Sic 'em" to your dog, if it comes to that.)*
- *Tip #3: Yawn in the guest's face. Loudly, and often. This is an easy hint for your guest to take. If not, a quick blast of buckshot from your rifle will do the trick.*

IT'S ON THE TELEVISION NOW.

The executioner is declaring President Chiffray "a coward! He would let a child die in his place!"

With a jerky motion, the camera swings over to a chair where Jeff sits. His hands are in his lap. His lower lip is trembling. His eyes are huge with anguish.

When he looks at the camera, he's looking at me.

I see you, my baby. I'm here.

But the realization that I should be there makes my legs collapse from under me.

Lee drops with me and holds me until he's sure I'm listening to him, until he's sure my breathing is normal again, and then he murmurs, "Donna, I–"

"No, Lee! Don't say it." Slowly, I rise to my feet.

If he wants to tell me he can't jeopardize the country, even if it means sacrificing Jeff, even if it means my hating him for the rest of my life, I don't want to hear it, because, yes, I will hate him. I could never forgive him for doing his duty and putting the country above everything else, especially the life of my son.

If he wants to tell me that he is willing to offer himself as a substitute for Jeff, I can't let him do it. After all, he is the president of the United States and the most powerful man in the free world. Jeff's life would always be shadowed by Lee's selfless act. He would always feel guilty about Lee's brave sacrifice. He would do what he could to honor it, and die trying.

Or die in disgrace for never being able to live up to it. No one could.

And I would have Lee's sacrifice on my conscience, too.

I let go of his hand. "We'll figure something out."

"Bingo," Mara exclaims.

She's standing beside a window and looking down.

Jack and I join her there. "What do you see?" I ask.

She grins. "Our way in." She points downward.

The window directly below us is open.

Jack calls Arnie. "Look for three hot dots at a window in the president's suite."

After a pause, Arnie says, "Found it."

"Ask Henry if the room below it is a guest room, and if so, whose it is."

The pause is longer this time, but finally he comes back on the phone. "It was registered to the Chinese security minister."

"Then, it's empty," I reason. Yes, there's still hope.

"Ah, makes sense," Dominic murmurs with a straight face. "Who wouldn't want a breath of fresh Los Angeles air after leaving mainland China?"

Mara comes in with a handful of sheets that she pulled off the beds. "Nine-hundred-count hand spun sateen cotton. Top of the line and beautiful. Let's hope these hold."

No shit. We're on the nineteenth story of a twenty-story building. Even with a slight breeze, clinging onto sheets to get out of one window and into another on the floor below won't be easy. But at this point, I'll do anything to save my son's life.

MARA IS CHOSEN TO CLIMB DOWN FIRST. I'M TO FOLLOW, THEN Jack, and finally Dominic.

Besides tying the sheets together with double knots, we've tied belts around the knots, so that they hold.

One end of the sheet rope is wrapped around Mara's waist. The other is tied around the leg of a heavy antique table, which the men shove up against the wall next to the window.

With Jack's help, Mara eases herself out of the window. She then takes the rope with both hands. We lower her down but we hold tight, as her counter-balance. The goal is to swing through the window immediately below, land as quietly as possible, secure the room, and help the rest of us climb down.

I wince as she slams into the side of the building. Soon, though, she finds the rhythm she needs as she scales down the wall.

When she's level with the window, we give a little more slack as she kicks off one more time for the added momentum needed to go through the window.

To our relief, she disappears into the room.

The sheet rope goes slack. We won't pull it up until we get the high-sign from her.

I hold my breath until she reappears. Her thumbs-up is accompanied by a smile.

We pull the rope up. It's my turn.

I follow the same procedure. I tie it around my waist–not at the end of the sheet, but leaving a tail that Mara can grab ahold of, in order to pull me into the room.

Before I go out the window, Jack hands me his backup gun: a Sig Sauer P226R, with a suppressor. Mara is carrying the same equipment.

Then, he kisses me. A million emotions wash over me: love, desire, regret–

But mostly determination.

Together, we will save our son.

I walk gently on the wall as Jack and Dominic lower me down–

But in the silence eighteen and a half stories above traffic, the rip of a sheet is as loud as a thunder clap.

I look up to survey the damage.

Yes, I am almost literally hanging by a thread.

The look on Jack's face is one I've never seen before: sheer terror.

Above me, the rope goes slack as it drops.

The second it takes to pass me is long enough for the images of those I love to rise to the surface of my consciousness: I'm embracing them, telling them how much I love them, telling them that they will always feel me beside them.

And then my mind's eye is filled with the vision of my son as I last saw him.

I've failed you, Jeff. Please forgive me.

In desperation, I claw at the air. The split second seems like an eternity.

The next thing I feel is Mara grabbing ahold of me at my knees, and pulling me through the window with all her might.

We land on the carpeted floor with a thud.

I'm about to thank her, but she puts her finger to her lips to silence me.

Footsteps can be heard coming from the hallway.

She rolls under the bed. I follow her lead.

The footsteps stop outside the door.

A long moment later, the door opens. At first, no one enters the room. When he finally does, it's with the stealth of a cat.

Mara reaches for one of the dead Chinese minister's slippers and throws it toward the bathroom door.

As the terrorist makes his move in that direction, I roll out from under the bed and pull Jack's gun from its holster.

The shot is a direct hit to the heart.

Four killers to go.

I pray Mara has it in her.

I know I do.

THERE ARE TWO SOLDIERS AT THE FAR END OF THE HALL, GUARDING the elevator and sharing a smoke. Mara hits the one on the left with a bullet to the head. I do the same with the one on the right.

I text Jack: *LION and cubs leave NOW on E Elev! U use C Elev to us.*

Mara and I move quickly but silently against the hallway's right wall, the one that will give us the most coverage, since it is against the deepest part of the room. As we get to each doorway, we look inside. All are empty.

We duck low to the ground as we reach the double-door entry, and peek around the corner to assess the situation. The rest of the hostages, bound and gagged, huddle together behind the sofa in full view of the camera. The Chinese minister's body, stiff and bloodless, lies on a thick Persian carpet near a window. Next to it is that of his German counterpart. There is also a woman's body–Walther's assistant, Gretta, I presume.

Thank God, Jeff is still alive–but not for long, if we don't move quickly.

There is just one ISIL guard left, and even he is mesmerized by what is about to take place: the beheading of a mere child.

Tatyana mans the camera that will show the world their next heinous crime.

Jeff is now kneeling in front of a coffee table. His head is bowed. His hands are bound behind his back. My son is not crying. In fact, he seems to be in a trance. The executioner declares, "The United States' president has failed his people. He would rather see another innocent executed than sacrifice his personal political agenda. This is your child, America! How do you feel?"

After nudging Mara, I point to myself and then make a slicing motion, to indicate that my target is the executioner. She nods, and waits for my three-count.

On one, the man lifts his sword.

On two, a bullet leaves my gun.

Before the three count, he reels backward from the force of a bullet right between the eyes.

Tatyana ducks down, just as Mara's bullet whizzes over her head.

She rolls to one side. When she rises, she is pointing a gun at Jeff. The gun goes off–

And hits the soft flesh below the ribcage.

Not Jeff's ribcage, but Mara's because she has leapt in front of him, shielding his body with hers.

Before Tatyana can get off another shot, I shoot at her–

But I miss. She runs down the hall.

I pull the blindfold off Jeff's eyes, and rip off the restraints on his hands and feet. Seeing that it is me, he throws his arms around me as if he never wants to let go.

That's fine with me. I feel exactly the same way.

I'm reluctant to set him down, but I have to in order to see what I can do for Mara. As her blood flows out of her, her bittersweet life ebbs away. I cradle her face as I whisper, "Thank you, Mara, for saving Jeff's life."

I can barely hear her as she whispers back, "You have every-thing I ever wanted, Donna. And you deserve it all…after…Carl."

The glazed look of death in her eyes tells me she is at peace.

The next thing I know, Jack and Dominic are there too.

Jeff runs up to Jack to be enveloped in a bear hug that lifts him off the floor.

Over my son's head, I ask, "Tatyana! Was she apprehended?"

Jack stares back at me. "We didn't see her! We came straight here!"

"She must have ducked into one of the guest rooms! Oh hell–the elevator!"

"It only goes up," Jack reminds me.

I run down the hall just in time to see the elevator doors opening, and Tatyana getting on the platform.

As she leaps into it, I get off one shot before the doors close completely.

When it comes back down for me, there is blood in it, but no Tatyana.

It is probably Ed's, but I hope it's her blood.

As silently as I can, I look in Lee's suite first. Thank goodness, it's empty.

So is Walther's suite. I presume he's on his way back to Germany. The invasion of the summit is one black eye on his political career. The death of his country's security minister is its knockout punch.

I find it hard to feel sorry for him.

On quiet feet, I walk through the concierge elevator platform to my suite. When I reach the threshold, I stop to listen for any noises.

Nothing.

I crouch down and look out–

No one.

I hear a noise. It's coming from the sunken living room.

Step by silent step, I make my way down the hall. When I get to the living room, I stop and raise my gun, then turn–

To see Walther. He's sitting on a couch. His hands are tied behind his back, and his mouth is gagged.

The sight gives me pause.

Big mistake. Tatyana kicks the gun out of my hand. Her gun is aimed at my head.

She chuckles. "I was hoping it would be you! Much better

than Jack Craig. I'll enjoy taking away his one prized possession—his little *hausfrau*."

"That is not a dirty word in my language," Walther reminds her. I notice that his hands are free, and he has pulled the gag from his mouth.

He stands up. Before smoothing his cuffs, I see a tattoo on his right wrist:

A half-moon.

Walther is the saboteur code-named Sin.

He clicks his tongue at Tatyana. "You made the bindings too tight, Tatyana, *meine liebster*."

"Sorry, my dear." She shrugs. "Usually, you love them that way."

"Not when I don't have much time to take my leave." He nods at me. "Or, as you Americans say, 'make a quick getaway.' The chancellor is sending a helicopter. It should be on the roof any moment."

So, Tatyana was the playmate in Walther's bed, not Gretta. And having seen Gretta's dead body, I now realize that Tatyana was also the voice on the hotel's house phone relaying the terrorists' terms to Walther.

I glare at him. "You are ISIL's inside man."

He puts a finger to his lips. "*Shhh.* Let's keep it our little secret, shall we?"

"But—but you're a cabinet secretary in the German government! Why would you betray your country—and the world—in this manner?"

He shrugs. "The price was right. The moment the abduction was broadcast, fifty million was transferred into my Swiss bank account—a pittance to ISIL, considering the publicity! Hostages on American soil—and one is President Chiffray! It's priceless! Not to mention the number of eager new recruits!" He laughs.

"And now, being offered our dearly departed security minister's appointment is an added bonus."

I mutter, "Considering this major faux pas, I'm surprised your chancellor would trust you to walk her dog, let alone with the country's security."

He backhands me across the face. Noting that I don't flinch, he shrugs. "After Franz's grisly demise, I don't think there will be many takers."

Good point.

I turn to Tatyana. "You're a 'show me the money' kind of girl. What's your stake in this?"

She raises a brow. "As you know very well, the Quorum has also had a recent death in the family. But as much as we all mourn the demise of our fearless leader–your ex-husband–the show must go on. For this mission to be a success, ISIL needed an onsite consultant–you know, to make the necessary arrangements for getting their A-Team God Squad into the country without raising any red flags, and out again as soon as possible." She shrugs. "The executioners were worried that the mission might be too easy. You proved them wrong. That's okay. They were ready to meet their virgins."

"So happy we were able to accommodate them," I murmur. "By the way, how did you get ahold of Jeff?"

"He'd walked up eighteen stories on the fire exit, in order to get to your suite. When his security key let him into the concierge level, *voilà*! We had our perfect hostage," she sneers. "The fact that he's your son made it that much sweeter."

The thwack-thwack-thwack of a helicopter's propellers is faint, but getting louder. "*Auf wiedersehen, meine liebster*! So sad I can't take you with me, but you know how it is–we must keep up appearances." Walther pecks her on the cheek. "I'll see you back in Berlin."

Tatyana blows him an air kiss as he strolls through the elevator platform back to his suite, then jabs her gun into my back. "Walk with me. I'm using you as my human shield"–she shrugs–"for as long as you're needed. But better you than Jack or Jeff, eh, mama?"

SHE DOESN'T PUSH ME TOWARD THE CONCIERGE ELEVATOR. INSTEAD, she shoves me in front of my penthouse's private elevator and inserts a security card. "I held on to your son's card," she explains. "He's such a sweet, polite boy! Gave it right to 'the maid' when I asked for it." She fakes a sigh. "I'm happy my scars didn't scare him. Aren't you glad I didn't tell him that your loving Jack gave them to me?"

No bell rings when the elevator door opens. I know this is because there is no car.

But not Tatyana.

Before she has a chance to realize it, I shove her into darkness.

Instinctively, she grabs onto the only thing she can–me.

I try to push her off, but she has momentum on her side. Together we fall.

When I was hanging off the side of the building, I summoned my favorite memories of my family, and said my prayers.

This time, however, I do some math. An average floor is about ten feet. We're falling from the nineteenth floor. Since velocity is about thirty-two feet per second, I've only got five, maybe six seconds, to survive this fall.

You see? This is why you need to help your kids with their math problems–*you'll learn something too.*

It helps that Tatyana fell first. I stay vertical, then I lift my knees together and let loose with a kick that should keep her below me.

Next, I lunge toward a corner and grapple at anything on the walls that can break my fall, like the elevator cables that hang loosely on all sides. The oil on them makes this a slippery task, but I'm able to grasp one. Instinctively, I wrap a leg around it too–

Which is a good thing because my hand loses its grip–

And I find myself hanging upside down, about twenty feet from the bottom of the shaft.

You see? It pays to go to clown camp with your son's scout troop. *You may learn something too.*

I'm in a better position than Tatyana, who looks like a broken rag doll. Her head sits in a halo of blood. She died with her eyes wide open, and her mouth frozen in a scream.

In fact, it was her long echoing scream that summoned Jack. With the help of Abu and Dominic, he has pried open the lobby level doors of Elevator A.

He sees Tatyana first, below him at the base of the shaft on the garage level. When he doesn't see me, he looks skyward.

I wave.

Then I unfurl my leg so that I can drop into his arms.

I wish I could stay there forever, but I can't. "Walther was in on it," I tell him.

Jack makes the call that will ensure that Walther never makes it outside the confines of U.S. airspace. The closest he'll get to Germany is a black site in Poland.

I'll request a visit, every now and then. After what he did to Jeff, I'll enjoy making him cry.

22

And a Good Time Was Had by All!

All hostesses are anxious to learn if their parties were enjoyed by their guests. Well, guess what? You'll know instantly if:

1. *Everyone is talking about something that happened there. Except, perhaps an altar sacrifice. Save that for a more select group—say, your weekend Wiccan coven.*
2. *No one runs out of the house screaming and on fire. Terror is never great for word of mouth.*
3. *Everyone wants to come back for your next event. Giving out one-hundred-dollar gift cards as party favors truly works!*

BONNIE RAMSEY, THE FAMILY COUNSELOR, SMILES BROADLY AND shakes everyone's hand as Mary, Jeff, Trisha, Jack, Evan, and I file into her large, homey living room. There is no standing at attention. "Sit anywhere you like," she insists. "And please, call me Bonnie."

Evan and Mary look around warily before deciding on the two easy chairs flanking the open-hearth fireplace. Trisha plops down next to Bonnie's dog–an old Labrador named Louis–and pets it gently before hugging the old boy's neck too.

Jack sits on one side of the large settee. I take the other. Jeff burrows between us. He clasps our hands, but holds them down, next to his thighs. He wants us to see him as strong again, but he still has that post-traumatic stress twilight where he realizes he's safe, but he doubts what he sees with his own eyes.

Everyone is the enemy.

Yes, I've been there. I feel for him. I want him to trust again.

It's why we're here.

Bonnie explains that the one rule is that there are no rules. "No one should be afraid to speak their mind. You can cry or laugh. You can blame and accuse. That way, those who are the catalysts of your feelings can respond to you, and the dialogue you so strongly need will begin."

My children have borne the brunt of my actions. From what I know of Evan's life, I played a bigger part in it than I could have imagined.

I expect a tsunami of pain to come my way, and I brace myself for it.

Thank God I have Jack to hold onto.

It takes a while for Bonnie to get my children to open up. No one is surprised that Trisha is first, least of all me.

"Mary is mad at Mommy because of our other daddy. But I didn't like him, so I'm glad he's gone." Trisha's pronouncement is made with her eyes firmly on the dog, because she doesn't know if her words will hurt Mary, Jeff, or me. "Other people have two daddies, and they don't mind it at all. But our other daddy made Mommy angry. I didn't like that."

"Maybe you would have, if you'd gotten the chance to know him better," Mary points out. "You had already made up your mind because of"–she looks over at the couch–"Jack."

"He ran away from us, remember?" Jeff speaks so softly that everyone leans in. "He hurt people! And now we have to live with that. People hate us because of the things he did! They want to…to hurt us."

Mary can't argue with that, since she's experienced it herself. She scowls as she slumps down in her chair.

"Hey, at least your mother didn't kill your father," Evan offers.

Mary's head swings around. It's the only time I've seen her angry with Evan. She opens her mouth to say something, but holds herself back. Instead, she forces herself to turn her head away again.

Evan is so caught up in his own pain that he is oblivious to hers. "My father loved my mother, but it wasn't enough for her! He just wanted to get away from her lies–and I did, too. I was glad he was going to divorce her! At least that way, he'd have had the option of never seeing her again." He stops because he's choking on his sobs. "But she's my mother! Despite having taken him from me, as long as she's alive, I'll have her in my life."

Mary's frown softens. She reaches out in order to put her hand over his. "Somewhere along the way, my father must have quit loving my mother," she murmurs. "Why else would he have left her…and the rest of us?"

Hearing her say this is the crack in my emotional dam. I let my head drop to my chest so that I can cry.

Jeff turns and hugs me. "Don't cry, Mom, please! We don't miss him, really! We miss the idea of him. And you did, too. But eventually, you did the right thing. You learned to love someone who will always love us, too, and be there for us." He grasps Jack's hand again.

Jack squeezes it tight.

Mary goes over and takes hold of Jack's other hand. He looks up at her. His eyes glimmer with dampness. Her tears fall into her long hair as she smiles down at him.

Trisha is as transfixed at the tableau in front of her as I am.

But it doesn't last forever. Mary asks, "Mom, did you mean it when you said you're quitting?"

Jeff's damp smile fades. "Don't," he implores me. "Then who will protect us?"

"I will," I swear to him. "And so will Jack–always!"

"No! ...I mean, I know that. What I'm trying to say is"–he takes a deep breath before he continues–"if you quit your job, they'll always be out there. They'll always be able to do this– not just to us, but to everyone! We can't be scared of them–or they win."

Jeff is no longer crying.

Jeff is no longer afraid.

My Jeff is back.

Mary is nodding. Despite their sibling squabbles and teasing, they've always shared an unbreakable bond. Jeff's death would have shattered his sister. Instead, the harsh reality of his abduction brings a sharp clarity to the bittersweet blur of her childhood memories of Carl.

The love she had for her father cannot negate his bad deeds.

She bends over me to give me a kiss on my forehead. Finally, she forgives me for the role I played–the role I *had* to play–in Carl's death.

I had expected our session with Bonnie to go on all afternoon, but the way she rises, I realize that she agrees with me that we've accomplished what we set out to do today:

My family will heal.

As we walk out, Trisha asks if we can take Louis with us.

I shake my head no. "Bonnie has given us so much already." I give her a hug.

23

Thank-You Notes

After attending a party, most guests send thank-you notes. However, if you don't receive them, here's why:

- *Reason One: The note got lost in the mail. That being said, let the appreciative guest know as soon as possible. If (quelle horreur!) he or she admits to not having sent one, refer to Reason Two.*
- *Reason Two: The guest is not at all well mannered. If this is the case, cross him or her off your next invitation list! If you want to be around baboons, you know the way to the local zoo.*
- *Reason Three: The guest had a lousy time. Not that you'd know it by the way he gobbled down your canapés, swilled your liquor, and tried on your best pair of Louboutins. (You know this, because you have a videocam in your closet.)*

If this is the case, feel free to excommunicate him as a friend. Tell him he can have the Louboutins, too, now that he's stretched them out. He will also have to buy you a new pair. Otherwise, he'll be the latest sensation on YouTube when others realize he does a mean rumba in five-inch pointy stilettos.

THE MEMORIAL SERVICE FOR MARA PORTNOY TAKES PLACE AT sunrise, on Acme's rooftop. Not everyone in the organization knew her. Still, all of Acme has turned out for it.

Her name has been carved in the wall next to that of the love of her life, Kiril.

Those who shared missions with her speak out about her bravery, her sense of humor, and her love of life.

In Jack's case, his anecdote is one of levity. I join the others gathered here in wiping away tears of sorrow as we roar with laughter about the rainstorm in Prague and its bloody aftermath.

The tears flow again when it's my turn. I keep my voice level as I describe her selfless act in saving Jeff. Then I read the note my son wrote her, in which he describes his sadness at facing death without getting to say goodbye to those he loved, and his resignation when he saw the bullet coming his way, and how Mara's arms around him felt like angel's wings.

When I can no longer speak because the memory has become a hard knot in my throat, I place Jeff's heartfelt note beside her urn.

Mara will not be alone in her vault deep within the Wall. Jack had hoped to surprise her with the deed that would help right the wrong he did to her. Sometime last week he'd contacted Nikolay Krastevich, the Bulgarian covert operative Jack had charged with disposing of Kiril's body. Nikolay tracked down her lover's cremated remains, which had been interred in a Bulgarian mausoleum.

Kiril's ashes now share Mara's urn.

Together they will rest in peace for eternity.

RYAN IS KEEN TO MEET ME FOR LUNCH. I SUGGEST A LITTLE CAFÉ near his office, one we both know well from way back when I was young and innocent and nudging him for news on Carl's killers when my husband was supposedly dead.

It was also where he nudged me to consider joining Acme.

I wonder how he'll feel this time, as I prod him to consider my doing so once again.

I wait until he settles into a three-inch-thick corned beef sandwich on rye. It's only because his mouth is full that I'm able to make my case so fully. I point out that the world's terrorist organizations are getting more sophisticated, and that they're getting better funded–to that extent, thanks to the Quorum, whose players I know well.

Worse yet, they're getting closer.

"I know you've had your issues with me in the past," I concede. "But we both know my skill set is as good as you'll find anywhere, and my track record speaks for itself–"

He gulps down the food in his mouth. "Let me get this straight–are you saying you want to come out of retirement?"

"Yes. Exactly. And I hope you feel I'm not being presumptuous to–"

"Presumptuous? Who ...*you?*" He's laughing so hard that he begins to choke on his corned beef.

His face is so red that I stand up and jerk him under the arms with the Heimlich maneuver.

"You saved my life," he gasps.

"Only because I can't have everyone snickering over my

killing another Acme agent," I sniff. "To your credit, you didn't place a bet in the office's black widow trainer pool."

His mouth opens, then shuts quickly. We both know the truth: he won the damn pool. He was the only one who felt certain that Tally would show, God rest her soul.

He picks up the check. "What took you so long to call?"

For that, he's earned a kiss on his bald spot.

I'M IN MY CAR HEADING HOME WHEN I GET A CALL. CALLER ID shows that it's Penelope, and it's marked urgent. Knowing her, she'll just keep calling if I don't take it now, so I hit the speaker. "What is it now, Penelope?"

"I've got wonderful news, Donna!"

"Do tell."

"Despite the fire you started, the Hotel Savoy has decided not to sue the PTA after all."

"Nice to know," I exclaim. "And by the way, as for the fire, *you* started it. The proof is in the security feed. Don't you just love all those tiny little cameras?"

Penelope is quiet as that realization sinks in. "*Hmm.* You don't think a picture of me, practically naked and on fire, will end up online, do you?"

"Depends."

"On what?"

"On how I feel about what you're about to say next."

She chuckles as if I'm kidding. Little does she know I've already hacked the Savoy's security feed and downloaded the footage. Whenever I get low, I'll play it just for tickles and giggles. If–*oopsy!*–I hit a button that loads it onto FunnyOrDie.-com, well, hey, accidents do happen.

"Because of the fire, Henry has agreed to refund all of the

room fees. Between what we save there, and what we made on ticket sales, and what we'll make on sales of the bottles of liquor, the dance will have its biggest profit ever! I'm very proud right now."

"Well, thank you."

"What? ...Oh, you thought I meant *you*." I can imagine her shrugging at the thought. "In any case, today is your lucky day! The PTA steering committee took a vote and has decided to make your position as the prom committee chairperson a permanent one. What do you think of that?"

My response is a dial tone. I've got bigger fish to flambé.

As Trisha puts it, "I love, love, *love* my flower girl dress for Emma and Arnie's wedding!"

Of course, she would, since Emma instructed her to pick out any frock she wanted for her petal-strewing stroll down the lawn in front of Los Angeles' Griffith Observatory.

Her original choice was the Snow Queen Elsa's costume from *Frozen.* Noting my grimace, Trisha's new crush, Evan, made it a point to tell her how awesomely gorgeous she looked in the dress I'd suggested to her: the dusty lilac Zunie glittered tulle dress with a wide satin sash and a bow at the waist.

I blew him a kiss for that.

My own dress was chosen by the bride, who declared, "I want you to cut loose at my wedding! No elegant sheath and pearls! Something *fun*!"

I groaned. "We already had our 'fun'–last night at your bachelorette party, remember? I've got the tattoo to prove it."

"I'm sure Jack appreciated it," she giggled.

My blush told her she guessed right. Hey, what man

wouldn't appreciate a heart with his name on it, on his beloved's right butt cheek?

It hurt like hell. My consolation is that he kissed it–among other things–to make it better.

So, here I am, in a sleeveless ice blue Oscar de la Renta mini-dress overlaid with tea-length floral tulle, and making my way down the path in front of the crystal ball-topped obelisk known as the Astronomers Monument, toward a very nervous Arnie and his best man, Jack.

Emma follows, escorted by Ryan. Her dress has the Goth edginess I'd expect: a white body-hugging below-the-knee sheath–really a pencil skirt and crop top with sleeveless cut-ins and a rounded neckline, held together by a sheer mesh overlay. Her white pillbox hat has a tiny veil. White elbow-length gloves complete her ensemble.

Aunt Phyllis is in the front row, along with Jeff, Evan, and Mary. She holds Nicky, who squirms and coos. His onesie resembles a tiny tuxedo.

The rest of the wedding party is small. Besides their closest Acme colleagues, there are some of Emma's biker pals and Arnie's hacker buddies. The reception in the jumbo-sized tent beside us should be quite a party.

In the final rays of the setting sun, as the minister invites them to say their vows, Jack's eyes catch mine. He mouths the question, *Will you marry me?*

Yes, I whisper, *and I will always love you, with all my heart.*

But, of course, I want to hear him ask that question out loud.

Perhaps later tonight, when we are hand in hand, dancing beneath the stars.

–THE END–

Next Up for Donna!

The Housewife Assassin's Garden of Deadly Delights

(Book 10)

Housewife assassin Donna Stone's green thumb--and for that matter, her trigger finger--is put to the test when she must stop the release of genetically enhanced corn containing a deadly brain-eating virus.

Other Books by Josie Brown

The True Hollywood Lies Series

Hollywood Hunk

Hollywood Whore

The Totlandia Series

The Onesies - Book 1 (Fall)

The Onesies - Book 2 (Winter)

The Onesies - Book 3 (Spring)

The Onesies - Book 4 (Summer)

The Twosies - Book 5 (Fall)

The Twosies – Book 6 (Winter)

The Twosies - Book 7 (Spring)

The Twosies - Book 8 (Summer)

More Josie Brown Novels

The Candidate

Secret Lives of Husbands and Wives

The Baby Planner

How to Reach Josie

To write Josie, go to:
mailfromjosie@gmail.com

To find out more about Josie, or to get on her eLetter list for book launch announcements, go to her website:
www.JosieBrown.com

You can also find her at:

www.AuthorProvocateur.com

twitter.com / JosieBrownCA

facebook.com / josiebrownauthor

pinterest.com / josiebrownca

instagram.com / josiebrownnovels

www.ingramcontent.com/pod-product-compliance
Lightning Source LLC
Chambersburg PA
CBHW070556170726
48291CB00003B/628